Praise for
MISS MELVILLE'S REVENGE

"It's difficult not to laugh aloud as Smith skewers the daily tribulations of life in New York as suffered by those of wealth and position, then turns her non-discriminatory wit on just about everything else within reach."

UPI

"One feels like cheering when Susan pulls the trigger. . . . The author is a New Yorker who knows her art as well as her literature. In MISS MELVILLE'S REVENGE she mixes her usual blend of mystery, suspense and wit with foreign intrigue to give the reader a highly enjoyable story."

Abiline Reporter-News

"Smith presents a colorful world of intrigue and espionage, as well as a multi-faceted side of life in New York amid the wacky world of highly paid artists, diplomats and business people. . . . Written with wit and a sophisticated flair for repartee, Smith's latest endeavor is sure to please her fans."

Macon Telegraph & News

"Smith's wry sense of humor highlights her ingeniously plotted novel."

Booklist

MISS MELVILLE'S REVENGE

Evelyn E. Smith

FAWCETT CREST • NEW YORK

A Fawcett Crest Book
Published by Ballantine Books
Copyright © 1989 by Evelyn E. Smith

Library of Congress Catalog Card Number: 88-45729

ISBN 0-449-21794-9

This edition published by arrangement with Donald I. Fine, Inc.

Manufactured in the United States of America

First Ballantine Books Edition: August 1990

To Jeff Warren, Cal von Reinhold, and Bill Arnholt

"I am never going to take you to a party again, Susan," Alex Tabor said, "if you're going to go around killing the guests."

"May I remind you," Susan Melville told him, "that it was I who took you to the party. And that was only because Peter decided to go to that conference in Katmandu, and the Kibandans take a dim view of ladies coming to their parties without male escorts. Not," she added, before Alex had a chance to say anything, "that I would put up with such an attitude from one of the western countries. But one must make allowances for the third world."

She was not telling the truth. If need be, she would have worn a grass skirt and a ring in her nose—or whatever the native costume of Kibanda was—in order to get to that particular reception. But she couldn't tell him that. She couldn't tell him anything anymore. They had grown as far apart as if they had been brother and sister in reality instead of by informal adoption.

When, some years before, at the outset of Susan's association with Alex, her girlhood friend Amy Patterson had happened to encounter the two together and assumed the handsome young man to be Susan's illegitimate half-brother, Susan had let the mistake stand. It had seemed the simplest way of explaining Alex's presence in her life. She could hardly have told Amy that she and the young man were involved together in certain extra-legal pursuits of a lethal nature.

Or so she had felt at the time. Now she sometimes wondered if she might not have been better off if she had told Amy the truth at the beginning.

Of course Amy would not have believed her. Amy would have thought it was some sort of sick joke. She would have assumed that Susan had taken herself a young lover. Alex would not have been able to weasel his way into Amy's daughter's affections; certainly he would never have been able to marry her. There would never have been the joint enterprises that ensued: Tabor, Tinsley & Tabor (the stock brokerage) and Buckley Alexander and Baldwin Patterson Tabor (the twins).

And where would I be now? Susan asked herself. Would I still have fired the shot that made me famous? Well, it was all water over the bridgework, as a former acquaintance of hers, now dead—as so many of her former connections were wont to be—used to say.

Certainly neither she nor Alex would be sitting at breakfast in the Tabors' Fifth Avenue condominium, with the radio dispensing the news, more or less as background accompaniment, until the news of the death at the Kibandan Mission claimed their full attention. She was sorry she hadn't had the forethought to turn the radio off, or at least switch it to an all-music station, before they sat down to eat. She preferred not to hear about executions—particularly those she'd carried out herself—while she was eating.

"Actually it wasn't one of the guests who was killed," she pointed out to Alex, "it was the host's son, and he definitely was not one of the guests. Under the circumstances, it would have been in the worst possible taste for him to make an appearance at the reception."

There were those who had held that it was in the worst possible taste for the Kibandans to have held their reception at all under the circumstances. However, although Ambassador Upele had bowed to the quaint prejudices of the local natives to the extent of confining his son to quarters until the young man could be returned to Kibanda, he was not going to have his long-planned-for party spoiled by any such foolishness. He could not understand, he told a reporter from the news magazine *Today*, whom, because they shared a similar skin color, he mistakenly assumed to be sympathetic, why the Americans were making such a fuss over the rapes and, in one case, death (''accidental,'' the ambassador claimed, ''she should not have struggled'') of a few young women of such negligible importance, ''waitresses, word processors, women like that. It is sheer hypocrisy, of course, this to-do the Americans are making. The women were all black, like ourselves, and we know how Americans really feel about blacks. It is outrageous for us to be treated this way.''

The ambassador was even further outraged when his remarks appeared in *Today* (as well as in its Spanish language counterpart, *Hoy*, in which they sounded even worse) and were immediately picked up by the daily press and the broadcast media. ''It just goes to show that you cannot trust an American, no matter what the color of his skin,'' he said in another ill-advised interview.

The American public on its part had also been outraged; first when it learned of the rapes and murder; second when, even worse from its point of view, neither Willy Upele nor his father had the decency to evince the least sign of remorse. And Ambassador Upele's insult to American civil righteousness—that was the ultimate outrage.

Demonstrations were held outside the United Nations and candlelight vigils outside the Kibandan Mission, to the great inconvenience of the other inhabitants of that posh block in the East Sixties. What deterred them from their usual practice of protesting any threat to the comfortable course of their high-tax-paying lives was an understandable reluctance to let themselves be exposed to the charge of callous indifference toward human rights. It spoiled their image and made them especially vulnerable to attacks from members of the left-wing press like the New York *Times*.

''Although really,'' a sable-coated woman who had been walking her Sharpei said, when accosted by a reporter from Channel Seven, ''one would think we didn't have human rights, the same as anyone else.'' When he came home that evening and saw her on the eleven o'clock news, her husband, a prominent Wall Street lawyer, beat her so severely she needed medical attention, thus compromising his hopes for future political office. The Metropolitan Area—and, to a lesser degree, the nation, which was otherwise inclined to think of UN affairs as primarily the responsibility of New York and Washington and good riddance—demanded that Willy Upele be brought to justice.

But there was no way that Willy Upele could be brought to justice. As the son of Kibanda's ambassador to the United Nations, he could do anything he liked—rape, kill, steal, trade inside information, evade paying the fare on public transit—no matter how heinous the crime, the law was powerless to act against him. The most that could be done, except for candlelight vigils, demonstrations, and the odd rock thrown at mission limousines, was for the State Department to have him declared *persona non grata* and order him expelled from the country.

This was finally done—with great reluctance on the part of the State Department, which was anxious to keep on the good side of Kibanda, for that small third-world nation was of some strategic importance that was not immediately apparent to the ordinary citizen. Willy Upele was scheduled to fly back to Kibanda the day after the grand reception at the Mission. Which meant that this would be Susan's last chance to act.

There had been no problem in getting an invitation to the reception. As one of America's most distinguished living artists, Susan Melville was much in demand at top-level social occasions. She had only to pick and choose. She chose this one.

The day, rather, the evening, arrived. The handsome gray stone mansion in front of which Susan's rented limousine (insisted on by her business manager as necessary to her status) drew up had once, she recalled, as she and Alex got out, belonged to the Turloughs. In her youth she had suffered through many a soirée there. Now the last surviving member of that family had followed the rest into extinction, and, like so much American property, it had passed into the hands of aliens.

Currently it housed not only the Kibandan Mission to the United Nations, but also the ambassador's residence. This was not just for reasons of economy or even security, but also because it had proved impossible for the Kibandans to buy or even rent a suitable apartment for the ambassador anywhere in the city; and, presumably, they did not have the cash to expend on a townhouse. Few people, few countries even, did, the price of New York real estate being what it was these days.

No one, of course, would extend credit to the Kibandans. Diplomats, especially third-world diplomats, because of their extra-legal status, were not considered desirable debtors, tenants, or neighbors. If they did not choose to pay their rent or wrecked the place or held wild parties, they could not be held accountable. And so they had trouble finding suitable living quarters, unless they paid through the nose and in cash, and not always then. They claimed they were discriminated against. They were discriminated against, and rightly so.

The Kibandans put on an impressive show. On either side of the double doorway through which the guests were entering, there stood a Kibandan soldier, resplendent in a uniform that would have put a Park Avenue doorman to shame. Other decorative guards were posted inside, as the guests came into a reception area which, like that of so many impoverished third world nations, was a display of opulence run riot. They were announced by a functionary even more ornate than the soldiers, and herded toward the receiving line along which they must pass before they could get at the bar.

As soon as Alex's attention was engaged elsewhere, Susan slipped away. The place was as heavily guarded upstairs as it was down, but the guards in both areas seemed more for show than for protection. And she knew that no Kibandan guard, conditioned to regard all women except the young and nubile as invisible, would pay any attention to a well-dressed middle-aged lady blundering into the family's private quarters in search of a convenient ladies' room—which was the excuse she had prepared in case anyone challenged her.

No one did. The whole thing was ridiculously easy. Her only difficulty was how to determine which of the doors in the bedroom wing led to the young man's room, and that proved simple after all. No sooner had she slipped inside the wing behind the back of a guard who was engaged in making advances (or so she assumed, since she did not understand the language) to one of the Kibandan maids, when the strains of hard rock issuing at high volume from behind one of the closed doors left Susan in no doubt as to where her quarry lurked.

She opened the door and went inside. The young man—instantly recognizable from his photographs in the papers—was reclining on a pile of cushions, a dreamy expression on his face, a cigarette in his hand, the sweet scent of something that was not tobacco in the air. He didn't look up when she came in, but said something in Kibandan.

She said nothing in reply. The occasion, she felt, did not call for any exchange of the usual amenities. She simply took the gun out of her handbag and shot him.

It was all over so fast that when she rejoined Alex downstairs she knew he didn't have any suspicion that she had done anything more than powder her nose. Not then, anyhow. It was only the next morning, as she and Alex listened to the radio as they breakfasted that they heard the news of Willy Upele's demise; and Alex had leaped—jocularly, or so she hoped—to an all-too-accurate conclusion.

Susan was staying at Alex's apartment while her own place was being renovated. This was out of necessity rather than choice. For years she had resisted having her apartment redone to conform with her new status in life. She disliked being discommoded. However, the previous superintendent of the building in which she lived had been killed by a hit-and-run driver two years before; and, after several replacements that ranged from inadequate to catastrophic, the co-op board had engaged Adolfo Reyes, who certainly seemed better than his immediate predecessor, who had spoken little English and was given to physical attacks upon residents when he was under the influence of alcohol, which was often.

Just the same, Susan took an instant dislike to him. "Adolfo, indeed!" she complained to the chairman of the board. "The way he acts, he's more like an Adolph. Have you seen those little manifestoes he's started putting under the apartment doors?"

And she flourished a sheaf of papers under the long-suffering Mrs. Acacia's nose. "Attention, residents!" the uppermost one read, "It is forbidden to deposit garbages in front of the service entries except during ordained hours. Transgressors will be unflinchingly reported to the broad of directors."

"I know, I know," Mrs. Acacia said, waving them away. "I live here too, remember. Several of the other tenants have also spoken to me about these little memos of his. Personally, I think they're rather amusing; and, since I seem to be what he refers to as the broad of directors, I feel that, if I'm not bothered, no one else should be.''

Personally, Susan thought, Mrs. Acacia was easily amused.

''He told me he's only trying to instill some team spirit into the tenants,'' Mrs. Acacia said.

''I have no desire to be instilled with team spirit, no matter how the other tenants may feel.''

''Of course not, of course not. But after all, compromise is the name of the game, isn't it? He really is a superior employee, on the whole, although I grant you it does seem doubtful that he is, as he claims to be, a graduate of the University of La Pradera. Still, there isn't any reason for an apartment house superintendent to have a college degree, is there? In fact, it could be a drawback, because it would tend to make him dissatisfied with his position in life, and there's already too much of that going around.''

Even if the board had been interested in probing Adolfo's background, there was no way of proving or disproving his claim to a baccalaureate. The University of La Pradera had burned to the ground during a student revolt over a decade before, and all of its records, as well as a number of the students and a few faculty members, had perished in the flames. It had never been rebuilt. As Cristobal Herrero, El Gran Manumismo of La Pradera, had observed 130 years before, ''Education agitates the people; agitation educates the people.'' Mrs. Acacia couldn't have said it better herself.

''Remember,'' she told Susan, ''Adolfo is a refugee, an exile from his own country, a former freedom fighter against tyranny.''

''He told me he was a Marxist,'' Susan said.

''Oh dear, oh dear. Well, perhaps the word has a different connotation in Spanish. He has such splendid references, it's hard to believe. And you know it isn't easy to attract competent maintenance workers these days when there are so many good no-show jobs in private industry. Besides, Adolfo has so many capabilities. He's a plumber, an electrician, a carpenter, an air-conditioning expert. T̶̶̶̶̶̶̶̶̶̶̶̶̶̶ ̶̶̶̶ ̶̶en money he's going to save us."

But Susan didn't care how much mone̶̶̶̶ ̶̶̶̶̶̶̶̶ ̶̶g to save the co-op. There was something abou̶̶̶ ̶̶̶̶̶̶ ̶̶̶he didn't care for. A burly, black-mustached fello̶̶ ̶̶in his mid-fifties or thereabouts, he eyed each tenant as if he sensed a potential enemy (in which he was not, she supposed, far wrong; antagonism between resident and building superintendent was second only to antagonism between resident and landlord in the natural order of things, and this building had no landlord). Moreover, Adolfo lacked the deference appropriate to his station, although, at least at the start, he stopped short of actual rudeness.

He came close to it, though, when Susan (along with a number of the other tenants, as she found out later) refused to let him have a set of the keys to her apartment. She didn't like the way he'd demanded them as soon as he arrived. "If work needs to be done here, there will always be someone to let you in," she'd told him.

"But, Miss Melvilly, what if there should be an emergency event?"

"If there is an emergency event, you can break down the door and I'll pay for it. And the final *e* in Melville is silent."

He complained to Mrs. Acacia. "How can you call these cooperative apartments when the residents do not cooperate?"

"I tried to explain to him just what a co-op is," Mrs. Acacia said to Susan, "but it's hard to make it clear to someone whose first language isn't English. Sometimes it's hard to explain to someone whose first language is English."

Susan was not surprised when Adolfo's vaunted capabilities turned out to be not as great as advertised. Certainly they had not been up to the leaky pipe in the apartment above Susan's. It had burst while he was ministering to it, bringing down part of the ceiling and inundating a large part of the floor below.

Adolfo insisted that the fault was not his. "The pipe was

old. It was corroded. It should have been displaced long times before.''

"A licensed plumber would have realized the danger before he started working on the pipe," Susan told Mrs. Acacia.

Mrs. Acacia shook her head. "My dear, this is the third co-op board I've headed. I have had far more experience with plumbers than you. At least the accident isn't going to cost us as much as if we had been paying a plumber's hourly rate in addition to Adolfo's salary. And I'm sure your insurance will take care of any damages.''

"The building's insurance," Susan reminded her.

"Very well, then, our insurance." They smiled coldly at each other.

In any case, Susan's apartment was a wreck. Fortunately, some time before she had at long last given in to her business manager's importunities and rented space to use as a studio in one of the old loft buildings that still existed, though in ever diminishing numbers, on the fringes of the Upper East Side. Not for her the trendiness of Soho and adjacent areas, although she could well afford them. If she had to paint in a place other than her apartment, she wanted to be able to walk to work from there.

So her work in progress was safe (the main body of her work was stored in a fireproof, waterproof, bombproof Queens warehouse, again thanks to her business manager's insistence); and, although she wouldn't dream of saying as much to Mrs. Acacia, she had little else in the apartment that was of real value to her—little else that she could openly acknowledge, anyhow. Fortunately the locked suitcase on her closet shelf that contained the guns still remaining from her father's collection—together with a few state-of-the-art models she had picked up while attending a seminar on southern painters in Georgia; you never knew when a good gun might come in handy—was impervious to water and plaster dust.

She took it with her, along with her clothes, when she left for the Tabor apartment. The next day she came back to her own apartment and removed everything else personal she could salvage and stored it in her studio. The remainder she, with whatever assistance her housekeeper could give her in between bouts of hysteria, stuffed into boxes obtained from a local mover and left in the apartment. She tried to be careful, but she was in a hurry and, as she discovered later, she was not as careful as she should have been.

The furniture she left perforce. Much of it was damaged and would either have to be thrown out or taken away to be repaired. Anyhow, the really good old pieces had been sold in her days of penury; and what remained, together with the additions and replacements that she had been forced to make over the years, was not especially dear to her. The insurance would take care of all that. If only the co-op board would fire Adolfo, it would have been almost worth it.

But Mrs. Acacia made it plain that the board had no intention of firing Adolfo. Susan didn't want to push it, for fear that Mrs. Acacia would start wondering why the mild Miss Melville, who normally accepted all the co-op's decisions—rises in maintenance costs, new uniforms for the doormen, fish for the pool in the lobby (they kept disappearing, and it was suspected, though never proven, that old General Van Dongen in 14J was catching and eating them)—without a murmur, should take such a strong stand against someone who was after all nothing more than a head janitor, a servant, a menial.

She couldn't help wondering, herself: Would she have felt as strongly about Adolfo if he had not hailed from La Pradera? Could it be that his origin was prejudicing her in his disfavor?

She certainly hoped not, for she was opposed to prejudice, even when it was justified. Simply because a Praderan had killed her father didn't mean that all Praderans were murderers, any more than the fact that Adolfo was a Praderan meant that all Praderans were incompetent bumblers. Probably many Praderans were perfectly nice, decent people. For instance, that young painter who had introduced himself to her at the Art Students' League several months before the disaster to her apartment was a Praderan, and he turned out to be charming and intelligent and, she found out later, an accomplished artist as well.

She had gone down to the League to pick up her old friend Mimi von Schwabe (née Van Horn; then LaFleur, Livingston, Delvecchio, Tibbs, Carruthers, and Hunyadi, in increasingly rapid succession) for lunch. Mimi had been at the League to discuss plans for the Ball to Benefit Bulimic Artists which the Van Horn Foundation was sponsoring with a cohort of hers who was on the League's board. She and Susan were coming down the steps into Fifty-Seventh Street when the startlingly handsome young man had come up to them and hailed Susan by name: "Miss Melville—Susan Melville!"

And, when she had paused, not sure whether he might not be someone whom she had previously met and forgotten—although, as Mimi observed later, how could you possibly forget anyone who looked like that?—he had said, "My name is Gil Frias. I am an artist myself, and a great admirer of your work."

Oh, no, not another one of those, she thought. She gave him a courteous smile and was about to proceed on her way in spite of Mimi's tug on her sleeve, when he added, "I come from a little country called La Pradera; probably you've never heard of it," and she stopped dead in her tracks.

"But even there you are known and appreciated," he finished. They stood there for a moment, looking at each other.

"You come from La Pradera?" Mimi chirped, always ready to fill a conversational void. "Isn't that a coincidence. One of my maids comes from there. Or is it El Salvador? Some place like that, anyway."

The young man smiled. "Well, both countries are in the Southern Hemisphere, and Spanish is the official language of both."

"There, you see, Susan," Mimi said, "anyone might have mixed them up, so there's no reason for you to look daggers at me like that."

"No reason whatsoever," the young man said. "It's a perfectly natural error."

Oho, Susan thought, so it's Mimi he's after. The Van Horn

Foundation was known to give grants to deserving artists, and Mimi had been known to give further benefits to handsome young male artists, no matter what they deserved. A smooth operator like this one wouldn't walk up to her and say, "I've seen your picture in the society pages"—that would seem too obvious, to him, if not to Mimi—but he could say to Susan, as he was saying now, "I saw your picture in *Art News* last month, and I recognized you instantly, even though it didn't do you justice."

Her face must have shown that his last observation did not sit well with her, for he went on quickly, "I must apologize for the intrusion, but I'm such a fan of yours I couldn't help myself. I suppose you must hear that sort of thing all the time—such a bore for you."

Susan had been hearing that sort of thing ever since pictures of her began appearing in the art journals—and, occasionally the mass media. Not enough to be as troublesome as if she were a major celebrity, like a rock or movie star, but enough to be, as he put it, a bore.

Not in his case, however; not when it came to the second Praderan she had ever, to her knowledge, met. She was trying to think of something to say that would be encouraging without sounding eager, when once again Mimi took hold of the conversational reins. "I'm Mimi von Schwabe—the Van Horn Foundation, you know."

The young man gave her a polite smile, as if he had never heard of the Van Horn Foundation which was, of course, absurd. Anyone who had anything to do with art had heard of the Van Horn Foundation; anyone who had anything to do with money had heard of the Van Horn Foundation. Perhaps not a simple Praderan peasant, but he was hardly that. He was obviously an educated man. He spoke English almost without an accent and his manners were excellent. He had heard of the Van Horn Foundation all right.

"Susan and I were just going to lunch at Leatherstocking's, Señor . . . Frias, is it? . . . and we would be delighted if you would join us. As my guest, of course. Hands across the sea and all that."

"You are too kind," the young man said.

Susan was inclined to agree with him. "There isn't any sea between the United States and La Pradera," she pointed out.

"We could always hold hands across the Panama Canal," the young man said. "Ladies, I wish with all my heart that I could have lunch with you. There are so many things about this country that I find myself unable to understand and that you could perhaps explain to me." And he looked up at the rear end of the Cadillac that was hanging out over the entrance to the disco a few steps from where they were standing. I'm glad we won't be called upon to explain that, Susan thought. "However, to my infinite regret, I too have a luncheon engagement, for which I am already late."

"Couldn't you possibly postpone it?" Mimi suggested. She gave him an alluring smile.

He shook his beautiful head. "I would give anything if I could but, alas, duty calls. Perhaps another time." And he was off with a warm smile and a handclasp for each lady, leaving no time for any suggestion as to how that other time could be arranged. Perhaps she had misjudged him, Susan thought.

Both she and Mimi looked after him as he retreated. From the back he looked as good as he did from the front—tall, broad-shouldered, narrow-hipped, thoroughly wasted, Susan thought, on two middle-aged ladies, although Mimi would have been miffed to hear herself described in such terms after the fortunes she spent on plastic surgeons and cosmetologists. "Thank goodness he's not a hand-kisser," Susan said, forgetting for the moment that Gunther von Schwabe was a hand-kisser par excellence, but then he wore a monocle, so what could you expect? "He seems quite civilized," she added.

"And why shouldn't he be civilized?" Mimi demanded. "Just because he comes from some little South American country no one's ever heard of doesn't mean he has to be uncouth. Honestly, Susan, you're getting to be such a bigot. Some of my favorite people come from South America, although naturally they don't spend much time there."

"Naturally," Susan agreed.

◇◇◇ **III**

Maybe she was getting bigoted, Susan thought—about South America generally, about La Pradera specifically, about Adolfo Reyes emphatically. And she reminded herself that Adolfo, in spite of his drawbacks, was, as a refugee, perhaps as much an enemy of the country's president, the dreaded tyrant Relempago Martillo, as she was herself, although her enmity was personal and his political. However, as Cristobal Herrero had put it, "The friends of my enemies are always my enemies, but the enemies of my enemies are not always my friends."

She had come across Herrero's works after Alex, when in the mushy state peculiar to new fathers, had broken down and told her how her father had died some twenty-five years before. He had been killed in a South American country called La Pradera and it was that same Relempago Martillo who was said, on good authority, to have killed him.

Up until the time she joined Alex's organization, Susan never knew what had become of her father after he'd fled to Brazil in the late fifties, along with millions of U.S. dollars, most of which were not his own. His family had never heard from him again. Her mother had divorced him *in absentia*. He never tried to get in touch afterward. It seemed he had forgotten that he had a daughter, or, worse yet, remembered and didn't care.

That had hurt because she had been devoted to him. She had been so much more her father's child than her mother's. It was he who had taught her to shoot, and so it was to him she owed the skill with a gun that had led Alex to recruit her

15

as an assassin. At that time her prospective employer could not, of course, ask for references, but he had run a complete background check on her, using resources far beyond any that she (or any legitimate agency) could have commanded. They had known at the time how and why Buckley Melville had died, but all they had told her was that he was dead, without further details, probably not wanting to distract her from her work.

Buckley Melville had gotten to know Colonel (as he was then) Martillo while both were in exile in Brazil, and Martillo had somehow persuaded Melville to back his counter-revolution. Possibly he had convinced the American that it would be a sound financial investment—which it would have been had Melville lived to reclaim his IOUs, for the counter-revolution, which had been even bloodier than the precedent revolution, succeeded, leaving Martillo, who had promoted himself to general by this time, in sole and total control of the country.

As for Buckley Melville, he seemed to have vanished from the face of the earth. According to Martillo, in his book *Mi Lucha*, not published until the early seventies and not translated into English until some years later, Buckley Melville had died in the course of the fighting, "a true hero of the revolution."

But it was absurd, Susan knew, to think of her father as having espoused revolutionary principles; the only cause he had ever been known to espouse was that of his own self-interest. It was conceivable that he would have sponsored Martillo's revolution if he thought there was money to be made from it, but he would have been careful to stay well away from the fighting. In any case, by the time the English version of *Mi Lucha* came out, he had become so thoroughly forgotten that none of the media bothered to pick up on the brief reference to him. As for the book, like most books about South America, it had not sold well here, and was remaindered soon after its publication. It took a long time before a book search service could find her a copy and they charged the earth for it.

* * *

She discovered the book's existence when, as a sort of penance for the injustice she had done her parent in her mind, she went to the library and read all the books she could find which had anything about La Pradera past and present in them. She looked up La Pradera in the Almanac. Population, 17,652,000; area, 389,725 square miles; government, republic—in name, anyway; products, gold, gemstones, plastics, wool, fish, meat, cocoa, fertilizer; tourism, nil. She read as many magazines and newspapers as she could get through, scanning them for references to Martillo and La Pradera, all of which she carefully cut out. She did think of subscribing to a clipping service, but decided that she didn't want to draw attention to herself in this respect.

She also looked up early stories on him in back-issue periodicals and photocopied them. There hadn't been much direct material from La Pradera in the early years of the regime, for there had been a press blackout before the counter-revolution, during the counter-revolution, and for some years after the counter-revolution. Even today La Pradera did not subscribe to the principle of a free press. Foreign journalists who criticized the regime were still expelled from time to time, but with the utmost courtesy, especially if they hailed from the large western nations. Local journalists who attempted to do the same thing were given much shorter shrift.

Much more informative were the stories from exiles and escapees at the beginning, and later on, when enemies of the state were no longer exiled, from escapees only. They did not add up to a pretty picture of either the man or his regime. There was the story of how, soon after he had gained control of the country, there had been a revolt against the harshness of his rule by the very officers who had helped him return to power, and how it had been suppressed with equal harshness (a lie put forward by his political opponents, the Praderan press office said, and there was no way of disproving this, because all the officers concerned seemed to have disappeared). There was the story of how he had put down the uprising of the students (all communist agitators, the Praderan press office said) and built a plastics factory on the ashes of the university. There was the story of how he had exterminated (relocated, the press office said) the indigenous Indians (Marxists) and sold their land to developers (patriots). There was the story of how he had suppressed the revolt of the shepherds (KGB agents to a man) and confiscated the sheep (who appeared to be politically neutral, except for a few who were exposed as wolves).

Even if Martillo hadn't killed her father, he seemed to be responsible for the deaths of a lot of other, possibly more estimable, people. And the references to Melville that did occur in those earlier accounts all took it for granted that Martillo had murdered Melville. However, they were all very brief. There didn't seem to be too much interest in the gringo who had become mixed up with El General and presumably got what he deserved.

Although it seemed to her at first that she had amassed a great deal of material on Martillo, on reading it over she realized how scattered and scrappy and repetitive it was. Martillo was only one of a growing number of Latin American strongmen and most of the others were more colorful, with much more media appeal. If she learned Spanish and could read publications in that language, she might learn more about him but it seemed like too much of an effort for such a small potential gain.

She was curious to see the face of her father's killer. During the early years, photographs of Martillo were few and out of focus, for he always seemed to be on the move. As time went on and it became possible for him to stand still occasionally without being shot at, there were more and better pictures; but even the posed photographs had a curious blurriness about them, as if the earlier impressions by the camera had left the man himself slightly out of focus. He was tall, black-bearded, unsmiling—except when greeting visiting secretaries of state of the various U.S. presidents, to all of whom he was a devoted friend and ally, when he would expose a set of excellent teeth, or superb dentures. He always appeared in full, increasingly magnificent uniform, his eyes always veiled by dark glasses, as if he feared being blinded by his own effulgence.

All the pictures had been taken in La Pradera, for, once he regained power, he never left the country, probably remembering what had happened the last time he'd taken a vacation. At the time, he'd been a member of the ruling junta. He had gone to Brazil to enjoy the carnival festivities, leaving his wife and young family behind. While he was away, there had been a bloody revolution, in the course of which the other members of the junta were killed and the small country left in shambles, as it had so often been left ever since Herrero liberated it more than a century before.

Martillo had remained in exile in Brazil for several years before he returned to La Pradera in triumph. It seemed reasonable to assume that he did not choose to run the risk of a repeat performance by leaving the country again.

And so Buckley Melville's murderer prospered while he himself seemed to have been forgotten by everyone except his daughter. The CIA must have known what had happened to him (the CIA knows everything) and they might or might not have told the State Department. If they had, the State Department never let on. La Pradera was of strategic importance. The United States wanted General Martillo as an ally. And, for the twenty-five years that followed the counterrevolution, he had been one of the best friends the United States had in this hemisphere.

The United States had military and naval bases there. It used Praderan airstrips (most of which were U.S.-built) as freely as its own airstrips, Praderan harbors as freely as its own harbors. U.S. instructors trained the Praderan troops. U.S. troops held training exercises there. The CIA not only had its own building in downtown Ciudad Martillo but was even listed in the telephone directory. And Martillo's government pursued drug traffickers with a zeal that, as U.S. officials were wont to point out, put the other Latin American countries' anti-drug efforts to shame.

"Look at what Martillo's doing," one president was reported to have told the Colombian ambassador. "He not only arrests the drug dealers, he hangs, draws, and quarters 'em. That's what I call real cooperation." His press secretary later insisted that the president had said no such thing and that furthermore he had been quoted out of context.

Actually, if the president had said what had been claimed, he misspoke. Martillo did not hang, draw, and quarter his foes. He used even more colorful but indigenous methods. In the end, of course, the effect was the same.

All this time there was peace in La Pradera, except for the occasional student revolt (now only on the high-school level). Of course there were guerillas or freedom fighters in the mountains—there are guerillas or freedom fighters in the mountains of most Central and South American countries that have mountains—but nothing to speak of. Apparently they lacked the solid public relations infrastructure necessary for an effective guerilla movement.

The country thrived and its people multiplied. They would have multiplied even faster, except that anybody incautious enough to question the regime or offend it in some way or unfortunate enough to be related to someone who questioned the regime or offended it in some way was likely to disappear—to join the guerillas or to flee the country, if he or she were lucky, to disappear permanently, if he or she were not. Elections were held every few years and Relempago Martillo was always re-elected president by unanimous consent—no fiction, this, because over the years anyone who voted against him disappeared, thus doing away with the opposition.

Susan sympathized with the people of La Pradera, as any right-minded person should. But there were so many oppressed peoples these days, so many tyrannical rulers. It was impossible to feel personal distress over each one. So it was not for what he had done to La Pradera that Susan hated Martillo. Nor was it even for the fact that he had killed her father. A revolutionary must do what he has to do. No, Relempago Martillo had made her hate her father all these years, thinking he had forgotten her, when actually he had been dead all along. And that was why she hated Relempago Martillo.

One Christmas, Jill Turkel, formerly Susan's agent and now her business manager as well, had given Susan a set of leatherbound scrapbooks, companions to a more utilitarian file which Jill kept in her office, for Jill was a practical young woman and she did not trust her clients in mundane matters. Susan was supposed, Jill told her, to paste all the copies of clippings relating to herself and her works with which Jill would supply her in the books, together with any memorabilia that could be appropriately included, catalogues of exhibits, autographed photographs of anyone relevant and (more to the point) important, letters, memoranda, and the like. "It will enhance their value later," she said.

Jill was always thinking of the bottom line. Well, that's her job, Susan thought; that's why I'm paying her a substantial portion of my earnings. Just the same, I wish she wouldn't try to manage my life.

Jill had grown less troublesome in that respect since she'd married Andrew Mackay; not that marriage had mellowed her, but because she had more to distract her. Theirs was one of those commuter marriages so prevalent nowadays. He was based in Washington and she was based in New York; and, since his work called on him to be out of Washington as often as he was in it, he did not object to the arrangement—which otherwise he might have done, for he was a rather old-fashioned young man in many ways.

He had risen to become assistant director of the organization by which he was employed, an organization so hush-hush that few people knew of its existence, and nobody knew its name, except perhaps the people who worked for it, and Susan wasn't even sure of that. She knew about it only because she had first encountered Andy in his professional capacity. Otherwise she, like the rest of the world, would believe that he was employed by a nonprofit organization dealing with the problems of the homeless.

"When people hear that," Jill told Susan, "they don't want to hear any more, which is why he picked it as a cover." She sighed. "And now people think I went and married a do-gooder. The things one does for love."

At first Susan was going to stow the scrapbooks in the closet she reserved for unusable Christmas presents; then she had a better idea. She took them and pasted her Relempago Mar-

tillo clippings in them. It was, in its way, she supposed a
memorial to her father, the only memorial Buckley Melville
was likely to have. Unless . . . but she must not let herself
dream.

◇◇◇ **IV**

At any rate, thanks to Adolfo, Susan's apartment was now uninhabitable. If Peter had not been away attending that conference on the abominable snowman in Katmandu, the two of them probably would have taken a suite in a hotel for the duration of the repairs, despite her dislike of New York hotels; she had killed too many people there in her hit woman days to feel entirely comfortable as a guest. Even now, had she wished, she could have joined Peter in Nepal. The organization that was sponsoring the conference had extended a very cordial invitation for her to come to Katmandu.

An actual snowman she might have found of some interest, but she knew what conferences were like. Listening to a series of dull papers and looking at fuzzy slides was not her idea of a holiday, even though Peter told her Nepal had many other attractions, not the least of which was the weather. It was a delightful spot in which to spend the summer, he said, or so his prospective hosts informed him. "As the poem goes, 'Oh, to be in Nepal, now that August's here.' "

"It's, 'Oh, to be in England, now that April's here,' " she said indignantly.

"We must have been looking at different translations. Sure you won't change your mind? If you don't want to attend the actual sessions, you might like to paint the local flora. Or do a spot of mountain climbing. Mount Everest is right in the neighborhood."

"I'm strictly a studio painter. And mountain climbing has never been one of my hobbies."

"And I don't suppose the idea of yak rides would appeal to you either? No, I didn't think they would. Somehow I can't see you on a yak. I just thought I'd mention all these things since the people who are sponsoring this potlach, the—'' he consulted the letter in his hand ''—the Sasquatch Society, make such a point of them. Probably you wouldn't like it there.''

He kissed her goodbye and left. As he was leaving, she couldn't help notice that he was developing a bald spot at the back of his head.

Up until the time she had established Peter Franklin as head of the Melville Foundation for research into anthropology and whatever else he cared to investigate (a very small foundation designed mainly to keep him occupied and happy), the two of them had spent more time apart in the course of their long (nearly two decades) association than together. Peter was always going off on expeditions to remote areas of the world or taking posts at universities in equally remote spots, and their affection for one another had remained undiminished.

During the last year and a half, however, they had been together almost constantly, except for the time she spent at the studio and he at his offices; and, although her affection for him was still as strong as ever, the prospect of spending a few weeks without him did not disturb her unduly. She would miss him of course, and she did feel it would have been nice if he'd shown a little more regret at her refusal to accompany him. But then Peter had never been one for the social graces, at least, the graces of this society.

Had her apartment been destroyed before he left for Nepal, she might have gone with him no matter how she disliked conferences. Better the Katmandu Hilton with Peter than the New York Hilton alone. But there was no point following him at this late date. He must be getting ready to return to New York any day now. If she set out for Nepal, there was a good chance that their planes or trains or yaks would pass each other in the night, traveling in opposite directions. Much less trouble to accept Alex's offer to keep him company while Tinsley and the twins were away at a retreat in Northern California, endeavoring to find out who they had been in past lives—which scarcely seemed worthwhile in the case of the twins, since, being little more than a year old, they were barely aware of who they were now.

It would be for only a few weeks, she told herself. After all, her apartment wasn't being gutted, just restored to its original state, with a few added amenities. It didn't seem likely that a promising subject for termination would turn up during that time, at least not one who couldn't be tabled until after Peter's return. For she had been under no illusion that she would find it simple to carry out a mission under Alex's suspicious ex-professional eye or even behind his suspicious ex-professional back. It came as a shock to find herself faced with the need to kill Willy Upele almost immediately; but it never occurred to her to pass him up. It was not the Melville way to shirk one's duty, no matter what the inconvenience.

One of the reasons she'd accepted Alex's hospitality was that she'd felt sorry for him and wanted to offer what comfort her company could give. Motherhood had changed Tinsley even more than fatherhood had changed him. Under the influence of her younger sister Hebe, whom she had hitherto regarded with the affectionate contempt reserved for the family idiot, she had taken up New Age metaphysics with the same intensity she had hitherto devoted to supply-side economics.

Although away from home, she had left her aura behind in the shape of crystals of various sizes, most of them clear, but several in pastel tints of rose and topaz and aquamarine, hanging in the windows of the breakfast room—indeed, in all of the rooms—and all supposed to be radiating beneficent energies like mad, Alex explained.

"They're certainly very decorative," Susan said. "There is a grace in natural forms that art can seldom match. And the way some of them have been made into mobiles is quite ingenious, although the constant tinkling could become an irritant."

"It's driving me mad," Alex said. "Fée says that if one's spirit is harmoniously attuned the chiming balances the psyche."

"Well, my psyche is balanced," Susan said, "and I'm

sure yours is too, so why don't we take down the noisiest ones, just while Tinsley's not here.''

"Good idea," Alex said.

Apparently this simple solution had never occurred to him. Oh, Alex, Alex, what has happened to you, Susan thought, as he got up and took down the crystals.

"Just what are they supposed to do?" she asked, as he stored them in what she had supposed to be a particularly ugly piece of modern art, but which appeared to perform the function of an old-fashioned sideboard; she could see silverware and other appurtenances of the table inside.

"Heal, protect you from the evil eye or, as they put it, inharmonious influences, God knows," he said. "Whatever the New Agers want it to mean." He returned to his chair and contemplated his image in the polished side of the coffee pot without pleasure.

"By the way, who is this Fée you keep talking about?" she asked.

"Tinsley's guru or pet psychic. I don't know what you'd call her exactly. Definitions are unimportant, she said, when I tried to corner her. She channels.''

"Channels—how do you mean channels? Something to do with television?''

"She channels spirits of the past; in this case, the spirit of Nicolas Fouquet. He speaks through Fée like a medium. Only never call Fée a medium or she'll have a fit. This is New Age. Mediums are old hat. Tinsley's great-aunt used to consult a medium, she says.''

Susan smiled as old memories returned. "That's right, I remember old Miss Patterson. She used to wear tons of beads and skirts that never seemed to be the same length all round. Her medium used to summon up the spirit of Pocahontas— some Indian woman, anyway. They used to be very big on Indian spirit guides in those days. We used to think she was wacko. Old-fashioned term,'' she explained. "Before your time. And your place,'' she added.

She had nearly forgotten that Alex had been born someplace other than the United States—where, he always refused to say. By this time the last vestiges of accent had disappeared from his speech except once in a while when he got excited. But he was still not completely American; perhaps he never would be.

"But why Nicolas Fouquet, of all people?"

"He was Louis XIV's minister of finance. Jailed for looting the treasury, something like that."

"I know who he is, but why him? He's certainly not the type of person I'd think anyone would look to for spiritual guidance."

Alex shrugged. "I suppose Fée has to take what she can get by way of a spirit guide."

"Well, the whole thing sounds reasonably harmless to me. Unless this channeler has been bringing undue influence to bear on Tinsley." Difficult to think of anyone bringing undue influence to bear on Tinsley, but the tougher they were to crack on the outside, she knew, the mushier they were on the inside.

"Does Fouquet speak to Fée in French or in English?"

"English—with a French accent. I tried to talk to him—or her, depending on how you look at it—in French once, and I got thrown out. He—or she—said my aura was hostile."

He punctured a spear of asparagus with his fork. "Damn right it was. Because the whole thing isn't as harmless as it sounds. Fée's been giving Tinsley tips on the market; that is, Fouquet's been giving Tinsley tips on the market. And Tinsley's been following them."

"Oh, dear, that is serious. Have you—has the firm—lost a lot of money?"

"That's the hell of it; we've been making money hand over fist. Every stock Fouquet picked started soaring as soon as we bought it. How am I going to explain that to the Securities and Exchange Commission? It'll look to them as if we had inside information."

"Well, in a way you do."

He made a sound that was anything but harmoniously attuned.

* * *

It was at that point that the radio came out with the report of Willy Upele's death, and Alex, diverted from his domestic difficulties, accused his sister of having done the young man in. "You'll have to admit, it does seem rather a coincidence that he was killed at a reception where you were a guest."

"You were a guest there, too, Alex," she reminded him "and you've killed a lot more people than I have."

He winced. "I can't deny that, but I did it simply to make a living. I would kill anybody I was assigned to kill—without enthusiasm, without regret. It was a job. I wouldn't have killed anyone unless I was paid to do it. I may have been a criminal, but, by God, I was a professional."

"So was I."

"Professional? You! You were a rank amateur. You refused to kill anyone you didn't feel deserved to die; you call that professional? Frankly, at first I thought that moralistic attitude of yours was plain hypocrisy; you were just looking for some way to justify yourself in your own eyes so you could retain your self-image. Then, as time went on, and you turned down some perfectly good assignments, I began to realize that you actually had come to believe in what you were doing, that you thought of yourself as some sort of moral crusader."

"Nonsense," she said. "I was just doing my job, the same way you were doing yours."

Real crusaders, with armor and swords, were all right, particularly if they did their thing back in the Middle Ages. There had been a Melville at the Crusades with Richard Coeur de Lion, which made them acceptable. The Crusades, that was; the Melvilles were always acceptable. But moral crusades tended to be gross—earnest without necessarily being sincere. They didn't fit in at all with the Melville image.

"In fact, I had an idea that killing had become such a—a holy calling for you that you were almost sorry when you had to give it up; and that was why you went around yammering about needing fulfillment after you'd become successful as an artist, got everything you ever wanted, or what you claimed you ever wanted."

"Don't be ridiculous. I was glad when I found I could

earn my living with my brush instead of my gun. And I have never yammered in my life." She was insulted at the idea.

The housekeeper stalked in with a fresh batch of hot biscuits. Serenity was a New Age disciple, the previous housekeeper having left, because she couldn't, she said, stand the chiming and the howling. It wasn't clear whether the latter referred to the New Agers, who were given, Alex said, to chanting and other strange noises, or to the twins, who were merely given to strange noises.

Although somewhat outré in attire and otherworldly in manner, Serenity performed her duties satisfactorily; and, if her ways of working were sometimes strange—in order to clean the kitchen floor, for example, she would dance on it with small mops attached to her feet—at least she got the work done. Her own diet seemed to consist of various grasses, but she cooked whatever her employers desired without protest. "Each one of us has to work out his own nutritional destiny," she said.

"At least she's broad-minded about it," Alex said.

The previous housekeeper had not been broad-minded. She'd felt that there was only one way to do things: her way. Alex approved of Serenity, he told Susan. Having a servant who existed on another plane gave you privacy. And, thinking about Michelle, her own housekeeper, Susan was touched with envy.

In her youth, Susan had been accustomed to the ministrations of a full staff of servants. Then the family had lost its money along with its head and she had been reduced to the services of a part-time, off-the-books maid. When she became affluent again, she retired Nellie on a comfortable pension and took on a professional cleaning service. At first she welcomed its impersonality; however, she got fed up after a year or so of their doing things like taking all the bibelots from their various locations and grouping them together in one place, "For maximum dusting efficiency," the crew chief had explained when cornered. "Of course we could get through our work even faster if you didn't have any of this junk around at all. Minimalism is the key to happiness. Less is more.''

Whereupon, acting on that principle, she fired the lot of them and hired Michelle. Although adequate as housekeepers went these days, Michelle turned out to be far too inclined to think of herself as a member of the family, even a family of one, although it did bother her that Susan wasn't married to Peter. ''Just livin' together ain't right for high-class folks,'' she said.

Susan's affairs, she felt, were her affairs, Susan's income her income; at least she felt she deserved a larger share of it than she was getting. Unfortunately she had come across an art journal which had given the current prices Susan's work was getting. ''You mean you got two . . . hundred thousand dollars for that little pitcher, Miss Susan?'' she asked incredulously. ''Not that it's not a very nice pitcher, but two . . . hundred . . . thousand . . . dollars! And you're givin' me only four hundred dollars a week!''

Susan wanted to tell her that Jasper Johns got over four million dollars a picture, and she'd bet that his housekeeper didn't get any more than four hundred dollars a week, but she resisted the temptation. It would only lead to argument.

Michelle did have her advantages. She didn't move Susan's bric-a-brac around, largely because she never dusted it unless urged to do so, and she didn't steal, and she almost always remembered to call when she wasn't going to show up at work. She had a habit of turning the radio up full volume while she was working, regardless of whether Susan was at home or not, but she was finally persuaded, by a combination of bribes and threats, to wear a headset radio instead. The headset meant that she couldn't hear the telephone ring (not that she would when the radios were blasting away, anyhow), so Susan was forced to answer her own phone when she was home, or let the machine take all the calls when she was out or disinclined for conversation. Since Michelle had a habit of answering the phone with a snarled, ''Whaddya want,'' and tended to rely on a rather erratic memory to retain messages rather than write them down, this proved to be a plus rather than a minus in the long run.

Michelle didn't live in, but went home to her husband and family each evening, so Susan was able to retain a measure of privacy, although she never felt entirely free of Michelle, even when Michelle had left for the day. "It is bad to be alone in a crowd," Cristobal Herrero had written; "it is worse to feel crowded when alone." She knew exactly what he meant.

❖❖❖ **V**

Alex reached for a biscuit and started buttering it. He was still as handsome as ever, but it seemed to Susan that his once finely molded features were beginning to blur slightly. Was this actual fact or was she letting her perception of what he had been distort her view of what he had become?

"It might not have occurred to me that you could have anything to do with Willy Upele's death," Alex went on, as soon as Serenity padded out (she usually went barefoot, except on formal occasions or when she was mopping), "if it hadn't been for Lady Bellingham."

"Lady Bellingham?" Susan pretended to think. "Oh, that woman from one of the Caribbean islands—Epifania, wasn't it?—who was killed by her maid. What does she have to do with anything?"

"Come now, you're not going to tell me you don't remember the details? You were at that dinner where she was killed the same way Willy Upele was. Another coincidence, I suppose?"

Susan poured herself another cup of coffee with a steady hand. You needed to have a steady hand in her line of work. Painting. Of course Alex was bound to have taken note of her presence at the dinner—abortive dinner, that was, because Lady Bellingham had been discovered dead in her boudoir just before soup was due to be served, and naturally after that no one felt like eating. The guest list—at least its highlights—had been printed in all the papers.

"It doesn't seem like all that much of a coincidence to me," she said. "After all, I go to a lot of dinners. And there aren't that many ways of shooting a person."

32

"True. Just the same, it looks like your work somehow, especially considering what a monster Lady Bellingham seems to have been."

"But they know who killed her. That maid who disappeared. When the servants told people how badly Lady Bellingham had been treating them, they said she'd been especially brutal to that particular woman. And she never was found; don't you remember?"

"She must have gone back to Epifania," Alex said. "Or, more likely, vanished into the vast underground of illegal aliens here."

"Very probably," Susan agreed. But she knew better.

After Lady Bellingham's death, the press uncovered the nightmarish conditions prevailing below stairs in the Bellingham household. All the world now knew what Michelle had told her mistress some weeks before: Lady Bellingham had treated her servants like slaves, working them day and night, half-starving them, threatening them, beating them. They could not escape from the Bellingham townhouse, for Sir Robert (the title a relic of British colonial days) had kept their passports locked in the mission safe.

"For their own sakes," he told the media later. "They are such simple people, always losing things. I had no idea of what was going on at the house. I have been so busy with affairs of state, I hardly ever get home, except to sleep. Believe me, I am as shocked as you are."

The servants, having acquired a hotshot lawyer from one of the big Wall Street firms to take their case, *pro bono* for them, *pro gloria* for him, learned they had rights, and that their wrongs made their rights even more interesting to the great horror-loving American public. They talked. They talked their heads off. They told of all sorts of abominations . . . but apparently not one of them mentioned that the body of Belinda Cauldwell, the missing maid, lay buried beneath the cement floor of the mission sub-basement, whence she had been conveyed in the dead of night some weeks before; after Lady Bellingham, in a rage over the disappearance of an emerald bracelet (which later turned up in the toe of one of her 200 pairs of shoes) had battered her to death with a metal statuette. From Michelle's sketchy description of the murder weapon, Susan thought it might have been the Rodin bust of Norbert Rillieux, which had been one of the numerous items in the collection of the Epifanian Museum of Art that had disappeared twelve years before, during the overthrow of the previous regime.

"Reason they buried her in the mission is 'cause the townhouse don't have no diplomatic 'munity," Michelle said, "and the mission do. Even if folks knew for sure poor Linda's body was down there, ain't nothin' nobody can do 'bout it."

Although Michelle hailed from the Bronx, her husband was a man from Epifania. According to her, the whole Epifanian community was aware of what had been going on in the Bellingham townhouse, but were reluctant to speak up for fear they would jeopardize the safety not only of the Bellingham servants but their own relatives back on the island, and possibly themselves, many of whom were here illegally. Besides, Lady Bellingham was, as everyone conversant with such matters knew, a witch, and, if you were smart, "you didn't go 'round messin' with witches. You got to promise you won't say nothin' to nobody, Miss Susan," Michelle finished.

Susan promised and she kept her promise. She was not unaware that the story might have been completely fictitious, the kind of tale that servants fabricate about an unpopular employer. However, she felt instinctively that it was true. Not that she trusted her instincts—a Melville did not act on instinct—but she had already met Lady—"call me Clarice"—Bellingham at a cocktail party hosted by the Saul Steinbergs, and she was ready to believe anything of her, including the fact that she was a witch.

Lady Bellingham was an art collector of the worst sort, the kind who tries to get art for nothing or next to nothing by working on the artist's charitable instincts, compassion, religious beliefs, sense of fair play, thirst for publicity, love of country, fear of blackmail—whatever seems most likely to do the trick. "Epifania is a poor country, Susan—I may call you Susan, mayn't I? I feel as if we were old friends—and our little museum has such limited resources. We only dream of owning a Melville. But dreams sometimes do come true, don't they? Perhaps there is some early work on which you do not set so high a value that might fall within the limitations of our laughable little budget . . . ?"

"You'd have to talk to my business manager about that," Susan said. "I have an ironclad contract with her. She could sue me for everything I have if I so much as showed a picture to a prospective client without first consulting her."

"But I have spoken to your business manager," Lady Bellingham purred. "Such a charming girl. She said I might as well ask you to give me a painting, and I thought to myself: oh, what a splendid idea!"

Damn Jill, Susan thought between her teeth, doesn't she know better than to get sarcastic with the third world?

Lady Bellingham linked her arm through Susan's. The scent of *Opium* was strong. "I know how the Melvilles have always been noted for their altruism. Surely you can see how great the benefit of giving one of your pictures to the Epifanian Museum of Art would be, not only for Epifania but for you yourself. The publicity value alone would be beyond measure, believe me. Especially since you do have that Caribbean connection way back."

She was referring, Susan knew, to Black Buck Melville, the pirate, from whom the family fortunes had come. She wants me to feel guilty about him, Susan thought. But there's no reason as far as she's concerned. It hadn't been Epifanian ships Black Buck had looted and pillaged when he'd been one of the chief terrors of the Spanish Main. As a matter of fact, when you got right down to it, Lady Bellingham's ancestors had been part of the loot and pillage. Besides, whatever remained of the original Melville money had gone down the drain with Daddy. I am a self-made millionaire, Susan told herself, her pride tempered with the natural embarrassment of someone brought up on old money to find herself one of the *nouveau riche*.

She wasn't able to make her escape from Lady Bellingham

without giving her promise to attend the next dinner party at the Bellingham townhouse. I can always think of an excuse, she told herself—with regret, because she didn't like to be one of those people who accepted an invitation they had no intention of honoring.

The formal invitation had come several days later. Michelle saw the envelope with the Epifanian crest and that prompted her to tell Susan about Belinda's fate. "So you don't want to go to dinner parties with no folks like that, Miss Susan."

Oh, but I do, Susan thought. And she accepted the invitation, without saying anything to Michelle about it. No need for any explanation before the dinner and no occasion for explanation afterward.

Peter had been still in town then and pleased to escort her. As an anthropologist, he particularly enjoyed diplomatic "dos." It made him feel he was back in the field, he said.

Resplendent in crimson velvet, Lady Bellingham glittered with emeralds and diamonds as she greeted her guests. She declared herself overjoyed to see Susan. "I have something very special to show you that I do not want the rest of the guests to see," she whispered in Susan's ear, while Peter was shaking hands with Sir Robert and dismaying him with queries about reports of recent outbreaks of cannibalism in Epifania. "It's in my boudoir. As soon as Robert and I have finished receiving, you and I will slip upstairs and I'll show it to you."

"I can hardly wait," Susan said, trying not to pat the bulge in her evening bag.

Because of the spatial limitations of a Manhattan townhouse, Lady Bellingham's boudoir was smaller than it would have been at the palace of Versailles in Marie Antoinette's heyday, which was where it otherwise looked as if it belonged. Perhaps her decorator had gone a little overboard, but then Marie Antoinette's decorator hadn't been any slouch either.

What Lady Bellingham had to show Susan was a small painting by Renoir, which, she said, she had recently acquired on behalf of the Epifanian Museum of Art. "The reason I am being so hush-hush about it is that I don't want anybody to as much as know it exists until the official unveiling. It is my fondest hope that I could unveil a Susan Melville at the same time. It would really put the Epifanian Museum of Art on the cultural map, believe me.''

But the Epifanian Museum of Art had been solidly on the cultural map up until the present regime had come to power and so many of its treasures concurrently disappeared, thus reducing it to third-rate status. What was more, Susan recalled that Renoir's *Girl with Owl*, the picture now hanging on the brocaded wall of Lady Bellingham's boudoir, was one of the paintings that had vanished during the turbulence of the revolution. Some of the other art objects on view also looked suspiciously familiar.

Does she think I'm a fool, Susan wondered. Doesn't she know that there are reproductions of *Girl with Owl* in dozens of art books, as well as lists of all the art works that disappeared from the museum in archives everywhere? Apparently she thinks artists can't read. Or maybe it's that she never looks inside books herself.

Susan knew that there was small likelihood of either the actual Renoir's or the hoped-for Melville's ever reaching the walls of the Epifanian Museum. Both were destined to hang on the walls of the Bellingham townhouse until another coup overthrew the current Epifanian regime. Then the Bellinghams would seek asylum in the United States and most probably get it. They had many good friends in high places as well as vast private holdings here.

That might yet be Sir Robert's destiny, but Lady Bellingham had no destiny. Susan shot her in her own boudoir. Then she slipped downstairs, via the private stair through which they had gone up to the room, and returned to the other guests. Peter, dear Peter, was so absorbed in a conversation with the Swiss *chargé d'affaires*, he hadn't even noticed her absence.

After Lady Bellingham's body had been discovered, the police, treading carefully because all of the guests were important and a number had diplomatic immunity, took the guests' names and allowed them to leave. The next day it was discovered that the maid Belinda Cauldwell was missing. She was a person without importance or diplomatic immunity. It was taken for granted that she had committed the murder and fled.

Somehow, the police never learned that Belinda had been gone for weeks, not hours. Nor did they learn that her battered, bloodied body had been seen dead in Lady Bellingham's boudoir before her disappearance. Perhaps the servants' accounts were confused. Perhaps the servants felt that, if Belinda were known to have died long before Lady Bellingham, the police might start looking around for other people without importance and without diplomatic immunity on whom to pin the murder.

Or perhaps the servants had told the police what had happened to Belinda, and the police refused to hear. It was so much simpler and politically expedient (for Epifania, though small, was of strategic importance to the United States) to let the absent maid take the rap.

In any case, once the police and the press started poking into conditions at the Bellingham townhouse, the abysmal conditions under which the servants had been living could no longer be concealed. Neither could the existence of *Girl with Owl* and various other vanished Epifanian art treasures, which turned up all over the place. Sir Robert was recalled by his embarrassed government (under the circumstances, he could hardly ask for asylum in the United States) and the townhouse was put up for sale—on whose behalf Susan did not know. Or care.

◇◇◇ VI

So far, no one but Alex had seemed to see any connection between those two diplomatic dispatches—at least, as far as Susan knew. And even Alex hadn't had any idea that the death of the cultural attaché of the Takatakan mission in the street outside his Murray Hill apartment had been more than a simple political assassination. Although the man had been a proven child molester, he also had many enemies in the Takatakan opposition, as well as in his own party. Nor had anyone seemed to suspect that the death of the third secretary of the Maragayan mission had been caused by anyone other than one of the dealers whom he had been supplying with cocaine, which he imported via the diplomatic pouch.

As for the ambassador from Nyagalika, no one doubted that he had committed suicide by shooting himself on the edge of the East river; and that the gun, tumbling in after his body, must have been swept away by the current. The supposed reason for this self-destruction was remorse over having had his wives back in Nyagalika killed, so that he could marry an American woman who, as a confirmed Presbyterian, was opposed to both polygamy and divorce. Strictly speaking, Susan supposed, the crime did not fall within her province, as the actual executions had taken place in Nyagalika; but its origins were in New York, and it would have gone unpunished had she not taken a hand. As for the Presbyterian herself, the fact that Nyagalika, as a Moslem country, did not recognize their marriage at St. Thomas's, which meant that she would not fall heir to any part of her husband's vast fortune, was, Susan felt, punishment enough.

The reason that no one besides Alex had as yet made a

connection between the killings might have been that so far she had not killed anyone on the actual premises of the United Nations or even in its vicinity. This was pure chance. When she started, Susan had simply taken it for granted that all she would need to do was walk into the UN and pick off the erring diplomats as their misdeeds presented themselves to her attention. Had she given the matter more thought, she would have realized the obstacles that lay in the way of such a direct course of action.

In the first place, many of the diplomats concerned seldom if ever made their appearance at the UN or, indeed, at their respective missions. Others had diplomatic immunity only by virtue of their personal relationships, and not only had no business at the UN, but, in several instances, were *persona non grata* on the premises.

Those who did have business there were not readily gotten at. The metal detector at the visitors' entrance presented no problem. A child, providing he were a well-dressed upper-class child, could have taken a handgun through that. But a handgun wouldn't be of much use against anyone there, except the guides and gift shop attendants and, of course, the tourists. Delegates, staff, and visitors each came into the building through different entrances. Once inside, they were kept vast distances apart. It might be possible, Susan thought, to pot a delegate from the visitors' balcony of the General Assembly Hall with a sniper's rifle, but it would not be so easy to get a rifle past the metal detectors. Even had there been no metal detectors, it would be difficult to carry a rifle unobtrusively, even if it were in a disassembled state.

At first, in her innocence, she had planned to stand in the crowd outside the delegates' entrance and shoot the Nyaga-likan ambassador as he went past. She was not worried about the crowd; their eyes would be fixed on the delegates. She was not worried about the guards, either; their attention would be focused on the more sinister-looking elements in the crowd. She would just have to make sure that she was not standing next to anyone with a beard.

She picked a day when a demonstration was scheduled—

either the Israelis demonstrating against the Arabs or the Arabs demonstrating against the Israelis—so there was sure to be plenty of noise and distraction. She had anticipated the fact that the Nyagalikan ambassador might not show up on that particular day, or that he might be so surrounded by bodyguards or other delegates that she would not be able to get a clear shot at him. What she had not anticipated was that, owing to her extensive social life, a lot of the delegates would recognize her as they went past, and greet her: *"Jolly good to see you again, Miss Melville. . . ." "Ah, Mlle. Melville, que je suis ravi de vous voir. . . ." "Que maravillosa sorpresa encontrarme con usted, Srta. Melville. . . ." "Das trifft sich gut, Fraulein Melville. . . ." "Signorina Melville, còme sta?" "Apko yahan achanak deka kar bari khushi huee, Jenab Melville."*

Whereupon several tourists had asked for her autograph, on the principle that, if she knew all these important people, she must be someone important herself. Simplest to sign, so Susan signed. Later on they might find out, if they were lucky, what a prize they had captured. Chances were they wouldn't.

Since the purlieux of the UN were out, she had to kill her chosen diplomats here and there around town as each opportunity presented itself. She carried a gun with her all the time now, on the chance that an erring diplomat would come her way. From now on, however, she would have to be especially careful.

It did not matter so much that Alex's suspicions had been aroused; she had nothing to worry about from him except expostulation and impedance. He would not dare to expose her. He had too much to lose himself if she were exposed. It was the fact that he was suspicious that disturbed her. Sooner or later, other people were bound to get the idea that there was a serial killer of diplomats at work in the city. It was possible that this would make diplomats more careful about how they comported themselves, at least while they were in the city and its environs, and there might be no need for her further services.

On the other hand, if a connection between the killings

were made and it did not deter the diplomats from their evil ways, the police might try to determine—perhaps with a computer (she understood the police were getting very scientific these days)—who the killer's targets were likely to be in advance. She might get caught. She didn't want to get caught. She preferred not to become a martyr to her cause. It could be embarrassing.

She knew that any time she felt things starting to get hot, she could give up her good works, but she was reluctant to do that. The results made her feel good about herself in a way that the products she saw advertised on television as having that potential—hair coloring, cereals, soap—never could.

She had not been feeling good about herself for quite some time before she started moonlighting. She had felt uneasy ever since she had become successful as an artist. Although she knew that she merited her success, she also knew she had not achieved it through merit but hype; and, even though that's the way most success is achieved these days, she felt she must compensate somehow. Lady Bellingham would be right later when she would say that the Melvilles always had been noted for their altruism. Public spirit had been bred into Susan's bones. Giving large sums of money to charitable organizations which siphoned off a goodly share for their own support had been enough for her forebears. It was not enough for her. She wanted more than tax deductions, substantial though they might be. She wanted to serve humanity, directly, unequivocally, and personally.

And then Sam, the superintendent at her apartment house— old Sam, whom she had known since she was a girl—had been hit by a drunken driver one evening as he was out walking his dog. The dog had been so badly injured it had to be put away. Sam had been killed outright.

The driver turned out to be an attaché of the Boronian Mission. He could not be put in jail. He could not even have his driver's license revoked. "There's nothing anybody can do about it," Fred Burney, the lawyer who lived on the third floor of Susan's building and was reputed to have something to do with civil liberties although no one had ever caught him at it, told her. "He has diplomatic immunity."

"But that's monstrous! Surely they can't just let him go on killing people with his car."

Burney shrugged. "If there's enough of an outcry, the State Department could ask to have him sent back to Boronia. Or his government might be so embarrassed they'll recall or transfer him. That's the most you can hope for. It happens all the time."

And he told her of the many crimes diplomats had committed over the years with impunity. She had been aware of the worst of these, of course—the media had made much of them—but she had never appreciated the full scope of these misdeeds, nor had it occurred to her to add them all up. The cumulative total was chilling.

Nothing that can be done about it, eh? she thought. We'll see about that.

That night she took down the locked suitcase from the closet shelf and looked over the guns inside. All of them seemed to be in good working order. Pity she had no way of getting in some practice, but to join a local gun club might draw attention to herself, and she could hardly pot at a target in her apartment or even her studio. Once again, she couldn't ask Alex to go target shooting with her. He might have the time now, but he was bound to get suspicious of her motives. The old camaraderie was gone. She would be alone in this. Which was sad. Even the Lone Ranger, in spite of his name, had a Tonto.

She selected a gun and loaded it. She would have to trust to luck. After all, she hadn't shot a gun for some years before she made her first kill. But then, of course, landlords were easier to hit than diplomats, who were accustomed to evasive action. Luck was with her, although not in the way she had anticipated. Several weeks after Sam's death, that same attaché, barreling down Second Avenue in his Mercedes, ran a red light and crashed into an oncoming crosstown bus. None of the riders on the bus was injured, but the attaché was killed immediately. The bus was barely damaged, which was lucky because the Boronian Mission refused to pay the repair bill.

Fate had avenged Sam. But she felt let down. She had wanted to avenge him herself.

That was when the call came to her. Diplomats were always committing crimes. So were non-diplomats, of course, but it was no part of her plans to make up for the shortcomings of the police. It was up to them to do their jobs. That was what she paid taxes for. What she was going to do would be fill a vacuum. She was going to punish the otherwise unpunishable.

Where were the most diplomats to be found? In Washington, of course. She could move there, or take a place there. But she had always found Washington a singularly dreary city. She didn't want to live there, even on a part-time basis, and it would be difficult to work out of a hotel. The staff, all on the payroll of different government agencies as well as different governments—or so Andy Mackay had informed her—were always on the lookout for suspicious behavior. Even if she went to a different hotel each time she came to Washington, someone might notice that every time she came to stay in the city a diplomat died.

Andy had assured her that she would always be a welcome guest at his and Jill's Washington apartment whenever and for as long as she liked. "You have an inhibiting influence on Jill," he told her, "which is all to the good."

To which Jill made a face at him. The honeymoon was not yet over, but any minute it would be, and Susan didn't want to be caught in the thick of its aftermath. Moreover, it did not seem to her the wisest of ideas to operate out of the spare room of someone employed by an agency that, whatever its specific function, was definitely in the area of law enforcement.

So she decided to stay in New York and confine herself to United Nations personnel, although she would not rule out the possibility of taking pot shots at visiting diplomats from Washington who fitted her requirements, or of even going to

Washington, if an especially juicy target surfaced there. Above all, she wanted to remain flexible.

She made her plans. Minor crimes, such as shoplifting—frequent, since diplomats are a notably light-fingered lot—she would not attempt to deal with. Skill with the gun was her only form of expertise in this area; and she could hardly kill, say, a Bulgarian political officer for attempting to make off with a set of ladies' lingerie from Bloomingdale's or a Yemeni attaché for slipping a few ties under his burnoose at Brooks Brothers. And traffic violations, although the most common crime of all, didn't quite deserve the death penalty.

She did toy with the idea of sticking sharp objects in the tires of diplomats who left their cars where natives feared to park—but, no, that would be childish. The same applied to attaching hard-to-remove stickers that said, "Diplo, go home." It was death, not dirty tricks, that was going to be her area of operations.

VII

She read the papers. She listened to the news on the radio and watched it on television. She went to as many diplomatic gatherings as she could gain access to, although she was already, as she had learned, familiar with most of the ranking diplomats in the city, and she kept running into them at the usual party places, like the Metropolitan Museum of Art, the Forty-second Street Library, and the General Assembly Hall of the United Nations itself, for there was no institution in New York City that could not be used as the setting for a gala, given the appropriate inducements. In fact, Gisela Pfifferling, Gunther's niece, and a diplomatic spouse in her own right, had expressed surprise that the Forty-second Street Library was also a functioning book repository. "I thought it was just a place where they held parties," she said.

Susan had long since given up her early scruples about killing people with whom she was personally acquainted. If she met her potential targets while they were presumed innocent, it would be easier to sneak up on them when they were found guilty. But, although she met a lot more diplomats, many from countries she had never heard of, she did not succeed in meeting any diplomats from La Pradera. They were, or appeared to be, a quiet, sober, diligent lot, who behaved with the utmost correctness toward their host city. They never, so she was told, got drunk or misbehaved at the diplomatic functions of other countries, and their own parties were such models of restraint that nobody went to them unless protocol made it obligatory. They seldom mixed with the ruling social circles of New York, and were never seen at benefits and galas; although, Mimi informed Susan later, when the Praderan question came up, the Praderan Government always sent a generous check every time they were solicited for funds.

Even though it didn't seem likely that Susan would ever have reason to kill one of these exemplary individuals, she was anxious to meet them. Through them, she felt, she might be able to meet, or at least reach, their president, for, she finally had to admit to herself, her secret heart's desire was to kill him. True, she had taken a stand in her mind against killing for personal reasons. So far, she'd been lucky. On both occasions when she had lapsed, she had advanced her career. But it was too easy to go astray. You started with the building superintendent, then the postman, then the supermarket clerk, and before long you found yourself walking down Madison Avenue guns blazing. But surely Martillo's crimes against humanity were heinous enough so that she could stretch a point and knock him off, even though he had committed no crimes on American soil.

She was well aware that as long as he stayed in his own country she could become bosom buddies with Ambassador Yepez in New York (or Ambassador Nuñez in Washington) and it still wouldn't get her any closer to him. However, it would give her an in if she ever went to La Pradera, for it had occurred to her that, if all else failed, she could go down there on a shooting trip. At the same time, she knew that if she went simply as a tourist it was unlikely that she would have a chance to get near him. Foreigners were not allowed to move around freely in La Pradera; natives were not allowed to move around freely in La Pradera; in fact, nobody was allowed to move around freely in La Pradera.

On the other hand, if she traveled down there, armed with letters of introduction from his ambassador and other high-ranking Praderan diplomats, she was bound to be invited to the presidential palace for, at the very least, a reception, or, if she was lucky, a dinner. It was not equally certain though that she would be able to leave as unobtrusively as she came. And she was not ready for a suicide mission. There were too many paintings to be painted, too many diplomats to be killed.

* * *

Just the same, it was worthwhile getting to know the Praderan diplomats, even if she did not plan to go to La Pradera in the immediate future, even if she never went there at all. What if Martillo hadn't left the country for twenty-five years, she told herself. That didn't mean he would never leave it. One day he would come to New York (unless he was leaving La Pradera permanently, in which case he would head for Miami) where she, by then already entrenched in Praderan diplomatic circles, would be invited to a dinner or a reception or a grand ball in his honor, and be able to kill him at her convenience.

If anyone could arrange an introduction to the Praderan Ambassador to the UN, it would be Mimi. Ever since she had married Gunther, she had become one of the city's leading diplomatic hostesses, in fact, one of the nation's leading diplomatic hostesses, for she had bought a house in Georgetown simply to establish herself as a presence in the nation's capital. It was through Mimi that Susan had obtained her invitation to the Liberation Day Fête at the Zagrovian Mission, after which the senior delegate had been found in the garden, shot dead, people supposed, by a discarded lover or an unpaid debtor or an angry neighbor or a grieving parent, for he was a man of many vices.

It was unfortunate that Susan had had the bad luck to have Mimi run into her while Susan was having tea with Gil Frias at the Museum of Modern Art, one afternoon, the week after she and Mimi had met him outside the Art Students League. She could tell from Mimi's face that Mimi had leaped to one of two erroneous conclusions—either that Gil was sucking up (vile expression, but that was the way Mimi would think) to Susan, in order to get a sponsor with her prestige and wealth (modest affluence, in Mimi's eyes) or that Susan was attempting to entice the young man by dangling her prestige and wealth before his eyes. It would not have occurred to Mimi that Gil could possibly like Susan for herself alone, and, to tell the truth, it would not have occurred to Susan either. Just the same, she wished she could tell Mimi straight out what Gil had just told her, that he already had a wealthy and prestigious sponsor, none other than Relempago Martillo.

This did not come as the shock it might otherwise have been, because she had checked the young man out with Jill right after she'd met him; why, she didn't know, since she'd had no real expectation of ever seeing him again. Curiosity, perhaps.

Jill had come back with the information that he was quite well known as an artist, even beyond the borders of his own country. In fact, he was the only contemporary Praderan artist, to Jill's knowledge, to have made it beyond the borders of his own country, either by reputation or in person. In addition, next month he had a one-man show scheduled at the Fothergill, one of the oldest and most prestigious galleries in the city, "So somebody up there must like him—either God or that guy who runs the country, Murillo, or whatever his name is." Susan didn't correct her for fear of betraying too intimate a knowledge of the country and its affairs. Jill was not only sharp but nosy, a deadly combination.

"Why are you interested in this fellow, Susan? Thinking of adopting him? His bio (I got a look at an advance copy of the catalogue from Sonny Fothergill) says his parents were killed in one of those revolutions they're always having in those parts, which makes him an orphan; and, since it doesn't say anything about anybody having adopted him, he's presumably available."

"He picked Mimi and me up at the Art Students' League," Susan explained, "and I wanted to make sure he was on the level. You know how Mimi is about young artists."

"Especially young con artists. Good-looking guy, is he?"

"I suppose so. In a Latin way."

"Swarthy and sexy, eh?" Susan started to protest; then thought better of it. "Mimi better watch out," Jill said with relish. "That new husband of hers isn't the type to take kindly to having his wife play around. You know what these Mittel-Europeans are like. If he caught her making eyes at some pretty boy, he'd probably strangle her or run her through with his sword or something medieval like that."

She warmed to her topic. "And he could get away with it, too. He has diplomatic immunity. If he terminated his bride, the most the government—our government—could do is ask to have him recalled to Austria."

"But surely the Austrians would—?"

"Don't count on it. Look at what they didn't do about Waldheim. Bunch of Fascists. I wonder how far this diplomatic immunity goes," she went on cheerfully. "Do you suppose Gunther would inherit her money if he killed her, claimed diplomatic immunity, and went back to Austria?"

"Stop it, Jill. You sound positively ghoulish."

Jill patted her on the shoulder. "You mustn't be so sensitive, Susan. This is a brutal world we live in. If Gunther kills Mimi, maybe somebody will kill Gunther. There seems to be a lot of that going on nowadays in diplomatic circles."

Oh, dear, Susan thought. She'd known that sooner or later the public would start taking notice, but she had hoped it would be later.

VIII

Susan had not met Gil at the museum by chance that day. They had met by prearrangement. The previous afternoon her phone had rung, and, "This is Gil Frias," a slightly-accented voice said. "I'm sure you won't remember me, but I spoke to you at the Art Students' League last week."

And, when she did not reply immediately, "The artist from La Pradera . . . ?"

"Oh, yes, I remember you," Susan said.

"I know this is terribly presumptuous of me, but I know very few people in the New York art world. There is no one to whom I can turn for advice about my career. I wondered whether you would have tea with me at the Museum of Modern Art."

Susan knew why he had chosen the Museum of Modern Art. It seemed so respectable, so innocuous, a place where a middle-aged spinster would join a strange young man without a qualm, or just enough of a qualm to make the occasion intriguing.

And it certainly was presumptuous of him to call up a near stranger, let alone an artist of her stature, to ask for advice about his career. Why was he doing it, anyway? He was an established artist in his own country; he was being sponsored by his government; he had a show coming up at one of the most prestigious galleries in New York. As far as she could see, he stood in no need of her or anyone else's advice.

But she would have tea with him. If he knew General Martillo, if he had any kind of connection with General Martillo, she was as anxious to cultivate him as he seemed anxious to cultivate her. Pity he'd chosen that particular spot, though. MOMA was one of Mimi's regular stamping grounds. It would be awkward if Mimi came upon them there.

And her fears had been realized. Mimi had come upon them there. Now she would go around telling everyone Susan Melville had been keeping a rendezvous with a handsome young artist. Well, better than an ugly old one, like the one Mimi had in tow at that moment, Susan thought.

"You know you don't need me to give you any advice about your career," she told Gil, after Mimi had come and gone in a billow of pique. "You're already a famous artist, and you're having a show at the Fotheringay. What more could you want?"

He gave her a smile that would have turned Mimi into a quivering jelly. "I am honored that a busy and important person like you should have taken the trouble to investigate my background."

"My agent did that," Susan improvised. "I happened to mention you to her. She's always looking for business."

He gave her a searching glance. "And she convinced you that I am not a—a phony?"

"She convinced me that you're an established artist," Susan said with a smile.

After a moment, he smiled too. "It's true that I am not without appreciators in my own part of the globe. But New York is the art capital of the world, and here I am unknown. Until I establish myself in New York, I will feel that I am merely a provincial painter. Dare I hope that you will help me to establish myself in New York, dear Miss Melville— may I call you Susan in that charmingly informal way you North Americans have?"

And he looked at her so meltingly that a pair of young women who had been sitting at a table close by casting admiring glances at Gil snorted. Susan wished she could tell them in her charmingly informal way that her paintings were hanging on the museum's walls at that very minute, but that would impress them only if they were art lovers. And they did not look like art lovers. They looked like young women who had come to the museum to pick up young men.

Well, they're not going to pick up Gil, Susan thought. He wants something from me, and, whatever it is, he's not going to risk it by flirting with them. Not, to do him justice, that he seemed even to have noticed them.

She picked her words with care. "I understand that General Martillo himself is one of your appreciators."

"President Martillo," the young man corrected her. "Now that we are a democracy, he no longer uses his military title. Yes, he has been kind enough to take an interest in me and my work."

"I didn't know he was interested in the arts." There had been no mention of any cultural inclinations on Martillo's part in anything she had read. But then, there had been nothing to indicate that he was an uncivilized boor, either. A monster, yes, but not a boor.

"Oh, he is passionately interested in the arts," Gil declared, buttering a muffin with all the passion he had ascribed to his mentor, "and it has always made him sad that La Pradera has no culture of its own. We have no literature, no music, practically no art."

He should have thought of that before he got rid of the writers, the musicians, and the artists, she thought.

"So, when he discovered, when I was very young, that I had a talent for painting, he became my patron and saw to it that I had the best teachers available, which," he said with a rueful grin, "in La Pradera was not so very much. But later I was sent to study in Mexico City."

"How did he happen to come across you and your talent?" Susan asked.

Gil looked embarrassed. "He found me in an orphanage. He had me taken from there and made sure that I had a good home and a good education." His voice quivered with emotion. "He has been like a father to me." He picked up a tea sandwich.

But this was wonderful: the direct link she had wanted delivered right into her hands. She tried not to show her elation. "Then you must know him very well."

He swallowed the sandwich in a gulp. "Not well, not well

at all. That is, if you mean do I know him well personally.
When I said he was like a father to me I meant it more as
if—as if he was the father of his country and we are all his
children.''

Now she had to try not to show her disappointment. "Then
you don't know him personally?" She knew she should get
up and say, well, it was nice meeting him but she really had
to get back to the studio, but she felt reluctant somehow.

Then he said, "Oh, I've met him, of course, receptions,
openings, closings, things like that," and she settled back in
her mind. "What's he like?" she asked. "The media don't
paint a very flattering picture of him."

"The media! Always looking to make trouble. It seems to
me they are more interested in sensation than truth. Oh, I
won't deny that he can sometimes be a little harsh, but that
is necessary in a country that, in spite of all the advances
we've made, is still so backward, so primitive. But nowhere
near as backward and primitive as it used to be before he
took over. He has done so much for La Pradera, but there
are always those ready to bite the hand that feeds them."

He went on to tell her in more detail than she wished about
the wonderful things Martillo had done for the country. Natural enough he should feel that way, she supposed, considering how much Martillo had done for him. Probably one of
the reasons he'd been sent up here was as a public relations
ploy, to try to improve the country's image. And not a bad
idea either, sending up an orphan artist whom *El Presidente*
had taken under his wing. I suppose if he generates enough
goodwill, they'll send up an orphaned singer and an orphaned poet and then perhaps an orphaned tennis player.
God knows they have plenty of orphans there.

"I know they say terrible things about *El Presidente*, but
they are all lies, spread by his enemies, who will stop at
nothing to discredit him."

And I'm one of those enemies, she thought, although dis-
crediting him is not precisely my aim.

"He is such a good man," Gil persisted, "so kind, so
generous, so charming, so—so fond of children and animals."

She could hear the Praderan P.R. man say as he briefed Gil for his goodwill mission, "Tell them *El Presidente* likes children and animals. It's a sure way to make Americans roll over and wave their paws."

"I know that if only you knew him you would love him as much as we Praderans do," Gil concluded.

I'll bet, she thought. But he had given her an opening, and she took it. "Perhaps I would. Perhaps some day very soon I will visit La Pradera and you will introduce me to him, and I could start learning to love him the way the Praderans do. What I mean is," she went on quickly, fearing that last could be misconstrued as sarcasm, "I've heard so little about your country, I'd like to know more."

Gil drained his cup of tea as if it held a much stronger beverage. "It would be my pleasure to show you around one day, and take you to meet our president. But right now the country is not ready to welcome tourists. We don't have a really first-class hotel and the streets are dangerous—mudslides, crime, Communists—you know how it is with a developing country."

"Really, I'm not at all fussy. . . ."

He shook his head. "Not yet. Besides, if my show is a success, I myself will not be going back there for a long time."

He leaned forward. "I am so anxious for my show to be a success, Susan, for my country's sake, as well as my own, and I hope you will help me."

After that, it came as somewhat of an anticlimax to find out that all he wanted was for her to come to the opening of his show. She couldn't help remembering what had happened to Rafael Hoffmann when she had attended his opening. But she had attended many openings since then and none of the artists had died, except perhaps in the press. And Gil wasn't asking her to make a speech, just to be there.

She told him she'd be delighted to come. And she was telling the truth. The Praderan diplomats were bound to be there *en masse*, and she would be able to meet them all at once. She was happy to give him her address, so that he could send her a formal invitation. In a surge of benevolence, she suggested that he might also like to send an invitation to Mimi. "She's very influential in the art world." And she gave him the names of a few other people to whom he might like to send invitations, including Jill—not that Susan was especially anxious to have her there, but she didn't want her wondering why she hadn't been invited.

"You're very kind," Gil said, taking down the information with an air of polite gratitude that made it clear he had no idea of the enormous favor she was conferring on him. "We had better exchange phone numbers, too, in case you think of anyone else whom I should invite, or I should find it necessary to consult you for some reason. If you don't mind, that is."

"I don't mind," she said. She gave him her telephone number. It was only after they had parted that she remembered he already must have her number, or how else could he have called her to begin with. It was unlisted, too. Where could he have gotten it from? But that wasn't really too hard to explain; there were plenty of people in the art world who knew it.

To her disappointment, as far as she could tell, none of the Praderan diplomats showed up at Gil's opening. Only the usual art crowd was there—diplomats, yes, but the wrong ones.

She expressed her surprise. Gil shrugged and said no doubt the people from the mission would come and take a duty look in due course, but it still seemed odd to her. Another thing that seemed odd—"I thought you didn't know anyone in New York art circles . . . ?"

Gil laughed. "The gallery sent out all the invitations. I don't know anyone here except you, Susan. And, of course, Baroness von Schwabe."

Mimi had arrived in full fig, arrayed in a green gown topped by a strange construction of gold and emeralds that started on her shoulders, encircled her neck, and ended with a group of what looked like feelers springing from the top of her head and vibrating with every movement. She was alone; Gunther had been called to Washington, she said.

Jill also hadn't been able to make it; she hadn't been able to leave Washington, she told Susan on the phone. "Sorry to have to miss your protegé's opening, and so is Andy. He was very anxious to come; I don't know why. He's never made himself out to be an art lover before."

"He's not my protegé," Susan said.

Mimi immediately tried to take over Gil, as if by divine right, but he stayed so determinedly at Susan's side it was a little embarrassing. Finally, after Mimi's eyes had impaled her from a dozen different directions, Susan pleaded a dinner engagement, and left, leaving Gil to Mimi's mercies. He's a big boy, she thought; he can take care of himself. And I have to give Mimi her chance. Since the Praderan diplomats hadn't shown up at Gil's opening, it would have to be back to square one as far as getting to meet them was concerned. And square one was Mimi.

⬡⬡⬡ IX

She let a few days go by. Then, one evening at the conclusion of dinner with the von Schwabes at their apartment—Mimi's apartment, actually, which had taken on a subtly overstuffed Mittel-European look ever since her marriage to Gunther—she finally broached the topic.

"The Praderans!" Gunther repeated. "Why on earth would you want to meet them? They are barbarians, boors, *lumpen*. . . ." He popped an entire cream puff into his mouth and continued to speak, even more glutinously, "*Gott im Himmel*, they think books are for starting bonfires, and they cannot even speak their own language properly. I was posted in Ciudad Martillo years ago, when I was very junior, and the place was dead, I tell you, dead. Nothing to do but watch the public executions. Then the death penalty was eliminated and they went private. . . ."

He shook his head sadly and wiped cream off his mustache.

"She isn't interested in all the Praderans, dearest," Mimi said with malignant archness. "Only in one Praderan—that handsome young artist friend of hers. He is quite something, I must admit, but why you should feel you need to meet his ambassador, Susan, is beyond me. Unless you feel that you need his blessing before you—er—start anything with the young man."

"Don't be ridiculous, Mimi. I haven't the least desire to 'er—start anything,' as you put it, and, if I did, I wouldn't need anyone's blessing." So Mimi hadn't been able to make any time with Gil. Susan felt a sense of quiet satisfaction.

"I am surprised, Susan," Gunther said, with a heavy Teutonic smirk. "I would have thought you were too sensible a woman to make a fool of yourself over a young man, at your time of life especially."

Susan wanted to kick Gunther. She wanted to point out to him that not only was she personally not interested in Gil— at least, not in that way—but that she was at exactly the same time of life as Mimi, and that Mimi's last husband and the penultimate one before that both had been considerably Mimi's junior.

But she wanted to conciliate both of the von Schwabes; she needed them. "Oh, Gunther, you're being as ridiculous as Mimi," she said, with a coyness worthy of Mimi herself.

"And what does the good Peter think of this?"

"The good Peter flew out to Katmandu for a conference last week," Mimi told him.

"Aha!" Gunther cried. Susan wanted to do more than kick him. "But even if you are interested in this young man, why do you want to meet his ambassador? When I met Mimi at the Hapsburg Hop in Toronto and fell instantly in love with her, I did not immediately seek out the acquaintance of the American ambassador. It is true that I was already acquainted with him, but, if I had not been, I should not have wished to know him. As a matter of fact—" he paused "—well, I am a diplomat; I must be diplomatic." He surveyed the pastry plate through his monocle, and, after some deliberation, chose an éclair.

"My interest in La Pradera has nothing to do with Gil Frias," Susan said. "It's . . ." She tried to think of a good reason for being interested in La Pradera. ". . . it's just that Mimi made me feel bad right after we met Señor Frias, when she said I was bigoted about South Americans, just because I had some rather unpleasant experiences with some of them. And I determined to do something about it."

"Did I make you feel bad?" Mimi beamed. "I'm so glad. What I mean is, I'm glad you took my words to heart. Sometimes I feel you don't pay attention to anything I say."

"But why shouldn't Susan be bigoted about South Americans?" Gunther demanded. "She is not a diplomat. She lives in a democracy, in a country that has a Bill of Rights, freedom of speech, and all that *schnitzel*."

"It doesn't give me the right to be bigoted," Susan said.

Gunther took a large wedge of Sachertorte. Really, Susan thought, the man is going to swell up like a balloon and burst and I hope I'm there to see it. "You mean that you're allowed to say whatever you like, but you are not allowed to think whatever you like?"

Mimi and Susan exchanged glances. There were some things that foreigners never seemed to be able to understand.

"I decided it was my duty to find out more about—about our Latin American friends," Susan said (Gunther snorted), "and, since both the superintendent of the building I live in and Señor Frias come from La Pradera, and I discovered I knew nothing whatsoever about that country, I thought it was as good a place to start as any. And I'd hoped that you'd be able to help me, since you know everybody."

"Brazil or Argentina would be easier," Mimi mused. "I know so many more people from there; but then, of course, you know most of them too. I understand, you want a country you can really get your teeth into. Well, I'll see what I can do."

A couple of days later she called, and, after telling Susan about Ariel Slocum's latest exploit, which gave even Susan pause, she said, "You remember you wanted to meet some Praderan diplomats? Well, you know Margarita Labarca?"

"The woman who designs that weird—jewelry, I suppose you'd call it? Is she a Praderan?"

"She's Argentinian, and I think her stuff is lovely. That construction I wore to Señor Frias's opening was a Labarca."

"I must have been thinking of someone else," Susan said.

"She and her husband, Florencio—he's either an importer or exporter, I'm not sure which—pots of money, though— have an apartment in the same building as the Praderan ambassador. And not only does he have a lot to do with La Pradera in a business way, but Margarita and the ambassador's wife are second cousins—which is how the Yepezes came to get the apartment. And I think you're being unfair to Margarita. She's won all kinds of awards for her work, and she's a great admirer of yours. I know that if you ordered a piece from her, you could get it for next to nothing.'' Like most rich people, Mimi had deep pockets of cheapness.

"Then Sra. Yepez is an Argentinian?''

"Maybe. Or maybe her family is. I've never met her, so I wouldn't know. Anyhow, I have a wonderful idea. I'll ask Margarita and Florencio to dinner, and I'll also ask Ambassador Yepez and his wife and a few more people to make the evening interesting.''

She paused and went on, sounding very casual, "Perhaps you'd like to bring Señor Frias along, since he is a Praderan. What do you say?''

Susan suppressed her excitement. It would not do for Mimi to know how important this was to her. "That would be very nice. And it's kind of you to ask Señor Frias. Every young artist needs a helping hand, and I'm sure he'll be very grateful to you.''

There was no guarantee that the Yepezes would accept, Susan knew, but, even if they didn't, making the acquaintance of Margarita Labarca would be an in of a sort. If I order a dress from her, Susan thought, I don't see how, if I express an interest, she can avoid introducing me to her cousin. Then I can give a dinner to which I'll invite the Yepezes as well as the Labarcas (and, I suppose, the von Schwabes, unless I can manage to pick a date on which they'll be in Washington). Little by little I should become solidly entrenched in Praderan circles, and ready for the kill.

But, of course, her apartment disaster occurred before she could do any entertaining, so she had to postpone her plans. There's no hurry, she told herself, not realizing that there was all the hurry in the world.

The Yepezes did accept Mimi's invitation, much to Gunther's surprise, for he had tried to discourage Mimi, telling her the Praderans never went anywhere. "They must have heard what a wonderful hostess my Mimmchen is,'' he told Susan.

They turned out to be a small and undistinguished looking middle-aged couple, and Sra. Yepez seemed to speak very

little English. To Susan's surprise, Gil greeted not only the
Yepezes but the Labarcas as old friends. But why should I
be surprised? she thought. As his country's foremost, per-
haps only, artist, he was bound to have encountered them
before at official occasions. And, if both Sra. Yepez and
Margarita Labarca kissed him—well—that was only because
Latin Americans were effusive. She had a feeling that, if
Gunther hadn't been there, Mimi would have kissed Gil, too.

Florencio Labarca had the manners of a Spanish grandee
and the appearance of a gangster. Margarita Labarca was
much younger than her husband and handsome in what struck
Susan as a flashy looking way. She spoke with an American
accent. "Mama's second husband was an American," she
explained to Susan, "and I was educated up here." It seemed
to Susan that there was some kind of understanding between
Margarita and Gil, but probably it was only her imagination.
Certainly Margarita devoted most of her attention to Susan,
whom she seemed so anxious to cultivate Susan found it
difficult to get a chance to talk with Ambassador Yepez.

After dinner, however, he came up to Susan and thanked
her for taking an interest in Gil. "It means so much for a
young artist from a small country to be the protegé of an
artist of worldwide eminence like yourself."

"But he's hardly my protegé. Just a fellow artist in whom
I. . . ." In whom I what? Am taking an interest? That sounds
worse than protegé. "Just a fellow artist," she said. "But I
understand he is a protegé of your president's."

"Protegé? Is that what Gil told you?" Ambassador Yepez
looked a little surprised, almost amused.

Susan hoped she hadn't gotten Gil into any trouble. "The
young are apt to exaggerate. I'm sure all he wanted was to
impress me by claiming a special relationship with your president."

"Oh, he does have a special relationship, no doubt of it,"
Señor Yepez smiled. "It's just that we didn't want to publi-
cize it. It's so important for a young man to make it on his
own, don't you agree?"

But the exhibit catalogue had made it clear that Gil was
being sponsored by his government. Perhaps Señor Yepez

hadn't even seen the catalogue, any more than he had seen the show itself. Wasn't that just like a diplomat?

"I was surprised not to see anyone from your mission at the opening of Señor Frias's show," Susan said.

Señor Yepez looked a little embarrassed. "We had intended to go," he said, "but Isabella was taken ill. She suffers a great deal from the atmosphere of your city—not that I'm criticizing it," he added; "it's just that she is so sensitive. And the first secretary was in Washington and we couldn't reach him in time. However, we are planning to go next week. I understand the show was very successful."

"Yes, it was," Susan said. "He got excellent reviews."

"President Martillo will be very pleased," the ambassador told her.

The day that Susan found out Relempago Martillo was planning to come to New York to speak before the United Nations was the same day that she moved back into her apartment. The two events were not connected. Susan's immediate return to her apartment was precipitated by Tinsley's return from the coast.

Susan had not been aware that Tinsley and the children were expected back that Monday evening until, after an afternoon spent painting at her studio, she opened the door to the Tabor apartment, and heard howling and chanting, backed by what sounded like Muzak; saw the naked man with his eyes closed sitting cross-legged in the foyer on what appeared to be a pile of rags. He seemed to be responsible for the chanting; the rest of the sounds were coming from further inside the apartment.

Susan was about to retreat quietly into the outside hall and disappear, when Alex materialized in the doorway of the living room, a pair of brimming glasses in his hands, a glazed expression on his face. "No, you're in the right apartment," he said. "Tinsley and the twins are back. Along with some of—" he shuddered "—her New Age pals."

Susan tried not to make her voice sound accusing. "You didn't tell me she was coming back today."

"I didn't know she was coming back today. She swears she phoned Serenity last week, when we were both out, and told her to tell us. Serenity claims she doesn't remember any call, but she admits that she might have been in communion with the absolute at the time and above such worldly considerations. At this point Tinsley lost her sense of harmonious

balance and let her have it, and now Serenity's having a pro-
longed out-of-body experience strongly resembling a fit, so
there's not much hope of an early dinner—or any dinner at
all, in fact. It all depends on how long Serenity stays out of
her body."

He looked appealingly at Susan.

If he thinks I'm going to offer to cook dinner, she thought,
he's having an out-of-mind experience. "That's too bad,"
she said.

"Your maid—what's her name? Michelle—showed up a
little while ago with your mail. I offered her princely sums
if she would stay and cook for us, but she refused. Unfortunately she ran into Fée before I got to her, and she said she
wasn't going to come back here again as long as those
witches—her word, not mine—were here. Only wish I could
do the same."

"Just as well," Susan said. "Cooking is not one of Michelle's strong points." She was glad not to be asked what
Michelle's strong points were, because she would have had
difficulty finding an answer.

Michelle's duties while the apartment was being renovated
had been reduced to stopping in every day to pick up the
mail, see how matters were going, and deliver both the mail
and progress reports to Susan. At first Susan had wanted
Michelle to stay in the apartment all day, overseeing the work.
That way it wouldn't be necessary to give Adolfo the set of
keys he was demanding. But, when this scenario was laid
out before her, Michelle objected vociferously. "You mean
you want me to hang around all day doin' nothin'?"

"Indeed, I don't. There will be plenty to do. For one
thing, I want you to keep an eye on the workmen."

"While they stand around givin' me the eye? No way.
'Sides, I was hired as a housekeeper. You want an overseer,
you go get yourself some Simon LeGrinch, awright?"

"Are you quitting?"

Michelle's belligerence abated. Maybe good maids (sorry,
housekeepers) were hard to find, but so were good jobs.
" 'Course I'm not quittin'. I wooden leave you in the lurch

like that, Miss Susan. You want me to do it, I'll do it, but I tell you Lorenzo ain't gonna like me bein' alone with a bunch of sex-starved workmen all day one bit. And I'm not gonna be happy 'bout it neither, awright?''

Susan was not concerned about Michelle's husband. She'd met him on several occasions and she had an idea that he didn't care what Michelle did as long as she brought home a regular paycheck. Nor did she believe that Michelle truly feared the workmen's advances; in fact, one time when a porter (later fired for drunkenness) had taken a shine to her, she had seemed to welcome his attentions. Michelle just wanted to get out of as much work as she could.

But Susan didn't want Michelle to be unhappy, because Michelle's grievances never died; instead they tended to grow until they assumed mythic proportions. And, as far as Adolfo was concerned, Susan soon realized that he would have to be supplied with keys anyway, in case an emergency event arose during the evening or the weekend, when Michelle was officially off duty. She would simply have to have the locks changed when she came back.

Later she was sorry that she hadn't insisted that Michelle stay and supervise the work, because every time she went back to see how the work was progressing she found the place looking like an unreconstructed battlefield—a deserted battlefield, with not a workman in sight. She called the contractor, who insisted that she must have come during a lunch hour, a coffee break, a union meeting, for otherwise his workmen were on the job all the time.

''Then how is it that no work has been done on the apartment?''

''A lot of work has been done on the apartment,'' Mr. Levine said, ''but it's all structural, internal, as it were. I wouldn't expect the layman or, in this case, laywoman to appreciate—''

''You said it would be finished in three weeks. It's almost that now, and it doesn't look to me as if you had even begun.''

''Give us another week. Materials are hard to get, and the kind of skilled workmen needed for a tricky job like this are in great demand. When I first looked at the place and gave my estimate—just a ballpark figure, you understand—I had no idea of the actual extent of the damage.'' After which he plunged into a mingle-mangle of technical terms which sounded like gibberish and probably was. The only thing that emerged with any clarity was the fact that it was going to cost her a lot more money than he had indicated in his original prognostications.

"You'd think I was having the apartment gutted, instead of simply restored to its antediluvian state,'' she told Alex afterward.

"That's the way it is if you don't take charge yourself,'' Alex said. "I know that whenever I take a day off from the office I come back to chaos.''

Which wasn't true, Susan knew. The highly paid staff of Tinsley, Tabor & Tinsley were at least as competent as he was and almost as competent as Tinsley, but who was she to destroy his illusions so long as they did not interfere with her own? But he was right; it had been a mistake to leave Mr. Levine and his merry men to their own devices. No use trying to change the arrangement she had with Michelle at this point. Michelle believed that all promises that were made to her were carved in stone, whereas her own were written in water.

Therefore, even before Tinsley came back, Susan realized that, if she ever wanted to have her home again, she would have to go back and supervise the work herself, or at least go there to make sure the work was being done. And, if she had to stay there during the day, she might as well stay there during the night. It was a large apartment; surely one or two rooms could be made habitable. And, when Peter came back, he could stay there along with her. He shouldn't mind too much. It would remind him of his days with the Oupi.

But when was Peter coming back from Katmandu? The weeks had added up: He'd been in Nepal more than a month now, and still he seemed in no hurry to return. His letters spoke vaguely of joining an actual expedition that one of his fellow professors was trying to organize to search for the snowman, but as yet he seemed comfortably ensconced in his hotel. After the first week, he had stopped even suggesting that Susan fly out there to join him.

She couldn't help wondering what amenities beyond bed and board his hosts might be providing, or that Peter might be providing for himself, for he was adept at finding female companionship in the unlikeliest of places; in fact, that was one of his specialties. Each time in the past that he had come back from one of his expeditions, he had displayed an added expertise in the erotic arts that, she was immorally certain, could have come only from hands-on research; not that she hadn't thoroughly enjoyed the fruits of his labors of love. She hoped that if Peter did actually go on a search for the abominable snowman he would not run into an abominable snow-woman, or he might never come back.

◇◇◇ **XI**

Alex drained one glass and offered the other to Susan. She shook her head. Without opening his eyes or pausing in his intonations, the chanting man stretched out a hand toward the glass. Alex looked at him coldly and drank its contents himself.

"And who is this?" Susan asked, indicating their companion. "Tinsley's new secretary?"

"There really hasn't been time for introductions," Alex said.

The man sprang to his feet with an agility that belied his aging and unshapely body. His hair and beard were iron gray. He was not completely naked, she saw now, but wore a twist of cloth about his loins. "Allow me to introduce myself," he said. "I am the Professor."

He extended a hand. Alex made no move to take it. "Professor of what?" he asked.

The man shrugged. "This and that. Everything and nothing. Shadow and substance. No need to tell me who you are."

"I am your host, and it's priggish of me, I know, but I prefer my guests to wear clothes."

"One forgets how pettily restricted the earthbound mind is," the Professor said, unhurriedly draping the pile of rags, which proved to be a somewhat grimy robe, about his skinny form, and completing the ensemble with a pair of horn-rimmed spectacles behind which his small gray eyes gleamed alertly. "And I'm your guest only for the evening. I am, in fact, registered at the Plaza."

He didn't look like anyone whom the Plaza's doorman

would even let into the lobby, but, of course, now that Donald Trump owned the hotel things were bound to be different.

The Professor turned to Susan. "I am sure that you, dear lady, as an artist, must be above such foolish conventions as clothes."

"I believe that conventional surroundings require the application of conventional standards."

"You are right, of course," the Professor said. "Forgive me, mine host," he said to Alex. "It will not happen again."

Alex made a low growling sound in his throat. "Let's get out of here, Susan. Let's go to your apartment, no matter what condition it's in. Better yet, let's go to Nepal and join Peter. . . ."

"Nonsense," Tinsley said, coming into the foyer and taking her husband and her sister-in-law's arms in a firm grip from which there was no escaping. She was a sturdy young woman, in tiptop condition as a result of the physical fitness regimen which she had been relentlessly pursuing up to the time she saw the inner light. Susan wondered whether she were now in search of metaphysical fitness.

"You're not going anywhere," she said to her husband. And, to her sister-in-law, "You must come and meet the others, Susan; I know you're going to like them," in a tone of voice that indicated she knew very well Susan was not going to like them but, the conventions being what they were, she was going to have to lump them.

Susan tried to look on the bright side of things. At least Tinsley was wearing clothes—a flowing evening gown of some soft dull gold fabric that looked almost like a robe. Susan hoped for Alex's sake that Tinsley had merely acquired a new designer and had not become part of some formal quasi-religious group. Or even founded one. She did like to be in the forefront of things.

"I must go change," Susan said, thinking she would make a getaway by the back door. She hated to leave Alex in his hour of need, but she could see it was going to be every man for himself.

"No need to do that," Tinsley said, taking an even firmer grip on her arm, "it's going to be a very informal evening.

The only reason I changed was that Bucky threw up all over my Bill Blass. I'm not sure the stain will ever come out—'' she recollected her higher self ''—but what does such a trivial mishap matter when set against the immensity of the eternal omnipresence?''

''What indeed!'' Alex said.

''Poor lamb, he does hate to be kept up past his bedtime,'' she went on, presumably referring to Bucky, rather than the eternal omnipresence, ''but I knew you'd be anxious to see the babies the instant you got back, Susan.''

''Yes, of course, but I really have to change in my case. I have a dinner date.''

''A dinner date on my first evening back! Really, Susan, one would think you—''

''But I didn't know you were going to be back.''

Spiritual uplift had not brought logic in its wake. Tinsley seemed to feel that this was just an evasion—which, of course, it was, but she had no way of knowing that, unless she was truly psychic. For the sake of the peace, Susan agreed to break her mythical date, but that was the point at which she started making definite plans to go back to her own apartment . . . even before she saw what awaited her in the Tabors' living room.

The music stopped as they came in, but the howling continued. It came, as Susan had surmised, from the twins. The music appeared to have been coming from a group of string instruments being clutched by several ladies, of varying ages and modes of dress (they were all more or less conventionally clothed, thank God), but with an overriding sameness about them; perhaps it was the expression on their faces, which could be described as ineffable, and could also be described a lot less charitably. Also present were a few more women of the same stamp, but without instruments, and a middle-aged man wearing a Brooks Brothers suit with a turban. His features did not appear to be Asian. A convert, presumably. But to what?

Tinsley introduced them all, but gave their names so rapidly that Susan was not sure which was which, except that the man in the turban probably was the one named Herbert something or other. All of them expressed joy at meeting her, except Herbert who looked at her morosely. None of them seemed to fit into that ultramodern living room except Alex. Even Tinsley, with her flowing garments and intermittently beatific expression, seemed out of place.

Whom did they remind her of? Another group—the party-crashers with whom she had hung out (their kind of expression, but apt enough) before her serial metamorphoses from struggling artist to hit woman to successful artist and crypto-philanthropist. From time to time she ran into them at parties and greeted them as old acquaintances, but they avoided her. It was almost as if they felt she had been a spy unmasked in their midst.

These people were better-dressed, better-heeled, and undoubtedly better-connected. Probably they could afford to pay their own way to whatever social events they chose to attend, but there was an air about them, almost a vacancy, that seemed to indicate a detachment not only from the mainstream but from the more orthodox tributaries.

She allowed herself to be led over to the elaborate playpen in which the twins were caged, but refused to kiss them. The last time she had been persuaded into such an auntly gesture, one of them had bit her. "Hello, Buckley," she said. "Hello, Baldwin." Rather weighty designations for such small beings, but if she called Buckley, Bucky, she would have to call Baldwin, Baldy.

Buckley continued to howl, while Baldwin gnashed his teeth, ready to bite again. She placed herself out of their reach. The howling rose to a crescendo as, deprived of his prey, Baldwin stopped gnashing and joined in.

"We must do something," said a woman with long blonde hair that swung girlishly on either side of an aging equine face (had she been introduced as Alice something or was it just the hair?). "Otherwise the air will be too full of hostile vibrations for us to energize."

Energize. Wasn't that what the crew of the Starship *Enterprise* did when they left the mother ship in order to beam to another planet? Maybe—happy thought—they were all planning to beam to another planet. If so, Susan hoped they would do so immediately, or at least beam up the twins.

Herbert clapped his hands. A young woman materialized like a genie. Unlike a genie—at least, a conventional genie—she was wearing a voluminous chartreuse shirt, shiny red tights lopped off at the ankles, and Reeboks. Her hair was cut in a series of spikes like a cockscomb. Each ear had three earrings—two studs and one that dangled nearly to her shoulders. In other words, a typical teenager.

"This is Sister," Tinsley said. "She's the twins' new nanny."

"Shalom, you all," Sister said and bore the twins off. Although thin to the point of knobbiness, she seemed strong. And determined.

"Herbert, I wish you wouldn't clap your hands like that to call her," Tinsley said. "It seems so—so imperious."

"Would ringing for her or yelling be better?" Alex asked.

"Yelling would be more democratic, at least," the Professor offered.

"Is Sister from Israel?" Susan asked, wondering whether it was the girl's name or an appellation.

"She's from California," Tinsley said. "Originally, I believe she's from North Carolina or South Carolina, but she was studying at Berkeley when she experienced a new awareness and ran out of tuition money."

"What happened to Miss Briggs?" Susan asked.

Tinsley lost her beatific expression. "Some lousy, stinking, cutthroat family in Beverly Hills lured her away. People out there are absolutely ruthless. They'll stop at nothing to get a good nanny!" Her face convulsed in rage.

"Hatred is a pothole in the path to perfection," a plump woman in pink—Celeste or Paloma, last name ungrasped—said.

Tinsley struggled for mastery over herself. "I don't expect perfection to come all at once," she said. "No doubt there will be many a stumble on the way."

"But what if you break a leg?" Alex asked. "Will they shoot you—spiritually, that is?"

Tinsley gave him a long look. "Alex, why don't you get

everybody drinks? . . . Do sit down, Susan. And you, too, Professor. Nothing's going to happen until after dinner.''

"The higher spiritual consciousness is laid low by liquor,'' the small woman in pink said.

The Professor gave her an evil look. "On the contrary, my dear Celeste, alcohol liberates the spirit and frees the consciousness. When taken in moderation, of course.''

But what was going to happen after dinner, Susan wondered. What was she in for? Try to think of this as an amusing evening, she told herself. After all, it couldn't be worse than one of the Panethnic Society's Folkloric Benefits.

"If nothing's going to happen until after dinner,'' Alex said, "nothing's going to happen, because there isn't going to be any dinner, what with Serenity still under the weather, so to speak.''

"Oh, Alex,'' Tinsley said, "you're such a slave to your stomach.''

"Why don't we all go out to dinner?'' he proposed. "Even though we are rather a large party, I'm sure we can still get reservations somewhere.'' He looked dubiously at the Professor. "Maybe at Burger King.''

"Why don't we send out for pizza?'' the Professor said. "A very spiritual food if you omit the anchovies.''

"Everything's being taken care of,'' Tinsley said. "Mom's coming over for dinner before the session. When she heard what happened, she said she'd bring Matilda, along with dinner. Matilda is her cook,'' she explained to those not in the know.

Alex brightened faintly. His mother-in-law set a notable table.

Susan saw no reason for brightening. "Session?'' she repeated. "What do you mean by session?''

"A session with Fée, of course,'' the woman with the Alice blonde hair said. "You've never been to one of Fée's sessions? What a treat you have in store!''

"By session, do you mean séance?''

There was a shocked silence, as if, Susan thought, she had uttered an obscenity, no, a blasphemy. An obscenity wouldn't have bothered them as much.

* * *

"You must not be upset, my dears," a voice behind them said. "She is unenlightened. It will be our joy to enlighten her."

Susan turned. A tall woman stood posed in the doorway in an attitude that said: I am an imposing presence and don't you forget it. Her head was topped by a kind of crown made up of multicolored jeweled rays that glittered and trembled with every move. It looked like one of Margarita Labarca's constructions. If it was, then channeling must be a very lucrative line of work. A Labarca did not come cheap. Her evening gown was purple and so draped about her ample body that it looked like an imperial robe. Around her neck hung a snarl of gold chains bearing so many medallions that she clanked as she moved forward, with a gliding motion that gave the impression that she moved on wheels rather than feet, like a Ukranian folk dancer.

There was something familiar about her, something Susan couldn't put her mental finger on. I must have run into her at some benefit, Susan thought.

"This is Fée," Tinsley announced, a flourish of trumpets in her voice. "Fée, my sister-in-law, Susan Melville."

"How do you do," Susan said warily.

Fée took both of Susan's hands in hers. Susan resisted the impulse to wrench herself free. "What a joy to meet you, my dear Susan. I have been looking forward to this moment." Her voice was high and shrill, surprising in a woman of such majestic proportions. One would have expected rolling organ tones to issue from a chest of that size.

Fée peered intently into Susan's eyes. She smelled of expensive perfume applied with a cheap hand. "Yours is an old soul, a very old soul," she informed Susan.

"Like Old King Cole?" Alex asked with a giggle. "Only he was a merry, rather than a very old soul."

Tinsley emitted a sharp sound between her teeth. She was about to speak. The Professor forestalled her. "That means you've been reincarnated many times," he explained to Susan.

"We must forgive him," Fée said. "He is still at the threshold."

Everyone looked at Alex with a forgiving smile. He looked as though he were about to throw up.

"I see great power in your aura," Fée told Susan. "You have led many rich and vibrant past lives, but none so rich and vibrant as the present one."

The woman holding what looked like a zither sighed enviously.

"You have the ability to make things happen by willing them to happen."

Susan willed very hard for her to stop, better yet, for all the New Agers to vanish.

Nothing happened. Not that she had expected anything to happen. Alex was regarding her with a faint smile.

"But I thought we all had the power to make things happen by willing them," a tall, thin woman who, since she was not Celeste, must be Paloma, said.

"We all have the potential, but Susan has the power." Fée returned to Susan. "You have an overwhelming purpose—a goal that is more attainable than you realize. You are surrounded by forces that could stop at nothing to thwart you or could smooth the way toward your heart's desire. But you must be wary. To beguile the time, look like the time. . . . But that's a lesson you've already learned. . . ."

Suddenly Susan remembered where she had seen the woman before. "Weren't you a member of that acting troupe that used to come and put on Shakespearean plays every term at the European-American Academy some years ago, when I was teaching there? I seem to remember you as Lady Macbeth." But not with a squeaky voice like that, she thought. Maybe something had happened to her vocal chords—polyps, perhaps—that made her give up the stage and take up mysticism. Or perhaps it was the profit motive.

"I have led so many lives," Fée said, "I can hardly be expected to remember them all."

"But this couldn't have been more than eight or ten years ago. It couldn't have been a previous life."

"The chosen ones live multiple lives synchronously," the Professor, who seemed to have constituted himself Fée's exegetist, explained.

Fée gave Susan a gracious smile. "When you have achieved enlightenment, you will understand."

"Quite a coincidence your running into each other, just the same," Celeste said.

"There are no such things as coincidences," the Professor told her. "Everything has its purpose."

"Freud said something similar," Alex observed.

"Ah, Freud," the Professor said. He shook his head sadly. Apparently, as far as he was concerned, Freud had never achieved enlightenment.

Chimes sounded. Alex started to get up, but Tinsley said, "No, let me. It'll probably be Mother and Matilda." She went out into the foyer. Voices, and then Amy appeared alone.

"Well, everything's under control," she announced. She was wearing a pale blue evening gown which did not flatter her increasing amplitude. She pecked the air next to Susan's and Alex's cheeks. "Sorry I'm late," she said, "but I knew you wouldn't be able to start without me." And she gave her braying laugh.

Tinsley returned and went through the introductions again. This time Susan was able to get a few more of the names. But all Amy's interest was for Fée. "I've heard so much about you," she said.

Fée smiled. "Of course you have," she said.

"Shall we have more music until dinner's ready?" Tinsley suggested.

The ladies took up their instruments with expressions of joy that were not warranted by the sounds they produced. This too shall pass, Susan thought. I've heard worse. But not much worse. And at least it's diverted Fée's attention from me. Verbally, anyhow, for Fée stared at her through the concert. So did the Professor. So, after a while, did everyone else. She began to feel like the chosen victim in some post-prandial rite.

Dinner was ready sooner than Susan had expected—either Matilda was a fast worker or she had brought the meal already prepared—but not soon enough. Apparently Serenity had not yet recovered, because Sister served it, in a well-meaning but rather slapdash way. To the dismay of several of the guests, the main course consisted of rack of lamb. Meat.

"But how can we eat the flesh of creatures that were once alive?" the woman with long blonde hair asked.

"By releasing them from their current bondage of flesh, we are freeing their souls to ascend higher in the evolutionary scale," Fée said, picking up her knife and fork. "It is the cow's karma to be eaten by man. The cow, if it has been a good cow, may then ascend to its next incarnation to become a man. The man, if he has been a bad man, may descend to be reincarnated as a cow."

"Bull," Alex said. Tinsley glared at him. "I mean, shouldn't that be a bull rather than a cow, since it was a man?"

"Gender has no significance in transmogrification," the Professor explained. "If you were, say, a pig in a previous life, you might as easily have been a sow as a boar."

"He's getting to be a bore now," Tinsley said. "Anyhow, this is lamb."

"You mean it is always lamb's ultimate destiny to be sacrificed?" Alex asked.

Tinsley descended to the lowest plane with a thump. "Shut up and eat, Alex."

Apparently Fée's pronouncement had been tantamount to a religious dispensation, for the others tucked into their meat with gusto. All except Herbert, who stuck to vegetables. He seemed to be a man of principle, Susan thought. Or maybe he just didn't like lamb.

◇◇◇ **XII**

After dinner they were all herded back into the living room, where Sister and a subdued-looking Serenity joined them. Apparently democracy ruled at these sessions. Only Amy's cook was missing and that, Susan suspected, was more a matter of personal preference than exclusion.

She was relieved to see that there had been no effort to set any kind of stage in the living room. The lights remained at their normal brightness; the position of the furniture was unaltered, except that the smaller chairs and some fetched from other rooms had been arranged into a rough semicircle, with a larger, more ornate chair set in front of them like a throne. Susan had never seen it before. It seemed to have been brought in for the occasion, and did not fit in with the rest of the furnishings, being of dark wood and vaguely Oriental design. Susan wondered whether there were places that rented furniture for occult occasions.

Fée seated herself upon the chair with a majesty marred only by a slight belch. She really shouldn't have had a second helping of praline mousse, Susan thought, not if she was planning to commune with spirits.

So far, so good. It didn't look as if there were any plans for spiritual manifestations, ectoplasm, disembodied faces, even rappings. Such things, Susan surmised, were out of date; and, in any case, difficult for a psychic to achieve in someone else's living room, at least, without considerable advance preparation. There was more music from the ladies with the instruments; then the Professor produced a tape recorder from somewhere on his person—the robe must have had pockets—and placed it on a small table close to Fée.

They must be very sure of themselves, Susan thought, to keep a record of the proceedings.

Tinsley touched a button on the wall. The lights dimmed, but not enough so that there could be any possibility of hocus-pocus. The music stopped with a skreek. "We are here," Fée announced in her high, thin voice, "to blend our personal energies so that jointly we can tap a source of ultimate enlightenment that is beyond time and space."

She paused, as if she expected some sort of reply but there was no sound except for the heavy breathing of some of her more ardent disciples. "Let us all meditate," Fée said.

She closed her eyes. Everyone but Alex and Susan followed suit. The Professor and Herbert began chanting; only Herbert said, "Oom," and the Professor said, "Ohm." It was not clear whether their intent was to chant the same syllable but their pronunciations differed or whether they were actually chanting different mantras. The effect was jarring.

"We will meditate silently," Fée piped, without opening her eyes.

They all meditated silently for what seemed to Susan like a very long time.

Suddenly Fée began to writhe in her chair. She opened her eyes, rolled them upward, and made gurgling sounds.

Susan sprang to her feet. "She's choking. We've got to call a doctor." She started toward the phone in the foyer.

The Professor raised a hand to halt her. "She's just going into a trance. Perfectly normal. But there must be absolute silence."

Apparently the restriction did not apply to Fée herself, for she gave a piercing shriek; then a low growl, followed by a series of moans. Really, Susan thought, as she returned to her chair, this is beginning to get embarrassing. She avoided Alex's eye. It would be awful if both of them burst into laughter. On the other hand, it would probably end the séance— the session.

A deep baritone voice emerged from Fée's throat, so suddenly that, in spite of herself, Susan uttered a faint cry. "Welcome, seekers after enlightenment," it said, in a strong

French accent. "I, Nicolas Fouquet, have returned to bring you word from a realm outside of physical reality."

"*Bon soir, Monsieur Fouquet,*" Alex began, "*je—*"

"Alex," his wife said, "I've told you before: it's discourteous to our guests to speak French to Monsieur Fouquet. Not everyone here is as multilingual as you are."

"Okay," Alex said. "Hiya Nick. How're you doing, old buddy?"

"*Alex!*"

"Sorry, Mrs. Tabor, but there must be silence," the Professor said, a little unfairly, Susan thought, since it was Alex who had initiated the disturbance.

Tinsley swallowed. "I understand. But it's hard to keep on a truly spiritual plane when your own husband is so hostile to the spirits."

"There are hostile auras here," the voice said, "but there are hostile auras everywhere. They are part of the great totality."

Somehow Susan expected the other guests to chorus, "Praise the great totality!" but they were silent, as befitted an upscale séance.

"So there, Tin," Alex said, "I'm just a normal part of the great totality."

Tinsley kept silent with a visible effort.

"There are those here who are other than they seem," the voice continued, "and those who seem other than they are."

Susan couldn't help wondering whether Cristobal Herrero might not have been an avatar of Nicolas Fouquet. Or vice versa.

"There are those here who are related not by the blood that runs through their veins but by the blood that stains their hands."

Again Susan avoided Alex's eye, but this time she did not fear his laughter. This is ordinary spiritualist stuff, she told herself. It's bound to hit the mark from time to time or people wouldn't go on believing in it.

Fée's eyes—but at the moment they did not look like Fée's eyes at all; some trick with contact lenses, Susan supposed—focused on Susan. "Susan Melville, you are a locus of primal forces,'' the deep voice said. ''You do not serve destiny; you make destiny. You have an overwhelming purpose—a goal that is less distant than you think, but the road there is not as direct as it will seem. And it is fraught with danger, not only physical danger, but spiritual danger. Danger not only to you but to others.''

Susan automatically distrusted anyone who used the word ''fraught,'' but then, of course, she'd had no reason to trust Fouquet—Fée—whatever—from the start. The Fouquet persona seemed to be repeating in essence what the Fée persona had already told her; but then, of course, he would. She would. I'm actually beginning to let myself be conned into thinking they're two persons, she thought. Whatever else Fée does, she certainly puts on a good performance.

''There are two men whose destinies are immediately intertwined with yours,'' Fée/Fouquet said, ''a young man and an older one. Both of them hail from a land far to the south, and both of them can bring either sorrow or happiness.''

''A young man from south of the border,'' Tinsley said. ''That must mean this young Latin American artist I hear you're becoming involved with, Susan. I'd meant to speak to you about it when I got the chance, but, since M. Fouquet has brought it up—''

''He could be referring to Alex,'' Amy objected, turning bright red.

She'd been talking to Mimi, Susan surmised, and passed the dirt derived therefrom on to her daughter. Bitches three. Silliness she could put up with, but impertinence. . . .

''Really, Tinsley,'' Amy said before Susan could speak, ''you could have chosen another occasion. . . .''

''Ladies, ladies,'' the Professor said, ''you're jangling the vibrations.''

''Sorry, everyone,'' Tinsley apologized. ''I got carried away. We'll talk about this later, Susan.''

Susan tried to make her voice light, amused, pleasant, leaving the snap to the words. ''We won't talk about it at all because my affairs—'' unfortunate choice of word, but let it pass ''—are none of your or anyone else's business.''

"I demand silence!" the Fouquet voice roared.

Tinsley primmed her lips, as if to say she was keeping quiet for Fée/Fouquet's sake, not Susan's. Susan primmed her lips to indicate she was keeping quiet for the sake of the proprieties. Alex got up and poured himself a drink. After a moment, the Professor did the same.

"Now, Susan, is there anything you want to ask me?" the voice asked.

Really, Susan thought. I think he ought to call me Miss Melville. We haven't even been introduced.

"Tell me, Susan," the voice persisted, "how may I help you? Open yourself to me. Let me guide you."

"Thank you," Susan said, "but that really won't be necessary." Pushy spirit, she thought.

"If you do not wish to consult with me, perhaps there is someone who has passed over whom you would like to speak to, someone who matters to you, because I warn you, Susan, someone in this room is in grave danger, and it could be you. . . ."

"I'm afraid I believe in letting the dead rest in their graves and leaving the living to their privacy," Susan said, trying very hard not to think of her father.

But Fée/Fouquet was not to be deterred. "There is a spirit of one who has passed over who is anxious to speak to you," the voice announced.

If only she had her answering machine, Susan thought, it could ask the spirit to leave a message on the tape. Although she knew this was all a lot of nonsense, she did not want to hear what the anxious spirit had to say—particularly not in front of all these people. Alex, she noted, had become very quiet and was listening intently.

Fée/Fouquet's voice took on a note of irritation. "He is speaking in a foreign tongue. It is—I think it is Spanish. He seems very upset, but I cannot understand what he is trying to tell me. . . ."

Don't they have any translators in the spirit world? Susan wondered. But she didn't say anything. She didn't want to encourage the spirit. The only dead people she had known who had spoken Spanish were not people with whom she cared to communicate.

Suddenly a voice that was neither Fouquet's nor Fée's spoke—a harsh rasping voice. It uttered a few words in what did sound like Spanish; then stopped suddenly as though something had cut it off. Susan felt a chill pass through her. Alex, she saw, had gone white. "Did you understand what he said?" she asked.

"Just gibberish," Alex said. Nobody contradicted him, but Susan fancied she saw a thoughtful expression cross the Professor's face.

Fée/Fouquet's voice made a few gargling sounds, then announced, "The spirit has left, but you must be on guard, Susan; your present is passing rapidly into your future. Do not act heedlessly. Consider, contemplate, consult. And sell your shares of Consolidated Adhesives."

Fée gave an unearthly shriek. She slumped in her chair. Her head fell forward on her ample chest and bounced slightly. Apparently the session was over.

Susan felt shaken. Silly of her. It was just a lot of hokum and, despite Fée's impressive performance, not even the best hokum. Old Miss Patterson's medium had been a lot more effective; but, of course, Susan had been at a more impressionable age then. That must be why Fée had gotten to her— a little—at the end. It was a throwback to her childhood.

"Do you own a lot of Consolidated Adhesives, Susan?" Amy asked.

"I have no idea. Jill Turkel handles all my investments."

"If I were you, I would call her tonight and tell her to sell," Tinsley advised.

Fée sat up and smoothed her hair. "Did Nicolas say anything interesting?" she asked in her normal voice—if that was her normal voice.

"He devoted himself to Susan," Amy complained. "Didn't talk to anybody but us. I think it's unfair."

"It happens that way sometimes," Fée said, "especially in the presence of a powerful personality, or someone whose life is at a crucial point."

She probably says that to everyone she picks on, Susan thought. But why did she pick on me to begin with?

Unlike most inward questions, this was destined to be answered immediately. Fée smiled at Susan. "Usually I don't let artists paint my portrait, but I will make an exception in your case."

"I don't do portraits," Susan said.

"You said you were beginning to work with the figure," Tinsley put in.

"Figure studies," Susan said. "Not portraits."

"Not yet," Fée said. "But you will. I only hope there may still be time in this continuum."

Susan had been afraid that, even if the Professor was staying at the Plaza, the rest of the New Agers, or at least some of them, were house guests. However, at the end of the evening, all of them except Fée took their leave. The Professor had changed into a business suit, complete with briefcase. If it hadn't been for his long hair and beard he would have looked like an accountant. Even if things hadn't changed at the Plaza, he would have no difficulty in getting past the doormen now.

"I'm surprised that your brother isn't handling your financial affairs," he said to Susan in a low voice as he was leaving.

"My business manager takes care of all my financial affairs."

"Very wise of you. It's a mistake to rely too much on one's family. Well, good night for now, I hope to see a lot more of you. I feel there is a strong empathy between us."

"Did you say antipathy?" Susan asked.

He laughed. "I don't blame you for feeling that way, Miss Melville, but I hope you'll change your mind after we've had an opportunity for a chat." Which would be when hell froze over, Susan thought.

As soon as all the visitors had gone, Susan drew Alex aside. "What did the Spanish-speaking spirit say? I know it wasn't gibberish. I could tell from your face."

"He—she, I mean—said, 'He is an imposter.' The voice

was a trick, of course. But how could Fée know that I wasn't your brother?''

"You're taking it for granted that the spirit was supposed to be Daddy. But that doesn't make sense. Daddy couldn't speak Spanish.''

"He spent some years down there before he—uh—passed on,'' Alex said, presumably in deference to any hovering spirit, for normally he was not one for euphemisms. "He could have learned it.''

"But he was living in Brazil—he only died in La Pradera—and they speak Portuguese in Brazil. And what makes you think she was talking about you, Alex? She could have been talking about the Professor, about Herbert, about anyone in the room, maybe even about someone who wasn't in the room. Probably she was talking at random, figuring she would hit some mark.''

She remembered then what Fée/Fouquet had said at the beginning, about those who were joined not by the blood that ran through their veins but by the blood that stained their hands. Hard to think of that as a random shot, too, but what else could it have been?

"She wasn't talking at random when she gave Tinsley those stock market tips,'' Alex pointed out.

"Probably she has some perfectly ordinary sources of inside information. Clients in brokerage houses and law firms, places like that. . . .''

Alex groaned. "Ordinary but not legal. That's all I need. Talk of hostile auras, I can feel the SEC breathing down my neck.''

"But they can't blame you for taking her advice, if you really believed the tips were coming from Nicolas Fouquet.''

"They won't believe I really believed the tips were coming from Fouquet. And I didn't.''

"Even so, it was actually Tinsley who got the tips and who bought the stock she pointed out.''

"They'll go easy on her. She's a mother.''

Susan gave up trying to console him. She had her own problems. "Alex, I can't stay here any longer. I'm leaving tomorrow. Tonight, if I have to.''

"But you'll hurt Tinsley's feelings if you leave just as soon as she gets back," he protested.

She couldn't believe her ears. "I'll hurt Tinsley's feelings? What about my feelings? How do you think I felt when she started spouting all that stuff about young Latin American artists in front of all those people?"

"Come on now, Susan, where's your sense of humor? I thought you'd just get a good laugh out of it. I know I did. Anyhow," he added quickly, "it was Fouquet who brought it up in the first place."

"It was Fée who brought it up," Susan pointed out, "although, to be fair, she wasn't specific; it was your wife who decided to narrow it down. Just the same, if I weren't leaving because of Tinsley, I'd leave because of Fée."

"If you leave tomorrow, Tinsley'll take it out on me, you know," Alex said,

"I know," Susan said cruelly.

"What are you planning to do? Take a hotel room?"

"I think I'd better go back to my apartment. You were right; it'll never get finished unless I'm there."

"At least wait a few days, get it fixed up enough so you'll have somewhere to sleep at night. Your maid told me there wasn't even a bed in the place."

He did have a point. The old beds had been among the first pieces of furniture she had thrown out, and the new ones, although long promised, hadn't been delivered yet. Maybe she was being a little silly in leaving the Tabors' premises so precipitately, as if she had allowed Fée to frighten her. Which was ridiculous. Fée hadn't frightened her; Fée had insulted her. Actually, Tinsley had insulted her.

All the more reason to leave. But the thought of the beds, or rather the lack of them, did deter her. And she wasn't too keen about the idea of going to a hotel, both because that would look bad and because she wasn't at all sure she could get a reservation at a decent place on such short notice. "Very well, I'll tell Tinsley I'd already made plans to leave the beginning of next week, and I'll try to stick it out here for the rest of this one, providing that she promises there will be no more sessions with Fée. I mean that I won't be expected to attend any more sessions; she can commune with the spirits as much as she likes, for all I care.''

"Okay," Alex said, "but don't expect me to break the news to Tinsley. You're going to have to do it yourself."

"Naturally," Susan said. "Please give me credit for having some sense of the proprieties. But I'll do it tomorrow. I don't trust myself to speak to her tonight." And she went to her room without saying good-night to her hostess, a solecism for which, under the circumstances, she felt she could be forgiven.

Since it was only a little after eleven and since she knew Michelle kept late hours (at least she arrived late on most mornings), she phoned and told her she would be returning to the apartment on Monday. However, she would expect Michelle to resume her duties right away. At least she would have to spend enough time in the apartment every day to make sure that at least a few of the rooms were made habitable by the time her employer returned. "And, if you're afraid to be alone with the workmen, you can bring a chaperone. For whom I am not going to pay," she added quickly.

Michelle knew when to back down. "I hear you," she said. "Okay, I guess I can defend my honor if I hafta. Jus' the same, I think maybe you oughta wait 'nother coupla weeks 'fore you move in, awright? Things are in pretty bad shape there."

"How much work have they actually done since I was there last?"

"Not a lot. In fack, it don' look to me like nothin's been done at all, but then I'm no expert."

"How come you didn't say anything about this to me before?"

"I didn' wanna worry you," Michelle said.

"I have a feeling that, if I'd insisted that you go there every day and keep an eye on things, the apartment would be finished by now. I've let you push me around too much."

"That ain't true," Michelle said. "You've been a regular slave driver, honest."

"Don't forget to tell Adolfo that I'm going to be back on Monday when you go there tomorrow."

"I hear you," Michelle said, "but I'm not gonna go up to your brother's apartment with the mail no more, not with all them witches hoppin' around, awright?"

There was no point pushing Michelle any further, particularly as, in this instance, Susan had a certain sympathy for her point of view. "Very well, for the rest of this week just leave my mail at the downstairs desk and phone me if there's anything I need to know. Anything important. Don't just call me up to complain."

"As if I'd ever do anythin' like that," Michelle said in an injured tone.

After she'd finished with Michelle—not that she'd ever finish with Michelle—Susan thought, feeling silly but unable to help herself, she phoned Jill in Washington. Jill's voice sounded sleepy. "Sorry," she said with a yawn, "but they keep early hours in this town. What's up?"

"Would you sell all my shares of Consolidated Adhesives right away?"

"Consolidated Adhesives?" Jill repeated. "What the hell—Oh, that's right, your brother is a stockbroker, isn't he? I'll call the broker first thing in the morning."

Two days later, Jill called, still from Washington. "Thought you'd be interested to know that the bottom fell out of Consolidated Adhesives. I got us out in the nick of time. No, don't tell me how you knew about it. If you have a source of inside information, I don't want to know about it. Just pass the information along."

XIII

That next week at the Tabor apartment was one of the worst weeks of Susan's life. Trouble started just before breakfast, when she informed Tinsley that she would be going back to her own apartment the following Monday. Tinsley was furious. It'll be a long time before she achieves tranquility of spirit, Susan thought.

"You can't pack up and go the moment I come back! It's insulting to me; it's insulting to my friends, who've been looking forward to meeting you."

"She's not walking out the moment you come back," Alex pointed out. "She's waiting almost a whole week."

"And your friends have met me," Susan added. "And I've met them."

"You can talk all you like about having to go back to your own apartment, but it certainly looks as if you were trying to get away from them."

Susan took a breath. She must not allow herself to be provoked into descending to Tinsley's level. "I'm sorry if it appears that way to you, but I really do have to go back home."

"But at least while you're here, you could participate in the sessions, as a matter of courtesy. Fée will be so hurt if you don't show up at them. And I've invited some people later in the week who're coming mainly on your account— Mimi von Schwabe and Margarita Labarca and—"

Susan was beginning to lose her temper. "I'm sorry, but it would have shown some courtesy on your part if you had consulted me before you invited them on my account; and, if you're going to carry on like this—"

"Carry on! *Carry on!*"

"—then I won't wait until Monday. I'll leave right now and go to a hotel."

"Hotel, indeed!" Tinsley sniffed. "A likely story. You're just looking for a good excuse to fly to the arms of your lover."

"To Nepal? Hardly worthwhile for just a few days. And I don't need any excuse for flying there, if I should decide to go."

"I'm not talking about Peter. I'm talking about that young artist 'friend' of yours. The one Mimi told Mother about, that you've been making such a fool of yourself with."

Now I could really descend to her level, Susan thought. I could start screaming. I could go even lower and start throwing things. But I must try to stick to some semblance of civilized behavior, for Alex's sake, if not for my own. "Just because I go to the opening of a promising young artist's show and have lunch with him a couple of times hardly makes us lovers. And, even if we were, it wouldn't be any of your— or anyone else's—business."

"That's telling her," Alex observed unwisely.

Tinsley turned on him. "That's right, stick up for her. She's your sister. I'm only your wife and the mother of your children."

"You're beginning to get more like your own mother every day," Susan said.

Alex looked at her in alarm.

A sound that was a cross between a muffled shriek and a loud groan came from the doorway. Fée stood there. Attired in a flowing white robe, with her black hair braided into the semblance of a coronet, she looked like one of the elder Greek goddesses. "I sense hostile auras," she said, "and hostile auras always give me a headache." Her morning voice, Susan noted, was at least half an octave lower than her evening voice.

"You said you sensed hostile auras last night," Alex reminded her, "and they didn't give you a headache then."

"Yes, they did," Fée said, "but I didn't like to say so and distress my hostess."

Tinsley managed a weak smile. "So thoughtful of you. And the hostility's all coming from Susan. I opened not only my home but my spirit to her, and she rejected them."

"How can you expect her to understand in her present unenlightened state?" Fée demanded. "And, if you were fully enlightened yourself, you would understand her lack of understanding."

"So there, Tinsley," Alex said. "Some breakfast, Fée?"

"I could eat a little something," Fée admitted, and put away several croissants with butter and jam and a double portion of eggs benedict with souffléd potatoes. "These sessions take a lot out of me," she said. "I need constant replenishment."

"In effect, you're eating for two," Alex said. "For yourself and M. Fouquet," he explained, when Fée seemed disposed to take umbrage. "For three, in fact, if we count that other spirit."

Fée paused in the act of lifting a forkful of eggs to her mouth. "What other spirit?"

"There was a strange Spanish-speaking spirit who tried to horn in," Tinsley said.

"Not horn in," Susan said. After all, one had to be fair to the other spirit. "M. Fouquet invited him to join us." Alex gave her a quizzical look. I'm going crazy, she thought. Of course Fée knows all this; she was responsible for the whole thing.

"How odd," Fée said. "Nothing like that's ever happened before, at least as far as I know."

"You never can tell what the spirits will be up to next," Alex said.

"That's very true," Fée said. She shook a sticky finger— she was in process of peeling an orange now—at him. "You are closer to us in perception, Alex, than you will admit. One day you, and Susan, too, will be one of us."

Alex snorted. Susan didn't feel entitled to snort, not after her *gaffe* (in her own eyes, at least) about Fouquet and the other spirit.

"As for you, Susan, if you don't wish to join our sessions while you are still staying here, then you must not come. Those who join us must come of their own accord—freely, gladly, joyously—or the basic principles of our being will be out of balance. And, if you feel you must leave this place next week or today or tomorrow, then no one should dare attempt to stop you. As I have said, your destiny is in your own hands, and it would be presumptuous for anyone to interfere in any way." Here she looked sternly at Tinsley, who glowered into her bowl of macrobiotic cereal.

For the rest of that week, Susan went out every evening, even making an appearance at the Luddite Society's Benefit for the Victims of Computer Technology, where she had vowed never to go again after what had happened the year before. Sometimes, when she did not get away early enough, she heard the strains of the New Agers' music emanating from the living room. But, although one or another of the members of the group would greet her in the hall, and sometimes look after her wistfully, no one, not even Tinsley, tried to pressure her into joining them for their psychic sessions, nor did she run into Mimi or anyone else she knew. The Professor did waylay her from time to time and attempt to make a date for lunch. "I know you're a busy and popular woman, but you can't be so busy and popular that you aren't free for lunch one day."

"Yes, I can," she said.

"How about a drink, then?"

"Sorry," Susan said.

"Let me assure you that this isn't entirely social. I have a business matter to discuss with you."

"Then discuss it with my agent. Or, if you prefer, my brother," she said, gesturing at Alex, who was slipping along the hall past them, hoping to escape unobserved.

"I don't think that would be such a good idea," the Professor said, and hurried off to join the others in the living room.

"I don't think he likes you," Susan said.

"The feeling is mutual," Alex assured her.

It was less easy to avoid Fée, who was, after all, a fellow house guest. Although she kept to her stated policy of not attempting to interfere with Susan, she kept looking at her and sighing, which, as Susan complained to Alex, quite put her off her feed.

One morning she presented Susan with a crystal, "as a farewell gift, if you will, but I prefer to think of it as more of a soul-warming gift. Carry it with you always, and gradually it will help open your spiritual eyes and expand your transcendental perceptions."

Susan thanked Fée politely. The "carry it with you always," had to be a figure of speech, for it was nearly a foot long and must weigh over ten pounds. It will make a good paperweight, she thought. Somehow, the thought of throwing—or even giving—it away, never occurred to her, until long afterward.

As the week drew to a close, Susan grew more and more anxious to be out of the place. She was tempted to set out on Sunday night, but she had too much baggage with her to be able to make a quiet departure by herself. She would have to have help. And Sunday night was a notoriously difficult time to secure paid assistance in Manhattan, even in the most opulent of Fifth Avenue apartment buildings. As for unpaid help, the one time the New Agers might have been of some material assistance, they were off at a giant mass meditation in Madison Square Garden. The twins were at the Pattersons' place in the Hamptons, along with their grandmother, not that they themselves could have been of any help, but that Sister—a willing young woman less interested, Susan had discovered, in her spiritual than her economic development—might have been pressed into service.

She and Alex were, once again, alone in the Tabor apartment. And he categorically refused to help her get back home. "I am not going anywhere tonight," he declared. "This is the first quiet evening I've been able to have in a long time, and I plan to relax and enjoy it. Even if this place should catch fire, I'm not sure I could bring myself to leave. Tomorrow morning we can start out early. I get up at the crack of dawn, for Tinsley, Tabor & Tinsley opens with the lark these days, now that Tinsley's on sabbatical.'' And he heaved a sigh, for more wealth—and, according to Amy, they were really raking the stuff in—had not brought him happiness.

Had Andy and Jill been in town, Andy would have helped her, she knew. He was a very obliging young man. However, when she had called Jill earlier in the day on another matter, she'd found they were still in Washington. ''But we hope to be back in New York some time next week,'' Jill said. ''And we'll see you then. Andy's very anxious to talk to you about something. I have no idea what. Probably some sinister crime in the art world. You will tell me what it is after he's told you, won't you? In strictest confidence, of course.''

''I'm sure he has no intention of consulting me on any criminal matters,'' Susan said. ''He's far too professional for that.''

''Meaning that, if he does consult you, you're far too professional to let me know what it is,'' Jill said. ''But, I'll get it out of you, never fear.'' She wouldn't be able to, of course, but she would try, and that was what Susan did fear, for her agent was a notable nag.

There was nobody else on whom Susan could call for assistance, for most of her friends were accustomed to having things done for them. They would be horrified at the idea of doing for themselves, let alone for someone else.

Well, she thought, tomorrow morning let it be.

XIV

Early as it was when they set out, the streets were already full of cars; not so full, however, that Susan didn't notice the blue Chevy that seemed to be accompanying their cab. She drew Alex's attention to it. "Probably the SEC," he said. "They're keeping a constant eye on me."

"I should think they'd be keeping an eye on Fée."

"For all I know, they are."

She and Alex arrived outside her door to find a copy of the *Times* lying on the mat. She saw the front page. Her heart skipped a beat. "Didn't you remember to cancel your subscription while you were gone?" Alex asked, as he deposited her luggage on the floor.

She put down the bag she was carrying and, at the same time, picked up the paper, tucking it securely under her arm, so that Alex couldn't see the front page. "I don't subscribe," she said, keeping her voice level. "I usually pick up a paper when I go out. It must belong to one of the neighbors and got delivered here by mistake."

She had caught only a glimpse of the picture on the front page. There it was, staring out at her, the face of Relempago Martillo—dark-bearded, dark-glassed; she had seen it so often that it had become as familiar to her as if she actually knew the man. She hadn't thought about him actively for some time—too occupied with present stresses to brood over past distresses—but he had been ever-present in the back of her mind. Now he sprang to the forefront again.

Her first reaction was to make sure that Alex didn't see the front page of the paper; that is, see it while he was with her. He was bound to see it later. Everybody looked at the

Times sooner or later, whether they wanted to or not. She had never mentioned Martillo's name to Alex after the time he had told her what had become of her father. And Alex had never spoken of Martillo to her again. But he must be aware that she couldn't have forgotten. Or forgiven.

As she unlocked the door to her apartment, there was a scurrying sound from inside. She and Alex looked at each other. "It could be a rat," she said.

"You have rats here?"

"I've never seen signs of any, but since Adolfo took over—"

"Whatever else your superintendent's shortcomings," Alex said, "he would hardly have introduced rats onto the premises."

"Maybe—" she began, without knowing how she was going to finish her sentence, when a door banged somewhere inside the apartment, which settled the question. Rats couldn't bang doors.

"Maybe Michelle got here early," she said, after a moment of silence. Ridiculous. Michelle had never gotten anywhere early in her life—and probably not in any of her previous lives either. I've stayed too long with Tinsley and her associates, Susan thought. I've become infected. Previous lives, indeed.

And, even if it had been a born-again Michelle arriving early why then would she leave? Because the next sound they heard was what sounded like her back door slamming.

Neither she nor Alex made a move toward the door in the hall that led to the service landing. It would be a relief, she thought, if they heard footsteps on the stairs or the sound of the elevator descending—anything to indicate that the intruder, if there was one, was leaving. But there was only more silence.

She and Alex waited outside her front door. Was there an intruder waiting outside the back door? She could hear the sound of Alex's breathing. Perhaps he could hear hers. Was there someone breathing heavily on the service landing? And why didn't Alex rush heroically to the service landing to confront whoever it was?

Because he was not a fool. If there was an intruder, he might be armed. And Alex presumably was not. But I am, she thought. There's a loaded gun in my bag, ready to take out misbehaving diplomats wherever I find them.

But if she confronted the hypothetical intruder and he had a gun, she might be forced to kill him. She didn't like the idea of killing someone on her own service landing. Even if she only winged him, it would entail tiresome explanations.

"We could call the police," Alex suggested without conviction. Although he had been a respectable citizen for some years now, he was still reluctant to believe that the police and he could ever be on the same side. She, herself, although not hampered by early criminal conditioning—for she had not turned to crime until she was mature and set in her ways—was not anxious to talk to the police either. Let sleeping cops lie, she believed, especially when there was a gun in your handbag.

"We're not even sure that anyone is—was—there," she said. "We'd look like idiots if we called the police and it turned out somebody—a workman—carelessly left the back door open and the wind banged it shut."

"That's right," he agreed. "It's what I've been thinking myself."

They avoided each other's eye. "Your superintendent lives on the premises, doesn't he? Maybe we should call him."

But supposing it was Adolfo himself they had heard. No, that was ridiculous. He had her keys. She'd been away for over a month. He could have snooped to his heart's content any time he wanted to. He knew she would be coming back this morning. Even if Michelle had forgotten to inform him, Susan herself had called to repeat the message. Adolfo hadn't been there but she had left the information with Wilfredo, his assistant. If it was Adolfo, why would he have waited until the last minute? Could it be someone else who had gotten hold of his keys, someone who, for some reason, couldn't get in the apartment at any other time? The first thing she would do after Michelle arrived would be to get the locks changed.

Alex made up his mind. He carried her luggage into the foyer and turned on the light. A sheet of white paper was lying on the floor. He picked it up. "Attention, residents," he read aloud, "it is forbidden to deposit cigarette butts in the potted plants. . . ."

"That could have been something personal," she said, taking the paper from him.

"Who would put a personal note under your door?"

"For all you know, I have an admirer living in the building. Well, let's see what's what." She started to go into the living room. He stopped her.

"You wait here while I go in and take a look around the rest of the place to make sure there's no one here. Leave the door to the hall open and if you hear me yell, you yell and run for the elevators."

She started to say, "Be careful, Alex," but bit the words back. She knew he would be careful. If he hadn't been a careful man, neither one of them would be alive today. She put the case she was carrying down on the floor, making sure the newspaper remained underneath. She would have liked to take a look at the paper, but she didn't want Alex to come back and find her reading it.

Alex was gone for such a long time that she was beginning to wonder whether she shouldn't go call the police after all, when he came back. He looked worried, but he closed the door to the outside hall, so she gathered that the coast was clear now even before he said, "Nobody here. But only the snap lock on the back door was closed; the top lock was open." Which meant that there must have been someone inside who either hadn't had a key to the back door or who hadn't a chance to use it. Or, of course, that there never had been anyone inside to begin with and someone really had left the back door open and the wind really had banged it shut. But both of them knew that there was no window on the service landing, and where there is no window, there is no wind.

"I looked outside the back door to see if anyone was on the landing," he said. "It was empty, but I thought I heard the service elevator going down."

"If it was the elevator, that would mean it must be somebody from the building. The elevator's not automatic. One of the staff has to run it."

"Anyone can run one of those elevators. If an outsider could get into your apartment, he could get into the elevator."

"But was there anything to show there actually *had* been an intruder?"

There was a pause. "Hard to tell," he said, "the place is in such a mess, but it does look as if it had been turned over, if not actually ransacked."

She was half-expecting this; yet it jolted her. "Ransacked—what's to ransack? I took away everything—everything that mattered, anyhow."

"But whoever it was wouldn't have known that, would they? Come take a look; see what you think."

Once she got a look at the living room, she saw what he meant. The ladders and paint cans and sawhorses, tools, paper bags, and plastic cups, crushed beer cans, crumpled papers, and general indescribable debris were the normal complement of renovation; the tarpaulins that covered those pieces of furniture which had not been removed for reupholstery or rejection, the boxes in which she and Michelle had stuffed everything they could, the normal complement of redecoration. But the tarpaulins had been pulled off, and the furniture, which had originally been bunched in the middle of the room, dragged out to its perimeters. Some of the smaller pieces sprawled on their sides. All drawers had been pulled out, all cabinet doors opened, all lids lifted.

The boxes had been tipped over on their sides and much of their contents scattered. All sorts of things were lying about that, no matter how innocuous they might be, she didn't care to have exposed to public view. Obviously there had been an intruder. How could Alex have had any doubt? Did he think she could possibly have left everything in this state?

"At least they could have put things back," she said, picking up a battered teddy bear and pushing it as casually as possible into a box, along with some large books that had survived the flood. Photograph albums, they seemed to be. They must have belonged to her mother; she herself kept photographs in brown paper envelopes. There were scrapbooks, too, some dating from her childhood. And those scrapbooks Jill had given her. She should have taken them to the studio, she supposed; they had been a gift, no matter what the giver's intent.

It was difficult to determine what the intruder might have been looking for, whether it was large or small, flat or protuberant—or whether he had been looking for anything in particular at all or just making a general search to see what he could find.

"I suppose the rest of the rooms are the same," she said.

"Not as bad. But then, most of the stuff's in here—the old stuff, anyway. On the bright side, you'll be happy to know that the beds seem to have arrived, so you'll have something to sleep on tonight."

She pushed the thought of having to spend the coming night alone there to the back of her mind. She had enough worries of the moment. And, as it turned out, she didn't have to spend the night alone after all.

XV

Alex seemed in no hurry to get to his office, but stayed with her while she waited for Adolfo to respond to her summons on the house phone. She was very glad, after all, that she had not gone back alone the night before, and that he had come with her now and was waiting with her. She did not want to confront Adolfo alone. She knew that somehow he would try to blame her for what had happened.

And he did. There could not possibly have been an intruder, he said. The havoc wrought had been entirely the contractor's fault, or, at least, the fault of his hirelings—which was what always happened when a tenant hired someone "not recommended," by which Adolfo meant someone not recommended by Adolfo himself.

"Nonetheless, I, personally, or Wilfredo, a man of the utmost integritude, overlooked the goings on." No workman, he claimed, had been allowed to enter the apartment without checking with Adolfo or his assistant. Even Mr. Levine, the contractor, could not get in without Adolfo's "so-say," which was one of the less fanciful reasons Mr. Levine gave Susan for the work's being so far behind schedule. Nobody else had access to the apartment, Adolfo claimed. Nobody at all was authorized to be there for any reason whatsoever over the weekend. And no outsider could have gained entrance to the house, for the doormen were always on hand, ever-vigilant, ever-fearful of losing their jobs should they relax that vigilance.

"Could somebody have stayed behind and hidden in the apartment after the workmen left?" Alex suggested. "Say—

oh—some homeless person looking for a warm place to spend the weekend?''

Adolfo was outraged by the suggestion, as, indeed, was Susan. "No homeless person would ever be so much as allowed to set toe in this house," he said. "Besides, Wilfredo and I checked every nook and cranberry before locking up each night. Not even a midge could conceal himself.''

He looked sternly at Susan. "It is just your imaginings, Miss Melvilly. Ladies of a certain age are liable to imaginings. And all this—'' he pointed to the scattered furniture and belongings ''—probably you were looking for something and forgot to put it back together.'' He nodded, as if satisfied that he had proven his case to everyone's satisfaction.

Alex managed not to laugh, but his voice was shaking as he asked, "Are gentlemen of—of uncertain age also liable to imaginings? Because I, too, heard the door slam. Furthermore, the place was like this when we got here, and my sister was with me all weekend. I always keep an eye on her in case she should get up to any middle-aged shenanigans— Ow!'' he finished as Susan kicked him in the shins.

Adolfo looked baffled. "Maybe we made a mistake in not calling the police right away,'' Alex went on. "Well, it's not too late to rectify that.'' He made as if to move toward the phone.

Adolfo put up a protesting hand. "No, no! I spoke without consideration. Miss Melvilly would not throw things around like that no matter how old she gets.''

Susan pressed her lips tightly together. If she left them open in the slightest degree, she was afraid she would make a sound like a teakettle about to boil. She felt like a teakettle about to boil.

Adolfo snapped his fingers. "Oho! It must have been that maid of yours, that Seashell who has done this.'' He and Michelle were antagonists of long standing. Nothing unusual about that since he got on with the servants in the co-op even less well than he did with their employers. They did not treat him, he complained to Mrs. Acacia, "with the respectfulness due to my authority.''

* * *

"I tried to explain to him that he has no authority over the residents' employees, only the house staff," Mrs. Acacia had said at a general meeting of the residents, "but I couldn't seem to get the concept through to him. He was once an officer in his country's army—at least he says he was—and he seems to have found it hard to adjust to civilian life. One thing I did find out, though—" and she turned to Susan with a glittering smile "—he is not a Marxist, as one of the residents, who I am sure does not mean to be a troublemaker, has been running around telling everybody."

Susan opened her mouth and shut it.

"He is, he tells me, a *Marzist*. The Revolution which sent him into exile, I don't know how many years ago—"

"Twenty-five," Susan said, adding, "That's what he told me," in case anyone should wonder how she came to be so well-informed.

"Thank you, twenty-five years ago—"

"Surely that's long enough for him to have adjusted to civilian life," said one of the younger residents whose name Susan did not know.

"Once an officer, always an officer," General Van Dongen said. Through some error he had been briefly commissioned a general during World War II and he had never forgotten it, or let anyone else forget it.

"As I was saying," Mrs. Acacia persisted, "the revolution in La Pradera took place in March—which is Marzo, in Spanish. Hence, he is a Marzist, not a Marxist."

"But I understand from the media," Miss Wolsey from the sixth floor, who prided herself on keeping up with world affairs, the obscurer the better, said, "that the current regime is Fascist. That would make him a Communist, wouldn't it?"

"Not in this case," Fred Burney said. "Both sides are Fascist."

"So, you see, there's nothing to worry about," Mrs. Acacia said, beaming all round.

"Do you think he's altogether reliable?" Burney asked. "A fellow I know who's something at the UN lives in one of those new high rises over by the river, and he swears the superintendent there bears an uncanny resemblance to

Adolfo, whom he met when he was over here one evening
and got stuck in the elevator.''

"Are you suggesting that Adolfo's moonlighting?'' Mrs.
Acacia said. "Nonsense!''

"Or double-dipping?'' another of the younger residents
suggested.

"That's impossible. He has more than enough work here
to keep him busy all the time.''

"Yes,'' Mrs. Posner from the tenth floor said, "but does it?
Keep him busy, I mean. Most of the time it's Wilfredo who
comes when something goes wrong, if anyone comes at all.''

Some of the other tenants murmured agreement. Susan
was somewhat surprised. Whenever anything went wrong—
which was often—it was always Adolfo who came to her
apartment.

"The very idea is ridiculous,'' Mrs. Acacia said. "Your
friend's superintendent is probably someone who resembles
Adolfo. All these Latin Americans look alike, you know. It's
an ethnic resemblance,'' she said, as she caught several liberal eyes. "I daresay we all look alike to them.''

"Whatever they are, they're bugging my phone and making funny noises at night,'' General Van Dongen said. "And
I insist that you put a stop to it.'' The residents smiled at one
another. General Van Dongen was well known to be off his
rocker.

General Van Dongen took offense. "I suppose you're going to try to tell me that that Rodolfo, or whatever his name
is, hasn't been slipping threatening notes under my door?''

"General Van Dongen,'' Mrs. Acacia said, "he's been
slipping threatening notes under everybody's door. It's just
his way.''

"Bad enough we should have to put up with the older
residents'—er—idiosyncrasies but, considering what we had
to pay for our apartments,'' the first younger resident said,
"and the ever-rising maintenance costs, at least we shouldn't
be asked to put up with the super's quirks.''

"If you live in New York you have to put up with quirks
no matter how much you pay,'' an intermediate-aged resident told him.

* * *

"I still don't think we should have hired a bachelor," Mrs. Posner said. "A married man would be much more stable."

Several of the younger residents snickered. Although all of them were coupled—the aforementioned maintenance costs being too high for most singles—quite a few were not married, at least not to each other, which distressed some of the older residents. On the other hand, the fact that Susan wasn't married to Peter disturbed the younger residents; they felt that she was usurping the privileges of another generation, while it didn't bother the older residents. Famous artists, like royalty, were allowed a certain latitude in their sex lives; besides, the apartment had belonged to Susan's family before she inherited it, which made her old apartment blood.

"Adolfo is not a bachelor," Mrs. Acacia said. "He is a widower, which is different. Besides, if he had a wife, he would be likely to have children. That would mean we would have to give him a larger apartment, which would mean our maintenance costs would rise even faster."

There was silence. Her last remark had really hit hard.

"Widowers can have children, too," Mrs. Posner pointed out.

"So can bachelors," one of the younger residents said. This time the other younger residents did not snicker. It wasn't something to joke about these days, now that genetic tests had superseded blood tests.

"I suppose Adolfo might have grown children," Mrs. Acacia conceded, "but since, if he does, they don't live with him, it's none of our business. His personal affairs don't concern us."

"As long as he doesn't concern himself with our personal affairs," Susan said.

"Has he been snooping around your place, too?" General Van Dongen said, with interest. "I know somebody's been going through my things and some very valuable magazines are missing."

Nobody said anything. Everybody knew that whenever the general went to his club, his housekeeper—an unpleasant woman hired by his daughter who, popular opinion said, was trying to push him into an early grave so she could sell the co-op for the half million dollars or so it was now worth—threw out anything that she felt complicated her life unduly. But they didn't say anything, because they didn't want to stir up labor-management friction, especially with decent help so hard to get nowadays. And several of the residents took the opportunity to complain, as they always did somewhere in the course of a board meeting, that Adolfo was going out of his way to make life difficult for their servants, and Mrs. Acacia assured them, as she always did, that she would speak to him about it. If she did, it appeared to have no perceptible effect.

Now Adolfo was trying to make life difficult for Michelle. "It must have been Seashell who came in over the weekend and threw things around," he said, and nodded, as if the entire question had been settled.

"Why would she throw things around?" Alex asked.

Adolfo shrugged. "Who knows? Maybe she has some grievous against Miss Melvilly. Or she is just crazy."

"More to the point," Susan said, "what would she have been doing here on her days off? She's not that crazy."

Adolfo considered this. "She and her friends probably hurled a riotous party over the weekend."

"This doesn't exactly look like the aftermath of a party," Alex observed. "Bag lunches and beer among the paint cans?"

Adolfo sniffed. Obviously there were parties and parties. "Likely they were shooting dopes," he offered.

"We can ask the doorman who was on duty then," Susan said. "If Michelle had been giving a party, he would have seen her and her friends going in and out."

"Not so. She is a servant; she would naturally have used the service entrance. There is no one on duty there weekends, except by special bequest. Otherwise, it must be accessed by keys. And she has a key. She has keys to everything."

"You go around giving keys to everyone, even those of the lowest integritude," his tone implied. "But to me, who am of the highest integritude, you don't give keys unless you are forced." Could he have turned the place upside down out of sheer spite? Susan wondered. No, if he had, he would have made a better job of it.

Michelle was indignant when she arrived, shortly before ten, and found out what she was being accused of. "I don't use no service entrance, awright? That's for tradespeople. I use the front door like regular folks, and nobody's gonna stop me!"

She glared defiantly at Adolfo and Susan in turn. "What's more, I ain't been here since last—" here she faltered and lost some of her righteousness "—since last Friday."

"If then," Susan said, correctly interpreting both the pause and the significant look Adolfo was giving her.

"Well, I was plannin' on comin' in on Friday. I got on the subway and then my tooth was hurtin' so much I couldn't stand it no more—awright?—so I went back to the Bronx because that's where Mr. Karfunkel, that's my dentist, is; and he cooden' squeeze me in until the afternoon, so I says to myself, 'Well, there's no point goin' all the way downtown and comin' right back again.' The only reason I didn' mention it was that I didn' wanna look like I was askin' for sympathy. . . ."

She paused. No sympathy was forthcoming. "But I sure as shootin' didn' come here on no Saturday or Sunday, awright? If I wanna th'ow a party I got me a nice three-room apartment completely fitted out in the latest furniture fashions where I could th'ow it. I ain't gonna entertain my guests in no mess like this."

Susan was afraid Adolfo would tell Michelle that you didn't need fancy furniture for shooting dopes, but even he had enough sense to know when to leave well enough alone. "Let us get down to the nutty grutty. You tell me, Miss Melvilly, is anything missing?"

"I won't be able to tell for sure until the mess is cleared up." She probably wouldn't be able to tell even then, because she couldn't remember what she had left in the apartment, but, naturally, she wasn't going to tell Adolfo that.

 ◇◇◇ **XVI**

It wasn't until later, after Adolfo and Alex had gone their separate ways, the workmen had arrived, and Michelle was screaming at them for the mess they had left, that Susan remembered the *Times*, with its front-page picture of Relempago Martillo; and, by that time, it was too late. In a belated effort at neatness, the workmen had spread the paper over as much of the floor as it would cover.

She felt a primitive urge to go around the apartment, gathering up sheets of newspaper, but that would have been undignified. And unnecessary. She could easily get another copy of the *Times* later.

But what could the story have been about? What had Martillo done to get himself on the front page of the *Times*? She hoped it wasn't an obituary. It would be a shame to have him die of natural causes.

Intermixed with her reawakened thirst for revenge was a hunger for something else, something even more primitive and basic. Food. She and Alex had left so early neither had had a chance to get any breakfast. He was probably rectifying the omission at that very moment; stuffing his face was the uncharitable way she characterized it in her thoughts—which was unfair, since the haste had been of her making. He would have been perfectly willing to stop and eat before they left.

There was, of course, nothing to eat in the apartment. The kitchen cabinets had been cleared before the work started, and the refrigerator was empty, except for some cans of beer which presumably belonged to the workmen.

At first she was going to send Michelle out to get food as well as another copy of the *Times*; then she came to her senses. If she sent Michelle out on these errands, Michelle would spin them out to encompass the entire morning. And what would she herself do, alone with the workmen? Unlike Michelle, she was unable to relieve her feelings by screaming at them. She could not scream at anyone. It was a serious handicap for anyone living in New York.

"You're going to have enough to do here," she told a visibly disappointed Michelle. "I'll get myself some breakfast outside; then I'll stop off at the locksmith's afterward and tell them to come over and change the locks. So you won't have to worry about anything except making as much of the apartment as habitable as possible before I get back." And, as Michelle opened her mouth to protest, "Oh, and if you're worried about being alone with the workmen, I'll ask General Van Dongen's housekeeper to stop in from time to time and I'll make it up to her later."

"I can manage, I can manage," Michelle said. "And, if you're going to make it up to anybody later, it better be me."

On her way out of the building, Susan stopped off at the mail room to see if there might be anything for her. There was—a surprising number of communications to have accumulated in just three days. Even before Michelle had let slip the fact that she had not reported for duty on Friday, Susan had begun to wonder whether, in spite of her instructions, Michelle had even bothered to go to the apartment since the previous Monday, since there hadn't been any mail left for her downstairs at the Tabors'.

I suppose I am not a trusting person, Susan thought. Well, in this paranoid city, this paranoid world, perhaps that was the only way to be. "To believe in your fellow man is to believe in God; to believe in God is to believe in your fellow man," Cristobal Herrero had said, in what would have seemed like a change of pace for him, if it hadn't been well known that he was an atheist.

Luckily, she had picked up a tote bag before she left the apartment, in case she did any shopping, so she could take the mail with her and look at it over breakfast. As she stuffed the mail inside, she noticed something in the bottom. Fée's crystal. She had shoved it in the bottom of the bag under her

already-worn lingerie (which was probably some sort of sacrilege) and forgotten to take it out when she'd given the clothes
to Michelle. Funny she hadn't noticed its weight when she
left the apartment. Well, she wasn't going to go back upstairs
just to put it away and she could hardly leave it with any of
the help; it would cause comment. She would just take it
along with her. It wasn't all that heavy—certainly nowhere
near as heavy as she'd expected it to be when she'd first seen
it—and she wasn't planning to do any serious shopping, anyway.

As she left the building, a black Mercedes started up. She
wouldn't have paid any attention, except that a green Dodge
sedan parked a few cars behind started up at the same time,
and nearly collided with the Mercedes as it pulled out. What
was strange was that neither driver opened the window to
hurl imprecations at the other. Both drove off quietly. And
yet she could have sworn both cars bore New York license
plates. Very strange.

She bought a copy of the *Times* at a stationery store on
Lexington Avenue. She also got the *News*, the *Post*, and
Newsday, and took the lot into the coffee shop next door,
where she frequently breakfasted.

As she went inside, she sensed that there was someone
behind her, but when she turned around, there was no one
there. But a blue Chevy coupe was pulling up outside, and a
man was getting into it. So what, she said to herself. There
are thousands of blue Chevys and green Dodges in New York
and hundreds of black Mercedes.

She sat down in a booth and ordered French toast and coffee;
then turned to the *Times*. Shock nearly jolted her out of her
seat. In place of the picture of Martillo, there was a photograph of a factory in New Jersey in flames. Could she have
imagined seeing Martillo's picture? Was she so obsessed with
the man that, even when she was not consciously thinking of
him, she saw his face in every burning factory?

No, there was the story: "Latin American leader to address UN." *Relempago Martillo is coming to the United
States!* She hadn't felt so elated since she had shot Haiti's

Deputy Permanent Representative outside the brothel in the East Eighties which he had stocked with zombis. At long last the general was going to put himself within her grasp. With any luck, this would be her last grasp, and his last gasp.

This called for some sort of celebration. Had it been later in the day, she would have had a drink, but it was still not even eleven. One must observe the niceties, even when planning an assassination. "I'll have some ice cream," she told the waiter.

"What flavor? We have chocolate, vanilla, strawberry, rum raisin, butter crunch and. . . ."

"Butter crunch," she said. What else?

She returned to the story in the *Times*. The dispute that had precipitated the general's plan to appear before the world body was the sort of thing that seemed endemic to the Latin American countries. She had taken note of it during the last few months only because she took note of anything involving La Pradera. A neighboring state claimed that Praderan troops had crossed its borders and then refused to withdraw. Shots had been exchanged. There had been casualties on both sides.

Martillo didn't deny that his troops were in the other country or that there had been gunfire. There was no way he could have done so, since a TV crew doing a documentary on migratory birds had filmed the whole thing. Martillo said his men had been in such hot pursuit of drug traffickers they hadn't realized that they'd crossed over into the other country until they were fired upon, whereupon his men had naturally fired back.

Moreover, now that his troops were there, he refused to withdraw them. He said the other country had not been doing a good job of policing the drug traffic; in fact, he suggested, the government of that other country was up to its corrupt ears in drug-dealing. It was, therefore, necessary, he told the press at a conference which he called in the audience room of the presidential palace in Ciudad Martillo (only still cameras allowed; his eyes were too weak to stand the hot TV lights, his press officer explained, as he had explained on earlier occasions) for the Praderan troops to stay on the other side of the border to keep the peace, curb the drug traffic, and preserve the democratic ideal.

The head of the neighboring state (who loved both hot lights and the limelight) had appeared on television and said something in Spanish which the translator rendered as ''President Martillo is full of bee pollen.'' If he truly wanted to keep the peace, curb the drug traffic, and preserve the democratic ideal, the neighboring head of state said, he could do it from his own side of the border.

Martillo didn't reply directly. Perhaps he considered not withdrawing his men was answer enough. The other president had then complained to the United Nations, which issued a number of warnings to General Martillo, which the general ignored, as he had ignored similar warnings over the years. Now they were threatening to take action. But they had threatened to take action before, and again he had paid no attention. This time he had asked permission to present his case before the United Nations himself and been invited to address the General Assembly.

The dispute itself didn't interest Susan particularly. Apparently it didn't particularly interest the *Times* either, which was why the main body of the story was continued on a back page. And, yes, there on the back page was the picture she had seen earlier. This was a later edition of the paper; that was all. Other events which the *Times* apparently felt were more deserving of the space, had occurred between the two editions. It was always nice to know she had not gone mad, but it wasn't important. What was important was that at long last she was going to have the opportunity to kill Martillo on her own home ground.

But even on her own ground it wasn't going to be easy. A lot of other people wanted to kill him, too. In the past, the press had reported at least four failed assassinations and, it was rumored, there had been at least that many more that had been kept out of the media, probably because the method of dealing with attempted assassins in La Pradera tended to upset liberal stomachs up north.

The *Times* recapitulated these and gave a brief history of

his regime, which ended suddenly, as if several paragraphs had been dropped at the end. The *News* and *Newsday* went into greater detail, but while their descriptions of what went on were more lurid, they were not more informative, *Newsday*'s piece wandering off into a general diatribe against dictators in general. Only the *Post* brought her father into the story at all, and, since it ended its piece with, "and it has been claimed that General Martillo was responsible for the death of the writer Herman Melville, whose strange disappearance in Mexico has long aroused speculation," she didn't feel she had to worry about her connection with the general being made public—at least not by the *Post*.

There was much she wanted to know that the papers did not tell her. She knew when Martillo was going to speak before the United Nations—next Monday. But when was he actually coming to New York? What was his schedule? Where would he be staying? Who would be coming with him? Did he have a family? Not that it was important. Usually she liked to know the nature of the relatives her targets would be leaving behind and just how bereaved they were likely to be and habits were habits.

She knew his first wife and children had disappeared during the revolution. Had he married again? Nobody seemed to have any idea. It seemed that General Martillo kept his private life very private—a luxury that only a dictator was allowed to enjoy these days. You'd never find the president of the United States being allowed to have a private life any more. The very idea would strike at the foundations of democracy.

But it was General Martillo's public life that concerned her. His government would be sending advance men ahead to make the arrangements. They might even be here now, making the plans for his visit. Somehow she had to find out what those plans were. Whom could she ask? Ambassador Yepez? No, if Martillo's plans were being kept secret, it was hardly likely he would tell them to her.

Perhaps Gunther could arrange something. Certainly he'd be in a position to get her a guest ticket for next Monday, but what use was that? She didn't want to hear the general or even see him. She wanted to kill him. Mimi might be persuaded to give a dinner for him, but it might not be easy, Susan thought, to persuade him to come.

Then she thought of Gil. Of course. He was General Martillo's protegé, one of La Pradera's most prominent citizens. He was bound to be invited to the official festivities. How appropriate it would be for him to bring as his guest a significant American artist, to impress the general and show him the government was getting value for its money. Too bad to have to use the young man as a stalking horse, but, after all, that was the price he had to pay for being a dictator's protegé.

◇◇◇ **XVII**

After she had finished eating, she finally got around to looking at her mail. There was, as she had already noted, a lot more than usual, but very little of it personal. No letter from Peter, which meant he must be having a good time. When he was not having a good time, he tended to write a lot of long letters designed for posterity. Dear Peter, she thought, how I miss him and how glad I am, after all, that he doesn't seem to be planning to come back from Nepal in the immediate future. Although in the past she'd had no trouble assassinating people while he was around, those had been run-of-the-mill jobs. This was different: No casual going out, shooting a diplomat, and coming home for a cozy evening by the fire. This was a head of state she was after, even if the state was very small. It would require all her concentration.

When she got back to the apartment, she would put through a call to Katmandu to make sure that he was going to stay put for the next week at least. How was she going to manage that? she considered. What she would do, she decided, was tell Peter that she had allowed herself to be persuaded into acting as chairman of a ball to raise funds for displaced aborigines, something like that, which would be right up his alley; and she was relying on him to help her. That should keep him away until after the ball was over, or, at least, up until the day it was scheduled. Peter liked parties; he simply didn't like having anything to do with putting them together. He also liked aborigines, but he believed that they should remain in context.

She riffled through her mail. Advertisements, solicitations, invitations. The only item that seemed of even remote interest was an invitation to an international arts conference and festival in Hawaii, sponsored by some organization she'd never heard of. She was always getting invitations from organizations she'd never heard of. The program sounded more appealing than the usual run of arts conferences, and she had never been to Hawaii. Had she received the invitation two weeks, even a week, before when her only thought had been to get away from the Tabors' apartment gracefully (yes, she had felt she should be getting back to her own place, but she hadn't really wanted to go back), she might have been tempted to accept, might already have been winging her way to Hawaii, might never have known that General Martillo was coming to New York until it was too late.

Strange that she should have been given such short notice for so elaborate an event. Or had the notice actually been that short? She looked at the envelope. According to the postage-meter cancellation, the letter had been dispatched from Washington, D.C., over three weeks before. And the previous Wednesday Michelle had left a large bundle of mail with the Tabors' concierge, which meant that the letter could not have arrived before then. The delay must have been the Post Office's fault. For the first time in her life—and possibly the last—Susan blessed the U.S. Post Office.

She was impatient to get in touch with Gil, but first things first. The locks had to be changed, unless she wanted to sleep with a gun under her pillow. She found a locksmith's down the street, presided over by an elderly man with a face like a moldy walnut. "I'll be there sometime this week without fail, I promise you," he said, with the air of one conferring a great favor.

"The locks in my apartment have got to be changed this afternoon."

He shook his head, as if in wonder at her innocence. "Lady, lady, you know how many customers I got backed up? All over the East Side people have been losing their keys or having them stolen or throwing out their roommates or getting their locks smashed by criminal elements, or so they say. I don't ask questions; I just fix locks. I got a waiting list as long as my arm." And he shook that member by way of illustration. Since he was almost a dwarf, with limbs in proportion to his size, this was not as effective a demonstration as it might have been.

He shifted gears. "The only reason I don't say next week is that you got such nice blue eyes I can't resist you." And he leered up at her.

"In that case," she said, "I'll try another locksmith." She turned to go—a feint, and both he and she knew it, but it was part of the interchange between workman and customer, as formalized a ritual as the bargaining process between Oriental rug dealer and Occidental tourist.

"I can assure you, you won't find another locksmith in the city who isn't up to his ears in customers." This time he shook a finger.

"I'll take my chances," she said, moving toward the door. "If need be, I'll call in someone from another borough." An empty threat. People in the outer boroughs were in as dire need of locksmiths as people on Manhattan's Upper East Side. That was one area where rich and poor were alike— they needed locks.

"I'll try to see if I maybe can squeeze you in today. But I'll be honest with you, I can't make any promises."

Something seemed to stir in her tote bag. Her mail. She'd thrown most of it away; the rest was simply shifting. Nothing odd about that; what was odd was hearing her own voice say, "But you've got to promise; you've got to swear by the eternal omnipresence that you'll be there this afternoon."

My God, she thought, what's gotten into me. He'll think I'm crazy. I am crazy. Those New Agers are infectious.

His face changed. It took on an ineffable expression. Before, he had shaken various portions of his anatomy. This time his whole body shook. "Why didn't you say so before? I'll be there before five. I swear by the eternal omnipresence." And he actually came out from behind the counter and opened the door for her.

On her way out, she noticed the crystals hanging in his window over the Medeco display and the sample security grilles and realized that her subconscious must have noted them and caused her to act accordingly. But that didn't cheer her. Once you let your subconscious take over, there was no telling what it would be up to next.

She looked at her watch. One o'clock. She had made no plans for the rest of the day or the evening, because she hadn't known how much work she herself would have to do in the apartment before she could settle down. Just as well that she hadn't made plans, or she would have had to break them when she found out about the general's impending arrival. From now until he was gone she wouldn't be able to do anything but think of how she could get to him.

If only she could be direct—load her gun, go out to Kennedy Airport and wait for him, no matter how long it took. But he might arrive at Newark; he might land at a private field; he might arrive by ship or submarine. There was no way she could ambush him. She would have to wait until he arrived and get him then. In the meantime, she would try to get hold of Gil—not such a simple matter, for, in spite of Tinsley's innuendos, she and Gil were by no means on the kind of social footing where she could simply call him up and ask him to have lunch with her. She would need to have a reason before she could approach him, she felt, or he might think she was following in Mimi's footsteps.

Of course she did have a reason, an excellent reason, but she could hardly say, "Gil, I would like you to introduce me to your president so that I can assassinate him." He might take this as a piece of convoluted North American humor, but it wasn't likely to bring her to the general.

No, she had to act casual. If only she could run into Gil accidentally . . . but you can't run into someone accidentally on purpose when you have no idea of where he's likely to hang out. She didn't even know in what part of town he was living; the days were long gone when it was possible to determine the neighborhood in which someone lived by the letters prefixed to his telephone number. Now it was all numbers and no neighborhoods, and people lived in the unlikeliest places.

Why shouldn't I call him up and ask him to lunch, even if

we're not on that kind of footing, she asked herself. What does it matter what he thinks? When you're planning an assassination, sometimes you have to overlook the conventions.

Although she disliked using an outdoor telephone, she had no choice, unless she wanted to go back to the apartment, and she didn't want to go back to the apartment. She dialed—no, there were no dials anymore—she pressed Gil's number. The phone rang and rang. No answer. It was a long time since she had rung a number that was not answered by a machine, if no human being was there—and sometimes even if one was, listening to make sure the call was a welcome one, before picking up the receiver.

At this point, she was glad there was no answer; otherwise, she would have to talk to Gil or leave her message within the hearing of a man who, either waiting for a chance at the instrument or a chance to snatch her bag, had come up and was standing much too close for courtesy. But then how could you expect courtesy from someone wearing baggy trousers and a baseball cap? As soon as she left the phone, he stepped up and put money in the slot. She looked back as she left. He was talking on the phone in Spanish, making no effort to keep his voice down; but then, she had observed, most speakers of Spanish made no effort to keep their voices down. Spanish seemed to be a loud language.

She would try to call Gil again when she could find a more private phone. In the meantime, she remembered having noted an announcement for a show of collages at the East End Gallery. She would take a look at them—as good a way of spending the afternoon as any. And the East End was just around the corner from the Fothergill. After she'd been to one, she might drop in at the other and have another look at Gil's pictures. He might even be in the gallery; young artists often spent their time hanging around their work. Perhaps she would even buy one of his pictures. What better way to win an artist's heart than by buying one of his pictures? Not that she wanted to win his heart, just his gratitude, but the operating principle was the same.

Since it was only ten blocks or so away, she decided to walk there. As she walked, she heard the blaring of horns and the screaming of insults behind her. There seemed to be some sort of traffic tie-up caused, as far as she could determine, by a green Dodge sedan that was proceeding too slowly for the tastes of the other drivers in the street. As she turned to look, she seemed to see a blue Chevy a few cars behind the Dodge, and farther up the street a black Mercedes. A perfectly ordinary combination of perfectly ordinary cars, she told herself.

As she reached the front door of the small gray building on Lexington Avenue in which the East End was housed atop a pet shop, an antique restorer, and a dentist's office, she heard running footsteps behind her, and a voice—Gil Frias's voice—calling breathlessly, "Miss Melville! Susan!"

She turned around, surprised. She had not expected to succeed so easily in her quest. Something in her tote bag bumped against her leg. Nonsense, she told herself, it had nothing to do with the crystal. I came to this neighborhood hoping to see Gil, so it's really not too much of a coincidence that he should appear. If the crystal really had powers, it would be General Martillo who was running after me.

For one crazy moment she waited expectantly. . . . Gil remained Gil—tall, dark, handsome, the answer to any woman's dreams but her own. But then there were dreams and dreams.

"I am so happy to see you," he gasped. "I am anxious to talk to you about something very important. I tried to reach you at your brother's apartment. Someone there said you had gone home but she wasn't sure whether that was to your temporal or your spiritual home. For a moment—" he gave a little laugh "—I thought she meant you might be dead."

She was startled. "You seem to take the idea very . . . casually."

"Oh, no, I would be very sorry if anything bad happened to you."

"So would I," she said.

"I called your apartment but only your machine answered." He made a movement with his shoulders that was a cross between a shrug and a shiver. "I still haven't gotten used to those machines. Do you realize that, if you had died, the machine would go on answering the phone in your voice for God knows how long?"

"Until the tape ran out," she said. "You seem preoccupied with my impending death."

"Praderans are always preoccupied with impending death," he said gloomily.

"I tried to phone you," she said, "but no one answered."

"If I had known you were going to call, I would have been sure to stay close to the phone," he said, with more gallantry, she felt, than sense.

A dog which had been sleeping in the pet shop window got to his feet and eyed them. He seemed to be a genetic miscellany, cobbled together from various breeds. Endearing but definitely downscale. What was he doing in the window of a pet shop in such a neighborhood, she wondered.

"Do you live around here?" she asked Gil. Not that Gil was at all downscale—definitely upscale so far as she could judge.

"Not too far," he said. "But I'm in the neighborhood because I wanted to see Mr. Fothergill about—about the way some of my pictures have been hung. How lucky I am to have run into you like this. Do you happen to have a couple of minutes to spare? I am really very anxious to talk to you."

Wouldn't it be wonderful if Gil's object were to invite her to some large party to honor the general, where she could kill him (the general) quietly and conveniently? That way she wouldn't have to ask him for an invitation. She hated to be pushy, even in a good cause.

"Well, I was just going to see the—" she looked at the sign outside under the gallery's name "—Gittelman collages."

"I have not seen them myself. Perhaps we could look at them together. I know I would be able to appreciate them more keenly if you were there to appreciate them with me."

"I'd be happy to have your company," she said, adding casually, "As a matter of fact, I've been wanting to talk to you myself.'' Which was silly; why else would she have tried to call him?

As they went inside the building, the dog gave a volley of barks, definitely directed at her. "He seems to have taken a fancy to you," Gil said. "He's saying goodbye."

She smiled. Somehow the barks had sounded less like a farewell than a warning.

The elevator that took them up to the fourth floor was claustrophobically small, bringing them very near to each other. How large and dark and liquid his eyes were, Susan thought, a lot like the eyes of the dog in the pet shop below. But the dog had been deliberately appealing. He wanted a home. What did Gil want?

The elevator door opened with a clash, on the opposite side from the one by which they had entered. She always found it a bit unnerving to have an elevator open on one side at ground level and on another when you reached your destination, as if it were admitting you to some other dimension in space and time. In the case of the East Side Gallery, it was a small, rather dingy dimension, kept from being the twilight zone by rather inadequate track lighting, supplemented by some skylights that seemed to be covered with grime—which did not mean that they had not been recently washed. In New York City, the fight against grime is like the fight against crime, constant and futile.

It was nearly empty, as galleries were wont to be at that time of day, containing just four persons—an individual of indeterminate sex who sat, sunk in boredom, at a desk just outside the elevator; a couple of well-dressed, middle-aged women who were looking alternately at the collages and their catalogues and conversing in low knowledgeable tones; and a fattish, balding young man in a pullover and blue jeans, who wandered about from collage to collage with a distracted air.

Susan and Gil picked up catalogues from the androgyne up front; then went and stared dutifully at the collages, whose

chief value seemed to her to be ecological, in that they re-
cycled materials that would otherwise have been thrown
away. Perhaps someone could start a new movement: Solve
the problem of waste disposal; turn garbage into collage. But
then the world would be overwhelmed by mountains of art
instead of mountains of trash, and the end result would be
the same.

And how would you handle toxic waste? She was ponder-
ing the feasibility of arranging a toxic waste exhibit exclu-
sively for critics, when Gil cleared his throat. "I don't want
to distract you from the—the art," he said, glancing at the
collages and wincing, "but I wanted to tell you about a letter
I have just received from a patron of mine."

"General Martillo!" she exclaimed, so loudly that the two
women visitors to the gallery looked up with raised eye-
brows. Susan felt embarrassed. She had raised her voice in
a public place. How unspeakably boorish of her.

Even Gil was staring at her in surprise. "No one so ex-
alted, I'm afraid," he said.

"But I thought he was your patron?"

"My official patron, of course. Without his sponsorship,
I would never have been able to—to—" He stopped, seem-
ingly at a loss for words.

"Leave La Pradera?" Susan suggested.

"No, no! Anyone who wishes to can leave La Pradera
whenever he or she desires. It is a free society."

"Of course, of course," she said.

"I can stay here as long as I like, as long as—" he gave
her a rueful grin "—my resources hold out. No one will try
to make me go back if I don't want to."

He was protesting too much. And what were his resources
anyhow? What was he living on? Government money? Martillo money? Or did he make enough money from his art to
support himself?

"I'm sure you can do whatever you want," she said.

"*El Presidente* is my patron in the sense that he—that is,
the government—buys my pictures for public buildings, but
that's a matter of national policy. If you have an artist, hang
him. But there are people outside my government, outside

my country, who buy my pictures for their private collections and—'' he smiled ''—pay a lot more for them than my government does.''

So that could account for where the money he was living on now came from. He was not necessarily government-subsidized.

''And some of my patrons are kind enough to take an interest in me personally.'' This was not unusual, Susan knew. Many collectors took an interest in the artists whose work they bought. Often it was part of the deal. They collected the artist along with the art.

''You will wonder why I am telling you all this? There is a Brazilian gentleman who owns a number of my pictures. He is very wealthy, with houses all over the world, in North America as well as South America. Europe, too. At the moment, I believe, he is in Italy. He has a villa near Rome.''

He paused. ''I hope he is enjoying his stay. I understand the weather in Italy is very fine this time of year. Are we going to discuss all of his residences?''

Gil gave a nervous laugh. ''I suppose I am taking a long time to get to the point but—but it is not easy for me to—to ask favors.'' He gave her a melting look that was supposed to disarm her. Instead, it put her on her guard. Whatever he's trying to do, he isn't very good at it, she thought.

''Senhor Ribeira has a place on Cape Cod—a cottage, he calls it, but I have seen pictures and it is rather more grand than such a name would indicate. It has eight rooms, four baths, a swimming pool, a tennis court, and—'' he caught her eye ''—let us say it is very well appointed. He will not be using it for the rest of the year, and he has offered it to me for as long as I like. Although it is past the season, he says, it is beautiful there and, right now, very quiet. Many artists go there to paint, he says.''

She could not see Gil as a painter of Cape Cod scenes. All of his work, at least all of his work that she had seen, had been figures—sensuous female nudes in lush tropical surroundings. You didn't need to go to Cape Cod to paint them. In fact, she thought, the atmosphere of Cape Cod could have a decidedly deterrent effect on his type of work. Besides, what would a wealthy Brazilian be doing with a Cape Cod cottage, no matter how grand?

And what did she care, anyway? What concerned her was that Gil seemed to be making some kind of extended farewell—why he bothered, she didn't know; a simple postcard with a picture of a whale would have been enough—and she needed him to get to General Martillo. Once that was arranged, he could go to Cape Cod to paint sensuous nude New England fishermen for all she cared.

It was time to change the subject. "I was reading the morning paper," she began, "and, quite by chance, I happened to notice that—"

"Senhor Ribeira suggested that I might like to bring an artist friend along to keep me company, and it is my dearest hope, Susan, that you will consent to be my guest."

And Gil drew a deep breath, as if relieved at having gotten that off his chest. Not the most gracious of invitations, she thought, trying not to laugh.

Gil misinterpreted the expression on her face. "Oh, it will be quite proper, I assure you. There is a resident housekeeper of the utmost respectability. Do say yes, Susan. I could learn so much from you. Not," he added, "that I would presume to invite you there as my teacher. I want you to come as my friend." And, with a sudden surge of boldness, he took her hand.

Why, the impertinent little snip, she thought. Then she reminded herself that, whatever he wanted out of her, there was something she wanted out of him, and slid her hand out of his grasp, instead of following her first impulse and jerking it away.

"How can you possibly think of leaving New York at a time like this?" she demanded.

"At a time like what?" He looked around him, as if he expected to find some answer in the collages. "What is so special about this time? Is there some holiday I don't know about? Or some important event?"

"General—President Martillo is coming to New York next week. Isn't that an important enough event? Surely you'll want to be here to greet him when he arrives?"

"How did you—? *El Presidente* coming here; that's impossible. Where did you get this piece of misinformation?"

"It was in this morning's *Times*."

"There must be some mistake."

"How can there be? The *Times* never makes a mistake." And when she saw that he did not appreciate the pleasantry (after all, one could hardly expect a foreigner to appreciate the fact that the daily Corrections column in the *Times* was many New Yorkers' favorite part of the paper), "It was in all the other papers, too." Not that they couldn't all make the same same mistake; they seemed to follow each other like lemmings. "What makes you think it's a mistake?" she asked. "Are you in the general's confidence?"

His laugh was so forced it was more like a hoot. "That's absurd. How could I, a—a mere artist, be in *El Presidente*'s confidence? But something like this, his coming to New York, I—any Praderan—would have heard. It isn't every day that *El Presidente* leaves the country."

"I understand that he hasn't been out of La Pradera for over twenty-five years," she said.

"That is what I said. Twenty-five years isn't every day." There were beads of perspiration on his forehead.

Why is he so upset about the general's coming to New York? she wondered. Rather, why is he so upset about my knowing that the general's coming to New York?

However, she was beginning to think she knew the answer. The invitation to Cape Cod was just one invitation too many. Somebody wanted to get her away from New York. And Gil had been chosen as the instrument of her removal—one of the instruments of her removal.

"Even if there is no mistake and *El Presidente* is coming here," Gil persisted, "there is no reason why I should be here in the city when he arrives. Undoubtedly, if he is coming, he is coming for matters of state. What do I have to do with matters of state?"

"The papers did say he was coming to speak before the United Nations, but you know how it is when a head of state visits another country. There are receptions, dinners, gala evenings at the opera, and I'm sure he'll want to visit the Fothergill to see your show.''

"He might do that, if conditions permit," Gil acknowledged, "but, even so—"

He was interrupted by a cough close by—a self-introductory rather than a respiratory sound.

They turned. The balding young man stood beside them, an insecure smile on his round pink face. "Forgive me, but aren't you Susan Melville, the artist?"

◇◇◇ **XIX**

She would have liked to deny her identity, but that could be productive of embarrassment later. "My name is Melville," she admitted, "and I do paint." Thank God, she thought, the other two visitors to the gallery had left a few minutes earlier. She could envision them pricking up their ears at the mention of her name.

The young man's face became suffused with joy. "I thought I couldn't be mistaken. I can't tell you how delighted, how honored, I am that you've come to see my collages."

"You must be Mr.—" she gave a quick look at her catalogue "—Gittelman."

The young man blushed even pinker. "Yes, yes, Quentin Gittelman. I'm always forgetting to introduce myself."

She indicated Gil with a wave of her hand. "This is Gil Frias, La Pradera's most eminent artist."

"Of course, of course." Clearly Mr. Gittelman had never heard of either La Pradera or of Gil. "It is an honor to meet you, sir," he said. But his eyes were fixed on Susan's face. He looked like a dog waiting for a bone.

For a moment she was without words. Gil came to her rescue. "Your work is truly remarkable, Mr. Gittelman. We have nothing like it in my country."

Mr. Gittelman beamed, but his gaze was still fixed on Susan. Clearly Gil's praise was only an appetizer. He wanted the main dish. She would have to give it to him or she would never be able to get away. "What I find most impressive is the subtle convergence of energies, the juxtaposition of forces so alike and yet so disparate as to create a harmonious bal-

ance. Each collage makes what appears on the surface to be
a single strong statement, but, upon closer inspection, sep-
arates into a multiplicity of divergent images, which, in the
end, all come together to form one comprehensive aspect of
the great totality.''

Gil looked at her with respect, Mr. Gittelman positively
glowed. How much the vocabulary of the art world seemed
to coincide with the vocabulary of the New Age, she thought,
and wondered whether there were any esoteric significance
there or whether it was all part of that same great totality.

''And now,'' she said to the ecstatic Mr. Gittelman, ''much
as I'd like to stay and—and savor your collages further, I do
have an urgent appointment. So nice to have met you.'' And
she made for the elevator, Gil hard on her heels.

''From now on,'' he said, as they were descending, ''I
will go only to exhibits of Old Masters. At least you will not
find Rembrandt or Renoir lurking about waiting to pounce
on you.''

''Don't be too sure,'' Susan said, without thinking.

He looked at her in surprise. Wishing she had kept her
mouth shut, she tried to explain to him about channelers and
channeling. She told him about Fée and Nicolas Fouquet,
trying to make a joke of the whole thing.

But he took it—or seemed to take it—seriously. ''Ah, *una
mistica*. In La Pradera we have many such.''

Had the New Age come to La Pradera, she wondered, or
were they still in the Old Age there, without the jargon and
contemporary flourishes that were supposed to transmute an-
cient beliefs into up-to-date credos?

''*El Presidente* has often spoken out against such things,''
Gil went on. ''He says it is all silly superstition. Why, he
does not even believe in astrology.''

''Do you?'' Susan asked.

He took his cue from the surprise that must have been
evident in her face. ''Of course not. I am not an ignorant
peasant. Still. . . .'' He hesitated. ''Peasants are in touch
with the earth. Sometimes they know things that sophisti-
cates are reluctant to believe.''

"The people I know who believe in channelers are hardly ignorant peasants," she said, smiling at the thought of how Tinsley would react to hear herself and her cronies described in such a way, even negatively.

"Of course not," Gil said. "Yet. . . ." He hesitated again. "Maybe in some way they are back in touch with the earth."

The elevator door opened. They came out into the lobby. A man in baggy trousers was waiting for the elevator. There was something familiar about him; however, she couldn't see his face, since most of it was obscured by the handkerchief he was holding to his jaw. Apparently one of the dentist's patients.

The dog in the pet shop window greeted their reappearance with another volley of barks. "He seems to recognize you," Gil said, disclaiming any previous acquaintance with the animal on his own part.

"He's looking for someone—anyone—to buy him and take him away from all this," she observed.

"There are worse places than this," Gil said; "at least from a dog's point of view." She wondered whether he was referring to the sad lot of underprivileged dogs, or whether he was referring to something—or someone—else.

"So will you come with me to Cape Cod?" he demanded suddenly, almost angrily.

"Cape Cod?" she repeated. It took her a moment to remember, to understand what he was talking about. "There's no hurry about that, is there? Senhor what's his name . . . ?"

"Ribeira."

"Senhor Ribeira said you could use the house whenever you liked, didn't he? And, since we've agreed that you can't possibly leave town when the general's due here so soon. . . ."

"We have not agreed on any such thing!" He was obviously having trouble controlling himself. "There is no reason why I should stay in town, none whatsoever. And soon it will be too cold to go to Cape Cod."

"Not for another month at least."

"For you, perhaps, but not for me. I do not like the cold."

"Then you won't like New York after a couple of months, because it gets cold here, too."

"In the end it gets cold everywhere," he said.

She was not going to let him lure her away from the topic at hand. "There's every reason for you to stay in New York right now. After all President Martillo has done for you, it would be most ungrateful of you not to be here to greet him. I am sure he, and also Ambassador Yepez, will expect you to attend whatever—er—festivities are planned for the occasion."

Gil opened his mouth and shut it.

"And, speaking of those festivities, I wondered whether you would take me to one of them as your guest. I've heard so much about the general—the president—from you and—and other sources, I'm anxious to meet him." There, she'd finally gotten it out.

And, really, it wasn't such an outrageous request. No reason for him to turn white, as if she had uttered some kind of blasphemy. "That would be very difficult to arrange; it would be impossible, in fact."

"You said once that if I knew him I would realize what a wonderful man he was. Well, here's my chance to meet him and talk to him. . . ."

"He doesn't speak English."

"The *Times* correspondent says he speaks fluent English."

"The *Times*, the *Times*, always the *Times*!" he declared passionately. "Thank God, we don't have a free press in La Pradera. And, forgive me, Susan, but it isn't a question of whether you want to meet him, but whether he wants to meet you. He is, after all, *El Presidente*. Your president doesn't meet with everyone who wants to meet him, does he?"

"I've been to dinner at the White House," she said. She didn't like to boast about it, but it was fact, and, if she was good enough to have dinner with the President of the United States Gil could hardly suggest that she wasn't good enough to have dinner with the President of La Pradera.

"I'm not political," Gil said, more to himself than her, "I never was political and I never will be political. Why does this have to happen to me?"

"Why don't you speak to the ambassador?" she urged. "Tell him you'd like to introduce me to President Martillo and see what he says. Or perhaps it would be better if I got in touch with Señor Yepez myself?"

"No, no, I'll talk to Leon—Señor Yepez myself. And then I'll call you and let you know what he says. I'll get started right away—trying to get hold of him I mean."

She'd been about to suggest that they have lunch, but she didn't want to stop him while he was headed in the right direction. Yet she was reluctant to let him go; it would be so easy for him to disappear completely. Why, she didn't even know where he lived.

"It just occurred to me that I don't have your address," she said, taking out a small, leatherbound pocket memorandum that someone had given her for Christmas or some similar occasion; it wasn't the kind of thing one bought for oneself. "I wanted to write you a thank you note after the opening, and I didn't know where to send it. Besides—" as he made a dismissive gesture with his hand to indicate that such niceties were unnecessary "—I'm associated with several organizations that sponsor events I'm sure would interest you, since you told me you were anxious to establish yourself in art circles here. I need to tell them where they should direct their literature."

"You are too kind," he said, running his hand through his thick dark hair, "but, at the moment I don't have a permanent address. I am staying with friends. After we come back from Cape Cod—"

"Well, what's your friends' address?" she asked, holding her pen poised over the paper.

He choked and sputtered, and finally, reluctantly gave an address in the East Sixties.

By this time Susan wasn't surprised to hear what it was. "That's the address of the Praderan Mission, isn't it?"

"Yes," he admitted. "They often put up visitors from home as guests."

Important visitors from home, she understood. As, for example, protegés of the President.

"Then how is it that when I tried to call you there, nobody answered. Doesn't the mission have a switchboard?"

"The guest suite has its own direct line so guests can have their privacy. That's another reason I will have to go to Cape Cod. I will have to vacate the guest suite so *El Presidente* will have his privacy."

"Oh, so he'll be staying at the mission," she said. At least that much was accomplished; she knew where he would be staying.

Gil said something to himself in Spanish that sounded like swearing.

"I should have thought he'd be' staying at the Waldorf or the Plaza." Too bad, hotels were much easier to crack than missions. "But that doesn't mean you have to leave New York," she added. "Surely you can find somewhere else to stay."

"I suppose I could go to a hotel," he said, "but I did so want to go to Cape Cod—with you," he added hastily.

"I'm afraid I wouldn't be able to leave town right now," she said, "and I do so want to meet General—I mean President—Martillo."

"I know," he said. "What I mean is, I'll speak to the ambassador about your request, although I'm afraid there isn't much hope of its' being granted."

"Will you call me and let me know what he says?" she asked.

He nodded. "I'll call you as soon as I can. If it's too late tonight—"

"I'll be up very late. You can call me at any hour. Promise me that you'll call, even if you can't reach the ambassador."

"I promise, I promise," he said.

She watched him trudge off, a despondent slouch to his shoulders, failure in his spine, the black Mercedes that had been parked across the street moving along slowly behind him, and she wondered whether she ever would see or hear from him again.

* * *

She was about to head uptown, when the dog in the pet shop window barked. Don't leave me here, the bark seemed to say. Probably he barked that way at everyone who appeared to show an interest; still, there was something appealing about him.

She had enough responsibilities; she was not about to take on the responsibility of an animal. But she couldn't leave him there. She had a happy thought. She did owe Tinsley a hostess gift; actually, she owed Alex a host gift, because he had borne the greater burden of hospitality. However, female liberation or no, it was still the hostess who got the gift. Susan went inside and opened negotiations for the dog. As she might have guessed from the shop's location, he was not a mutt at all. He was, the proprietor said, something purebred and unpronounceable.

"A purebred what?"

"A Tibetan yakhound, if you insist on a translation."

"I never heard of a Tibetan yakhound."

"You've heard of English sheepdogs, haven't you? They herd sheep. Well, Tibetan yakhounds herd yaks."

"Hounds don't herd," she told him. "They chase. Like foxhounds."

"So he chases yaks. There aren't that many yaks in Manhattan for him to cause a problem."

The dog cost a lot of money. Well, I can afford it, Susan thought. She bought the animal and directed the proprietor to deliver him to Tinsley—which, the man said, he would do immediately. He seemed anxious to get the dog out of the place. If she had wanted to bargain, she thought, she could have bought him for much less.

XX

She got herself a sandwich at a nondescript little restaurant on Third Avenue, more because she wanted to kill time than because she was particularly hungry; then she used up another couple of hours in taking care of some errands. She saw several blue Chevys in the street and a green Dodge, but no black Mercedes. She didn't see anyone she knew, but she did see a couple of people who looked vaguely familiar.

When she got back to her house there were several suspicious-looking characters loitering around the entrance, but then there were always suspicious characters loitering around the entrance. There were suspicious characters loitering around the entrances to most buildings in New York, even on the East Side. From time to time the doormen would go out and chase them away, but they eventually drifted back. She thought of complaining to the doorman now, so he would go and chase them away immediately, but she didn't want to draw attention to herself. Or to them.

By the time she arrived at her apartment, the workmen had gone, apparently taking a good deal of their debris with them. Michelle, dressed for departure, was waiting for her employer to return and heap the praises on her that she felt she deserved and which, for once—or so it seemed—she did deserve.

All things considered, large parts of the apartment had been made surprisingly habitable. The new kitchen appliances had all been installed or connected; and, if they worked, Susan would be able to make herself dinner, provided the food she had ordered from the supermarket arrived in good time. Life in New York was always predicated on the conditional. The dining room was more or less in usable shape, except for the miscellaneous objects heaped on the table and the sideboard—few of them having any relevance to the room's function. How much one amasses in the course of a lifetime, Susan thought, and how hard it is to let go of it.

"I was usin' the table to sort stuff and I didn't get a chance to finish," Michelle explained, "but all you have to do is clear away one end and you can eat like a lady." For ladies, according to Michelle's way of thinking, did not eat in the kitchen. Susan had no prejudice against eating in the kitchen but the kitchen furniture had mysteriously disappeared and she did have a prejudice against eating standing up at the counter.

At least she would be able to go to sleep that night on her new bed in her own bedroom, with only one small, really negligible hitch. "I looked and looked but I cooden find a matchin' set of sheets," Michelle said. "In fack, I had trouble findin' the sheets at all. Whoever messed up this place sure did a good job." From now on, Susan knew, whatever couldn't be found, whatever was out of place, whatever turned out to be damaged would be ascribed to the intruder. She surveyed her bed. Oh, for the good old days when all sheets were white and life wasn't so full of complications. The top sheet was a delicate pastel floral, the bottom sheet a bold geometric, the pillowcase . . .

"Where did that Snoopy pillowcase come from?" she demanded of her servitor.

Michelle looked at the pillowcase as if she were seeing it for the first time. "Maybe it was a present," she suggested. "That'd account for the matchin' towels. I put 'em in the bathroom."

"I would have remembered getting a gift like that," Susan said. "Maybe whoever broke into the apartment left me a matched set of Snoopy linens to make up for the intrusion."

"I guess maybe some time the laundry got mixed up with somebody else's, awright?" Unstated was the fact that, if the laundry had been mixed up, Michelle was the only one who could have done the mixing. "You don't know how long it took me to find any kind of pillowcase at all."

She rubbed her shoulder and groaned. "I been workin' like a dog and my arthritis is actin' up somethin' fierce. You know how many people there are in the world who don' even have pillows to lay their heads on at night, let alone Snoopy pillowcases?"

"Not as many as there are people who don't have housekeepers who are supposed to take care of such things for them," Susan said.

Michelle's mutter was so indistinct, Susan couldn't make out any words except "oppressed slaves," and she was too tired to make an issue out of that, at least at the moment. "Well," she said, "I'll sleep on Snoopy tonight and tomorrow, if you look hard, I'm sure you'll manage to find where the rest of the linens are."

"Whatever you say," Michelle agreed. Which should, Susan thought, go without saying, but, where Michelle was concerned, nothing went without saying. "And, now that I been worked to the bone, I guess I'll be gettin' along. It's half-past five awready, and, if I don' get home by six, which I'm not likely to do, the trains bein' what they are, Lorenzo's gonna worry hisself sick."

Susan had met Lorenzo, and he hadn't seemed the type to worry, but who was she to destroy another woman's illusions? "Goodnight then, Michelle, I'll see you bright and early in the morning."

"I kinda thought you might be sleepin' late." Here she rubbed her other shoulder and gave another groan.

"I might," Susan said, "but you won't. Nine o'clock sharp, please. Use your keys when you get here," she added cruelly, "in case I'm still asleep."

She was an early riser, but it was about time, she told herself, as she'd told herself before, that Michelle learned who was boss.

After Michelle had gone, with many a reproachful look and a few additional groans designed to fill Susan with enough guilt to last all night and spill over into morning, Susan checked her phone messages. None seemed important to her at the moment, although at the time nothing would have seemed important that did not offer direct hope of leading the way to General Martillo; for, by this time, she was beginning to suspect that Gil was more concerned with keeping her away from his president than with helping her gain access to him. Why he should want to keep her away, she did not understand, except that quite clearly it was not his own idea; someone was pulling his strings.

It occurred to her that, although her world might have forgotten Buckley Melville, it was quite possible that the Praderan world, particularly General Martillo, had not. After all, he had given him a mention in his book, which was more than he had accorded most of the other people he'd been accused of killing. The two men had been business partners, so to speak; they might have been friends as well. Maybe Daddy even showed him the picture of me he used to carry in his wallet, she thought. Not that I look much like that picture now; the main thing is that Martillo might very well know that Daddy had a daughter, and he would assume that she knew what had happened to her father.

Obviously, snug in his little South American realm, he would have had no need to worry about her over the years. But why should he start worrying about her now? Because he was planning to come to the United States, of course. Even so, what could he possibly think he had to fear from her? That she would kill him? Absurd. Upper-class American ladies did not go around avenging their parents as a rule; even a South American strongman should know that. And he would have no way of knowing that she was not one to follow the rules.

And, even if he did fear that she might attack him, he would come accompanied by bodyguards. He would be well protected—or so he would think. No, it could not be violence he was afraid of. A lawsuit? Again, no. If she'd wanted to sue him, if she'd thought she had grounds for a suit, she would have filed it long ago; she wouldn't have needed to wait for his arrival in the United States to start proceedings. Moreover, it would be the lawyers he would have to fear in such a case. Her presence in New York wouldn't make an iota of difference.

If she represented any kind of threat at all to him, it would be to his public image. The fact that he had killed Buckley Melville was known, but it was in the past, dismissed, no longer news. But if Susan Melville, one of America's most famous contemporary artists, made public the information that Relempago Martillo, who was going to speak before the United Nations, had killed her father, it could well become news again. The media would leap upon the story and make a three-ring circus out of it. It would cause him embarrassment and perhaps the president would suddenly find that all the guest rooms in the White House were full up, or that he was called away on some emergency. It could spoil his visit.

The whole picture seemed clear. Undoubtedly, Martillo had made his plans to come to the United States some time ago. Fearing that Susan Melville would make waves, he had sent his handsome young protegé up north with instructions to do whatever he could to keep her away from the city during his visit. In return, Gil would be given not only his government's gratitude, but a trip to New York and a show at the Fothergill, a handsome reward for any up-and-coming young artist. How far, Susan wondered, was Gil prepared to go in order to repay his obligations?

Of course, all this could be her imagination. Gil could simply be an innocent artist sent up north to give La Pradera a positive cultural image, in which case he might have no idea of the relationship, if you could call it that, between Martillo and herself; and that a confrontation with her would be the last thing Martillo would want. Although it seemed unlikely at this point that she would get any help from Gil, she didn't need to give up hope entirely.

But time was growing short. She had better look for a more promising means of access to Martillo. She called the von Schwabes at their New York apartment. The maid there said that Gunther and Mimi were in Washington. Whoever answered the phone in Washington said they were in New York. She left messages at both numbers. She hoped they had not gone out of town. It was just like Mimi to go off on a trip and forget to tell anyone, including the servants, where they had gone and how long they would be away.

Who else could get her a meeting with General Martillo? Ambassador Yepez was, of course, out of the question. If Gil wasn't his man, they were both working for the same agency. He would be as anxious to keep her away from his president as Gil was.

The downstairs doorbell rang. The voice of the porter on the intercom informed her that a delivery boy from the supermarket had arrived along with her groceries. Several minutes later, her back door buzzer sounded.

She opened the door. The delivery boy was not alone. He was accompanied by Adolfo. "I am acting as guardian," Adolfo explained, "because I know you are in a state of high nervousness. There was an intrusioner in her apartment early this morning," he explained to the delivery boy, "and Miss Melvilly is naturally wrought over."

"Did he—er—try anything?" the delivery boy asked, anxious for some tidbit to take back to the boys at Gristede's.

"He was gone before I got here."

The boy's face fell. "You were lucky, Miss Melville," he said sadly.

Adolfo followed him inside, ostensibly to help with the boxes. There was nothing she could do to stop him. He stayed behind after the boy left. She didn't close the back door. He didn't take the hint. "I am glad you are all serene, now, Miss Melvilly," he said. "You were all inside yourself this morning."

"I was naturally disturbed by the idea that there had been an intruder in my apartment, but I feel much safer now that I've had the locks changed."

Adolfo glowered. "You would feel even safer if you gave me a set of the new keys."

She let her silence drag out for a few seconds. His dark face flushed even darker. Then she said, "Well, thank you for coming up to make sure everything's all right. And now, if you'll excuse me, I have had rather a long day. . . ."

Instead of leaving, he came closer to her, so close she could smell the pungent odor of cologne or aftershave lotion. His manner was threatening; but then it was always threatening. He looked intently into her eyes. "You have seen today's paper?"

She stepped back a little, trying to appear unalarmed. After all, the back door was still open. People seldom went past on the service landing but there was always that possibility. "That's right, I was meaning to tell you. One of the neighbors' papers was left outside my door this morning and, before I could find out who it belonged to and return it, the workmen had spread it on the floor. If you'd give my apologies to—"

"No matter, no matter," Adolfo said, with an airy wave of his hand. "Papers come and go. Even in such a high-priced residence as this, it is an amazement how many papers disappear of a morning. Or little dogs without restraint do bad things upon them. I have told Mrs. Acacia time out and time in that dogs should be banned from this establishment, but she says—however, that is of small immediate moment." He advanced on her and she retreated. If anybody happened to be looking out of their window and into hers, she thought, it must look as if we're dancing. They would tell Mrs. Acacia, and she would say, "That Miss Melville. Goes on and on about wanting me to fire Adolfo and she secretly dances with him in her kitchen." And she would shake her head in the way she did whenever she discussed one of the residents, for, like most co-op board heads, she had a poor opinion of the whole lot.

"You tell me you have not read today's New York *Times*?" he asked. (He pronounced *Times* in two syllables—*Tim-es*. It took on a whole new identity that way.)

"Of course I've read today's *Times*. I got a copy of my own later in the day."

"And you saw nothing of strange interest there?"

"I saw many things of strange interest there. The *Times* is always full of things of strange interest, although not as full as the *Post*."

"You did not notice that the president of La Pradera is coming to speak before the United Nations?"

And why should he think I would find that of strange interest unless he knows of my connection with Martillo? Well, he's a Praderan. If Martillo knows I'm the daughter of Buckley Melville, why shouldn't Adolfo know?

Not having been a friend of Buckley Melville's—or so she assumed—he would find it more difficult to determine that Buckley Melville had left only one close living relative, his daughter, Susan. Even more difficult to determine that she herself was that same Susan Melville. *Who's Who* would tell him that her father had been named Buckley, but it would give the wrong year for his death (too embarrassed to admit when she had filled out the form that she did not know when he had died, she had given them an arbitrary year) and that could confuse him. He had to make sure she was the right Susan Melville; and, to do that, he had to search her apartment to see what evidence of her parentage he could find. Up until the time her apartment had been destroyed (had that been truly an accident?) he'd had no chance to do so, because he didn't have the keys to give him access. Now, of course, the family albums would have told him that she was the right Susan Melville, and the scrapbooks would have informed him that she was well aware of what had happened to her father.

No doubt in her mind now that he had not come to this particular apartment house by chance; no doubt that he had been her morning intruder. But why had he waited until the last possible moment to intrude? He'd had the whole weekend—and several weekends before that—to himself. He could have gone up there at his leisure and put everything back so she wouldn't have known anyone had been there. Had he timed it the way he had deliberately to frighten her? And what did he have to gain by frightening her? "It is easy for a wise man to understand the thinking of a wise man," Cristobal Herrero had written, "but not even a fool can understand the thinking of a fool."

The only thing to do was play it cool, pretend she had no

idea what he was talking about. "I'm afraid I only skimmed the paper. I must have overlooked the item about your president."

"He is not my president; he is a black-hearted usurper! But how could you have overlooked it when I saw with my very own eyes—"

He stopped. He could hardly say, "I saw with my very own eyes the scrapbooks you've been keeping on Martillo," without admitting that he had been the intruder in her apartment.

"—when I saw with my own eyes that it was on the front page of the *Tim-es*," he finished.

"I must have missed it," she said.

"I think you did not miss it. I think you know who he is."

No point going on fencing with him like this. "If you mean I know that he's the one who's supposed to have killed my father, yes I do know. I also know there's nothing I could do about it—even if I wanted to." She disliked the idea of discussing such personal matters with a building employee, but there didn't seem to be any alternative. "If my father chose to leave his wife and family and get mixed up in some tinpot revolution, then—" she steeled herself, "—I suppose he got what he deserved."

Adolfo was momentarily diverted. "It was not a teapot revolution; it was a glorious insurrection that putrefied because of the insect that became the head of it. And Martillo is not *supposed* to have killed your father; he *did* kill your father. I can swear to it."

She felt almost sick with excitement. She had known she cared, but she did not realize she cared so much. "How can you be so sure?" she demanded. *"Were you there?"*

Adolfo hesitated a long time before he answered. "No," he finally said, "I was not actually there, in the room. If I had been, I would not be alive today. But I spoke to those who were there, before they . . . disappeared. I could give you the details, but you would not want to hear them."

"Tell me," she said. "After all these years, I want to know exactly what did happen."

Adolfo shook his head. "It is not fit for a lady's ears. All you need to know is that that *chinche* killed the man who was his ally, his comrade, the man who had trusted him more than anyone else in the world.''

That did not ring true. Trust had never been Buckley Melville's long suit, especially when it came to his business partners. But Adolfo was hardly likely to be objective. ''Then you did know my father?'' she asked.

Adolfo swallowed. ''Yes,'' he said. ''A fine man.''

Well, of course he'd say that to me, even if he did know my father, she thought. He may have been an army officer once but he's a building superintendent now. Besides, he seems to want something out of me. What it was she could not tell. But, if he had any thought of gaining support from her for some project, she had better scotch that idea. ''All right, I believe you. Relempago Martillo killed my father. There's nothing I can do about it unless—'' she picked her words carefully—''you expect me to kill him in my turn.''

Adolfo laughed so long and loud she knew he didn't have the slightest suspicion of what she was planning. Perhaps he was laughing a little too long and a little too hard, but that was to be expected. ''No, no, Miss Melvilly, we would not expect a lady to do anything of such a nature. We—my associates and I—are planning a little demonstration outside the United Nations when he gets here. A big demonstration, if we can get enough people. With you at our side, we can attract much more medium attention.''

Of course, she thought. No wonder the Praderan government—or whoever—is so anxious to get me away. This could cause considerable embarrassment to their plans. It could also cause considerable embarrassment to my plans. ''I'm sorry,'' she said. ''I won't have anything to do with it.''

''Do you not want to denounce the man who killed your father?'' Adolfo demanded.

''As far as I'm concerned, my father died four years before the time he was killed, when he walked out on my mother and me.''

Adolfo tugged at his lip. Apparently he had not foreseen that this trivial circumstance would stand in the way of his plans. ''Still and all, the blood of your father is on his hands.

Doesn't that make you want to speak out on radio, appear on television, give interviews to the newspapers?''

"No," she said. "And, if you try to use me as a rallying point for your cause, I shall speak to Mrs. Acacia, and she will fire you.''

"My job is important to me, Miss Melvilly," he said. "But my country is more important. Besides, if there is a revolution, I will go back and assume an important position in the new government. I will not need this job.''

She hoped he did not tell this to any of the other residents, or he might get more support than he and his revolution deserved.

XXI

After Adolfo left, she felt totally exhausted; ready to flop down on her new bed and go to sleep. But there was so much to be done. First of all, she had to call Peter, to make sure of what his plans—if he had any plans—might be. He had stayed away so long; he might as well stay away a week or two longer. A little late, or, rather, a little early to be calling Nepal—approximately five A.M. there. But it wouldn't hurt Peter to be awakened. The eternal omnipotence knew he had done it to her often enough when he was out in the field or working far away.

Someone with a British accent undertook to connect her with his room. The phone rang and rang. No answer. "Sorry, madam, but there doesn't appear to be anyone in Professor Franklin's room."

She was alarmed. Supposing he was on his way back already, without having bothered to let her know. "He hasn't checked out, has he?"

"Oh, no, madam. He's still registered with us. Is there any message I could give him?"

None with which she would sully the ears of an innocent hotel clerk (not that she'd ever known a hotel clerk who was truly innocent). "Just tell him Susan Melville called," she said, and hung up with a click. Melvilles never banged receivers, but they sometimes felt like banging receivers.

After all, she told herself, she and Peter had no commitment toward each other. If he chose to disport himself with some big-breasted Himalayan hussy, as she'd half-suspected all along—why else would anyone want to stay in the Katmandu Hilton for over a month?—that was his own affair.

But he could forget about his expansion plans for the Melville Foundation. There was no reason why the foundation should occupy all five floors of a building in such an expensive neighborhood. She would do what Jill had been wanting her to do all along: rent out the first two floors. With real estate taxes going up the way they were, it was the only sensible thing to do; and it was about time she started being sensible as far as Peter was concerned.

Suddenly she didn't feel tired anymore. She felt full of energy. She went to work on the apartment. Michelle hadn't been as industrious as had first appeared. She seemed to have achieved her clearing-up effect by shoving as much as she could into closets (including most of the debris Susan thought the workmen had taken away); and there turned out to be a number of boxes she hadn't unpacked at all, but stacked behind screens and pushed under beds and into corners— wherever they would not be immediately perceived by her employer. The fact that her employer was bound to discover them in the course of the evening didn't seem to bother her. Michelle lived for the moment.

Susan started unpacking the suitcases she had brought back from the Tabors' apartment with her, and managed to cram their contents into the few drawers Michelle had left available and into closets, which she emptied by dint of removing the things Michelle had thrown into them and cramming their contents into other closets. Where had all this stuff come from? Probably a lot should simply be thrown out. She'd left in such a hurry she hadn't had a chance to do any real clearing out; she'd just taken the personal stuff to her studio. Her studio—how was she going to make room here for all the things she had temporarily stored there?

While I was having the apartment redone, she thought, I should have arranged to have more closets built in. It was not too late to have that done, but that would mean it would take even longer before the workmen finished. Perhaps I'll order a couple of armoires to help take care of some of the overflow, she thought; then she remembered she had already ordered a couple of armoires, which the store had promised to deliver the week before along with the new chairs and the couch. I'm lucky I have a bed, she thought.

She had done some shopping in the course of the afternoon—soap and toothpaste and shampoo, the kind of items that always disappeared whenever you took your eye off them. As she took the packages out of her tote bag, there at the bottom was the crystal Fée had given her, glowing smugly. She had almost forgotten it. She tried to push it into a drawer, but, although it had seemed to her she had made enough room, she was unable to cram it in. Finally she set it on the windowsill in her bedroom, where it would catch the morning sun. Even at night it seemed to have a luminous glow—from the moonlight, she told herself. She pulled the blind down and tried to pretend that the crystal wasn't still glowing.

She started to unpack the boxes. If she threw away things as she worked, or at least put them into the empty boxes so they could be donated to some charitable organization, she should ultimately be better off in terms of storage space. She was working away with an industry that she hoped—forlornly, she knew—would inspire Michelle the next day, and had come upon her missing linens, neatly folded under an incomplete and outdated set of the *Encyclopedia Britannica* and was about to take them to her bedroom, when the phone rang. She let the machine answer, so that she could hear who it might be, before she committed herself to answering it. It proved to be Alex. Oh, dear, she thought, maybe I was too impulsive about that dog. For a moment, she was tempted to let the machine take the message, but that would be the coward's way out. Besides, she would have to talk to Alex—and Tinsley—sooner or later.

But it seemed that Tinsley had been delighted with the animal. "She'll call you later or tomorrow to thank you herself. Right now she's busy with the twins. They're ecstatic over Tsung. I've never seen them so well-behaved."

"Ecstatic over what?"

"Tsung. That's what Fée named him. Or something like that, anyway."

"Fée? What does she have to do with the dog?"

"She took to him instantly; says he's a very old soul and the fact that you sent him to us proves your powers or his powers or someone's powers."

"The eternal omnipotence's perhaps."

"I wouldn't be surprised."

"But surely the eternal omnipotence's powers wouldn't have to be proved."

"You can discuss that with Fée," Alex said, "I have enough troubles of my own. The SEC have invited me to come down tomorrow and talk to them. They asked Fée to come down, too, but she said she wouldn't."

"Can't they make her?"

"I doubt that anyone can make Fée do anything she doesn't want to do," he said with a sigh. "Have you seen today's *Times*?"

"Yes," she said.

"You know that Relempago Martillo's coming to speak before the UN General Assembly?"

"I did happen to notice it, and if I hadn't, Adolfo very kindly brought it to my attention. Alex, I'm almost positive he must have been the intruder this morning." And she told him of her conversation with Adolfo, finishing, "I'm afraid he's going to drag me into this."

"Frankly, I was afraid you were going to drag yourself into it," Alex said.

"Alex, believe me, all I want to do is keep out of the whole thing. I don't want any publicity. I don't want people to remember what happened to my father, your father, too, as far as the world's concerned."

"I know," Alex said. "And Adolfo's probably right. Your name, if not your actual presence, would give them much more media coverage. But are you afraid of the publicity simply because you don't care for publicity, or because you don't want any attention drawn to you right now?"

She couldn't pretend she didn't know what he was talking about. "Alex, all that's over. All I want is to forget about the whole thing."

"I'm going to pretend that I believe you, because I want

to believe you," he said. "As I've said, I have enough to
worry about. If you like, I'll have a word with Adolfo, see
if I can get him to promise to keep you and your name out
of his plans. Maybe a little contribution to the cause would
do the trick. Wonder if it would be considered tax deduct-
ible?" he mused.

"That would be very good of you," she said. Here she
was, reverting to her mother's generation. If there was an
unpleasant task to be done, a burden to be shouldered, a
problem to be solved, let the man do it, shoulder it, solve it.
And, why not, after all, if you considered it simply as a
question of delegating authority to those best equipped to
handle the particular problem.

After she'd finished talking to Alex, she turned on the radio
to listen to the news. There were the usual robberies, mur-
ders, fires, and the like but nothing of importance—nothing
about Relempago Martillo. At any other time she would have
taken an interest in the Feracian diplomat who had beaten
two of his six resident children (there were four more in
Feracia) so severely that they required hospitalization; and
one seemed to be permanently brain-damaged, although it
was not clear whether this was the result of the beating or
simply that he took after his father. After she had disposed
of Martillo, then she would turn her attention to the Feracian
diplomat, but first things first.

At ten o'clock the phone rang. Mimi, perhaps, or someone else, some other friend, to whom she would force herself
to talk. She couldn't go on cutting herself off like this. Her
life would go on after Relempago Martillo's ended; that is,
if everything went according to plan. But I don't have a plan,
she said to herself. How can *I* make one when I don't know
what *his* plans are?

She picked up the phone. A click and then, "Susan?"
Gil's voice. No reason for her to feel so surprised. Or so
glad, either. After all the trouble they—whoever "they"
were—had taken to try to get her out of the way, she should
have known they wouldn't give up this easily. They would
keep on trying until the last possible moment.

But Gil must not suspect her suspicions, or she would lose any chance she still had—remote though it might be—of getting to his president through him. "Well, hello, Gil," she said in as bright and unsuspicious a manner as she could manage. "I'm so glad you called. I'd almost given up hope of hearing from you. Tonight, that is."

Was her voice too musical? It was. Would he notice? Probably not. He sounded a little overmelodious himself. "It is too late; I've disturbed you. Perhaps it would be better if I phoned you tomorrow or—"

"No, no!" she said. "I always stay up late. Sometimes I never go to sleep at all."

"Me, I need a lot of sleep," he said. "Sometimes I sleep all day. I suppose it is the difference in our—in our temperaments."

"In our ages," he'd been about to say, she thought. Older people don't need as much sleep as younger ones; but, after all, he's still hardly a growing boy, and I still have both feet out of the grave. Latin Americans had a tendency toward embonpoint. If he went on sleeping all day and eating a lot—and she had already noted at their meals together that he had a healthy appetite—he would get to look like Mr. Gittelman. And serve him right, she thought, though it was sad to think of all that beauty diminished by expansion.

Even in my mind, I'm attempting to avoid coming to grips with the issue, she thought. "Well, do I get to meet your president?" she demanded.

He made a bleating noise. He had not been prepared for such directness. "I—I am sorry," he faltered, "but it is as—as I thought. President Martillo is planning to keep himself very close, very private on his visit. He will not meet anybody in New York."

"Nobody at all? If he's going to speak before the General Assembly, then how . . . ?"

Gil sounded a little impatient. "Well, of course he'll have to meet the president of the General Assembly and the UN delegates and—and whoever else he has to meet as a matter of protocol. But otherwise he will see no one except a few close friends, not even members of the diplomatic community, except the Praderans, of course. There will be no gala evening at the opera, no grand ball at the museum, not even a La Pradera Day at Bloomingdale's.''

She was shocked. Not even a La Pradera Day at Bloomingdale's! He must really be running scared.

''He is, Ambassador Yepez tells me, just planning to come here, make his speech, run down to Washington to see the president; then go back to La Pradera.''

She didn't know whether to believe this or not. ''Then there's no way you can get me in to meet him?''

He was silent for a moment; then, ''Susan, I'd like to talk to you tonight. It's a little late for a restaurant; besides, I would like to talk to you in private. Could I come up to your apartment . . . ?''

''I'm afraid it's still being renovated. It's in no shape for visitors.''

''Susan, I've been through two revolutions; I'm used to that sort of thing. Look, let's not beat about the bush. I know you think *El Presidente* killed your father. You want to confront him. You want to accuse him. You want to revile him.''

One would think that by this time he would know me better than that, she thought. Me revile anyone indeed! All I want to do is kill him.

''But he did not kill your father, I assure you. Your father was his best friend, closer even than a brother. It happened during the revolution, the counter-revolution, I should say. One of President Martillo's—only he wasn't president then, of course—officers, a man whom my—whom Martillo loved and trusted turned on him and tried to kill him.''

''Are you going to tell me that my father—Buckley Melville—flung himself in front of Martillo and saved his life at the expense of his own?'' she asked, letting her disbelief show in every word.

''No, he accidentally got into the line of fire and was killed instead, by mistake. After which Pres—General Martillo killed the traitor.''

''How do you know all this?'' she asked. ''It wasn't in *Mi Lucha*. It wasn't in any of the refugees' books or articles. I've never read a word about it anywhere.''

"Nobody knows about it except him and me," he said. "The man who was killed left a family behind him. General Martillo did not want them to know that the head of their house had been a traitor."

"How is it then that you know it?"

"I know, because he himself told me. You see, Relempago Martillo is my father."

✧✧✧ **XXII**

She opened the door to him. They stared at each other dumbly for a moment. What do you say to the son of the man who killed your father? What do you say to the daughter of a man whom your father had killed? But his father had killed so many people, this sort of thing must come up for him all the time. And she must remember that he claimed that his father had not killed her father. Maybe he even believed it.

"Come into the dining room," she said. "It's the only place to sit because the new chairs for the other rooms haven't come yet, and the old ones are out being recovered. They were supposed to be here long ago, but you know furniture stores, how workmen are these days. Or maybe you wouldn't know."

As the son of a dictator, he probably wouldn't know. If he sent his chairs away to be recovered, they had better be back when promised if the upholsterer knew what was good for him. If he ordered furniture, she'd bet it would arrive on the promised day, if not before. She couldn't help feeling a pang of envy.

"I'm sorry the place looks like this," she went on. "As I mentioned before, it's being redecorated, and normally I wouldn't dream of asking anyone up while it's in this state, but under the circumstances. . . ." She was babbling, she knew, but it was difficult not to babble under the aforementioned circumstances. "I'll make tea and there are some sandwiches and things in case you're hungry. I know I'm hungry. I didn't feel like eating any dinner."

"Thank you," he said, following her into the dining room. "You're very kind. I couldn't eat much dinner myself." Had he eaten dinner at the mission, she wondered. Or with the Yepezes? Or by himself? And did they know he was coming here tonight? Was he here on his own or were his strings still being controlled?

He sat down at one end of the table that she'd cleared by sweeping everything that had been heaped on top into the boxes she'd emptied earlier, a technique she'd picked up from Michelle. "It is easier to learn a bad habit than to break one," Cristobal Herrero had written. "It is easier to break a good habit than to learn one."

In the center of the table she placed a hideous silver epergne that escaped the sales at Sotheby's, because it had been hidden on the back of a closet shelf, obscured by a pile of needlework pillows made by her mother, which had surfaced only in the course of the clearing out after the flood. It seemed right for the occasion, lending an appropriate touch of formality, if not of elegance.

Gil didn't offer to help her carry the tea things in from the kitchen, less, she felt, out of macho Latin reluctance to do anything that might be considered woman's work than because he seemed to be in the grip of a species of paralysis. Just as well, because, although she had cached guns in the oven and the sideboard, as well as in other parts of the kitchen and dining room and intervening spots, it would have been difficult to keep him covered at all points. There was a gun in her handbag, of course, but she could hardly carry her bag on her arm as she walked back and forth with plates of sandwiches and cookies, a teapot, and—should there be a need for something stronger—a decanter of brandy. No reason to think he was planning to kill her. He couldn't have the least idea that she was planning to kill his president, his father; but, just in case. . . . It would be ridiculous to be gunned down (or stabbed or poisoned) in her own apartment, like some amateur.

But why was he here to begin with? He'd said he wanted to talk to her. Did he want to talk her into something or out of something? Unlikely that he had just come for a cozy chat.

She poured tea into the cups. He refused milk, accepted

lemon, refused sugar; then changed his mind and put three heaping teaspoons in his cup. His hand was shaking. Good, she thought, in case he was planning to kill her after all— even though he hardly seemed the killer type. But do I seem the killer type? she thought. Her hand was steady as a rock.

She waited. He took a sandwich and bit into it. "This is very good. What is it?"

"Tuna tarragon. There's also curried chicken with lichis, if you prefer."

"This is fine."

She took a sandwich herself and discovered that she was, indeed, hungry. Famished, in fact. They chewed in silence. She was the hostess. It was up to her to break the ice. How to start?

Did you know that the superintendent of this building, who happens to be a Praderan, is planning a demonstration against your father, if not an actual revolution? Hardly the most tactful way to begin. Besides, numbers of people were probably planning demonstrations against him. That was one of the hazards of visiting New York for an official of a foreign government. For that matter, it was one of the hazards for an official of a local government.

More silence. "How is it that you don't have the same surname as your father?" she finally asked. "Did you have your name changed?"

"Frias is my real name. It's his, too—at least it was. He took the name of Martillo when he was a young revolutionary. It means 'hammer,' you know."

Susan didn't know, but she remembered vaguely having read in *Mi Lucha* that, when Martillo first went into active politics, or, as he (or his translator) put it, "devoted himself to the cause of freedom," it had been the custom for dissidents against the established order to take forceful *noms de guerre*, no doubt for good reason. Stalin, she believed, meant "man of steel," although he had been of an earlier generation and a different political persuasion. But she had never read anywhere what Martillo's real name had been. Now she knew. It didn't change anything.

* * *

Gil picked up his cup and took a sip of tea. He set it down, opened his mouth, and closed it again. He picked up the brandy bottle, poured a good measure into his tea, and drank deeply. Finally he spoke. "Forgive me if what I am going to say causes you distress—"

"Quite all right," she said encouragingly. "It's been such a long time; it seems so far away."

"For me it has been a long time, too, but it's still fresh in my mind, perhaps because I was little more than a baby and you—" he caught her eye "—you were a young girl, almost a woman, and—and girls are better able to handle such things than boys."

She opened her mouth; then shut it. She would take this up with him at another time. If there was another time, of course.

"Besides," Gil went on, "we—my mother and my sisters and brothers and I were hunted down like dogs, and you— you were not hunted down like dogs, were you?"

"No, we weren't," she said. Being dropped from the Social Register was not the same as being hunted down like dogs, although she had a feeling her mother might not have agreed.

"When we went into hiding after the revolution, I was only a year old, so I knew only what I was told later, when I was able to understand, how, for the next four years, we had to keep running all the time, for fear the government troops would find us. But they didn't catch up with us until after the counter-revolution started. My father and his men were fighting in the south and we were hiding in the north when they came. By that time, I was five years old, and I remember. There was a lot of noise and confusion. I remember my mother and sisters screaming and my brothers being very brave. They separated us. I didn't know then what had happened to them. It was only years later that I found out they had been shot, all five of them. Why they didn't shoot me too, I don't know."

He looked at her with those large, liquid doglike eyes of his. She was supposed to feel sorry for him. She would feel sorry for him if she could be sure it was the truth he was telling. He was a little too glib.

"The next thing I knew was that I found myself in a place that turned out to be an orphanage."

"Where they were very cruel to you, I suppose," she said, hardening her heart against an anticipated tale of woe.

"No, as a matter of fact, they were quite kind. We have excellent orphanages in La Pradera, all run by the State Bureau of Social Services with maximum efficiency and compassion."

"How long were you there?"

"I'm not sure. It seemed like a very long time, but you know how children are about time; it might not have been more than a year, maybe even less. Meanwhile my father came back into power and your father died—only I didn't know about him until just a few months ago."

"But he was mentioned in *Mi Lucha*."

Gil gave a rueful grin. "I must admit I only skimmed the book. It was very long and, although I would never have dreamed of telling my father so, a little dull in spots."

She poured a little brandy into her tea. He followed her example. "Go on," she said, still uncertain of whether to believe him or not. He certainly sounded convincing, but then he would have been well-rehearsed.

"After the revolution, my father searched all over the country for his family. Finally, after he had almost given up hope, he told me later, he found me, the only one left. I cried when he came to take me away. As far as I was concerned, he was a stranger, and I was frightened by his black beard. But I soon came to love him—as everyone who knows him loves him."

"I know; he's kind to children and animals. But is he kind to people—to grown-up people?"

"He is kind whenever circumstances permit it, and, whenever they do not, he is never cruel. He has assured me that he has never personally tortured anyone, and I believe him. I think I will try one of the chicken sandwiches. I didn't realize how hungry I was."

"Why didn't he acknowledge you as his son?" He

couldn't have, or surely she would have read about it somewhere. It had already occurred to her that Gil might be making the whole thing up, about being the dictator's son, that he was, in fact, an imposter. Hadn't the voice at the séance spoken of an imposter? Ridiculous of her even to so much as remember Fée and her performance, let alone pay any attention to it. Gil was too cozy with the Yepezes and the Labarcas to be anyone other than a member of the ruling circle of La Pradera. In fact, his being Martillo's son could explain a lot.

Gil took another sandwich. He ate as if he really were starving—perhaps a habit acquired in the old days when his family had been on the run—*if* those old days had ever really existed, she reminded herself. "No, he never did acknowledge me," Gil said. "At first he told me he felt it was too dangerous. The country was still in a very unsettled condition. His enemies were anxious to get to him in any way they could. If they knew I existed, they would try to get to him through me; a child is particularly vulnerable, you know."

"But surely the country is settled now. And you're not a child anymore."

"No," he said, "I'm not a child anymore." And he sighed, as if adulthood had brought burdens he would rather have done without.

He squirmed in his chair. The dining room chairs were not very comfortable. They were among the few pieces left over from the old days. Her mother had believed that people, particularly children, should sit up straight at meals and not dawdle; and the chairs were designed not so much as to facilitate this as to make it impossible to do otherwise. If she could have sold them in the days when she needed every penny she could lay her hands on, she would have, but the dealers didn't want them. Why she had kept them after she became affluent again, she didn't know. Inertia, probably. She didn't do much formal entertaining and so they were so seldom in use it hadn't occurred to her to get rid of them. When this is all over, she thought, I'll get new ones. Meanwhile, let him squirm.

''When things settled down and I started going to school, it was found that I had some small artistic talent—which seemed to please my father very much. We became closer after I began to study art. He taught me English and we used to speak it together. He was educated in the United States, you know.''

Susan was surprised. ''No, I didn't know. It wasn't in any of the biographies I read.''

''It isn't in any of the biographies. He felt it wouldn't look well if it were known that a revolutionary, a man of the people, had a degree from Harvard.''

She'd thought she'd known everything there was to be known about the man. It came as a shock to realize how little she did know. Not that the fact that he had gone to Harvard was going to stop her from killing him. She had killed several Harvard men in her day, as well as alumni of Princeton and Yale, and even disposed of graduates of Oxford and Cambridge and the Sorbonne. Several had even graduated with honors, but, although that caused her a certain amount of regret, it had not stopped her from killing them. Honor is more important than an honors degree.

''He told me that, although he would be proud to acknowledge me, I must realize that I would never be able to make a name for myself if it were known that I was Gil Frias, *El Presidente*'s son, rather than Gil Frias, the artist. Otherwise, when my pictures were exhibited, the critics would review his politics rather than my paintings.''

She wouldn't have expected a South American despot to reason so logically. But, of course, he was a Harvard man. ''You mean to tell me there's nobody in La Pradera who knows you're the president's son?''

''Of course there are people who know. It's not exactly a secret among—among—''

''The ruling circles?''

''Well, people like the Yepezes and the Labarcas, my father's friends and close associates, would naturally know, but we've managed to keep it out of the press. The media, I should say. People in La Pradera don't read the papers much

anymore. They all watch television—the way you do here."
Since President Martillo owned all of the Praderan media,
she could see how that would not have been difficult to do.
But how did he keep the people from talking? No doubt he
had ways.

✡ ✡ ✡ **XXIII**

Gil got up and rubbed his back. "Forgive me, but I feel a little stiff, and although your chairs are—are truly fine examples of the cabinetmaker's art, sometimes I have a little trouble with my back. I've had it ever since the time we had to hide in a swamp when I was a child. Isn't there anywhere we can sit that's a little more comfortable?"

"I'm afraid that not only are there no chairs in the other rooms, but they're crowded with all sorts of stuff that's been pushed there to keep them out of the way."

"Out of the way of what?"

"Who knows what goes on in the dark and devious minds of workmen? But you wouldn't want to sit on a packing box. I know I wouldn't."

Gil seemed to think anything would be preferable to the dining room chairs but politely forebore to voice the thought. "But where will you sleep, then?"

"I managed to get my maid to fix up one of the bedrooms enough so I'll have a place to sleep, but naturally . . ."

"Naturally," he agreed. "And I am glad that you will at least have a comfortable place in which to spend the night."

"So am I," she said.

He gave her a speculative look. Then he sat down again and poured more brandy into his teacup.

"Wouldn't you like some tea to go with that?"

"No, thank you, it's fine the way it is," he said, clutching the cup to him lest she forcibly attempt to dilute his brandy.

The conversation seemed to be at a standstill. "Tell me," she said, "how is it that your show opened and you came to

New York just before General—your father was scheduled to arrive? Don't tell me it was simply a coincidence?''

He didn't answer directly. ''It has always been my dearest desire to come to New York ever since I finished my studies at the university.''

She could not resist saying, ''Oh, you managed to finish before it was burned down''; a mistake, because it sent him off on another tangent about how his father was planning to rebuild it—as soon as he found a propitious moment—and how it was going to be the finest university in all of Latin America.

''I'm sure it will be,'' she said politely.

He picked up a cookie and nibbled on it. ''I kept asking my father if I could go to New York, and he kept putting me off. 'When I feel that you are ready,' he would say, 'I will send you to New York to arrange for an exhibition of your pictures in a big, important New York gallery. Meanwhile you can show your pictures in Ciudad Martillo, in Bogota, in Buenos Aires, in Rio, in—' ''

''In short, in all the capitals south of the border.''

''Right. And each time I did, the critics had good things to say about my work. And each time I would go to my father and show him the reviews and say, 'I am ready for New York now.' And each time he would say, 'Wait, my son, you are not ready yet.' Except that the last couple of times he said to me, 'If you don't stop nagging, you are never going to go to New York!' ''

She wondered why, once he was out of the country, Gil hadn't gone to New York on his own, but thought it might be tactless to ask.

Gil started to reach for another cookie. She slid the plate out of his reach. ''Later,'' she told him. ''After you finish telling me how you happen to be here right now.''

''Early this year he came to me and said, 'Gil, I think it is time for you to go to New York and try your wings there.' I embraced him and told him how grateful I was, which embarrassed him because he is not a demonstrative man. 'If only there were something I could do for you in return,' I told him.

" 'As a matter of fact, there *is* a small favor you can do for me. I am planning to go to the United States myself later this year, to speak before the United Nations.'

" 'Wonderful, Father!' I cried. 'We will go to New York together.' And again I tried to embrace him, and again he fended me off.

" 'No, I want you to go up there ahead of me,' he said. It was then that he told me about your father and how he had come to die and it made me very sad to hear about it. He went on to tell me that, although the rest of Buckley Melville's family was dead, he had left behind a daughter, who was living in New York. When he told me who you were, I was thrilled, of course, because I had heard of you. 'And you want me to go up there and prepare her for your arrival, Father?' I asked.

" 'No, if possible, I would prefer her not to know of my arrival at all. You see,' he explained, 'at the time Buckley Melville died, my enemies said it was I who had killed him. True, he was my friend, my comrade in arms, closer to me than a brother. But he was also my financial backer. Without his money, I could not have brought peace and prosperity to La Pradera. My enemies claimed that I killed him to avoid having to pay him back.'

" 'And you want me to go to New York now and tell his daughter what really happened, and make restitution to her?'

"At that point, he got a little testy, 'No need to make restitution. She is a rich and famous artist; she does not need the money, while the poor orphans of La Pradera have to beg for their bread.' "

"I thought all of your orphanages—"

"Not all of the orphans are in orphanages," Gil explained, adding, somewhat obscurely, "After all, we are only a small country. So I said to my father, 'Then you just want me to go there and tell her the truth about what really happened?'

" 'That would be useless,' he said, 'because she would not believe you.' And, when I protested, he said, 'Would you believe her if the cases were reversed and people said her father had killed me?' I had to admit that I would not. But, although I was very happy at the prospect of going to New York, I still did not understand what he wanted me to do there.

"He seemed to have great difficulty in getting to the point. 'When I arrive, Susan Melville is likely to confront me and accuse me of her father's death. She will go to the newspapers, the television networks, the radio stations, and they will rake up those old lies. They will give me a bad public image. My hour of glory will be ruined. The president may find himself called out of town and unable to receive me at the White House.' "

She remembered that the same idea had occurred to her. Either she was particularly perceptive, or she thought along the same lines as *El Presidente*.

" 'But surely you can tell the American people the truth about what really happened?' I said to my father.

" 'They are not likely to believe me any more than Señorita Melville is likely to believe me. They are always anxious to believe the worst, particularly when it concerns a Latin American. Besides, we must not forget the family of the traitor who actually *did* kill Buckley Melville, and whom I killed in his turn. His aged parents, as well as his widow and children are still living in La Pradera, honored and respected citizens. Why should they suffer for his guilt, as they assuredly would, if the truth came out, especially after all these years.' "

Gil paused, as if to give Susan a chance to express admiration for his father's nobility. When she was silent, he went on, "Incidentally there is something that has been puzzling me. My father told me that Buckley Melville had only one surviving relative—a daughter. But you have a brother. How is it that my father did not mention him?"

For a moment she felt a pang of apprehension, but it was short lived. Relempago Martillo was not going to be in any position to ask questions about Alex. "Perhaps he didn't know about his existence," she said. "My father was not married to his mother, so it's possible that he never told anyone about him for—for her sake."

"But my father was his good friend, his *buen compañero*," Gil said. "Still, I suppose you norteamericanos are even more different from us than you seem."

"My father was of another generation," she said.

"So is mine," he said.

"Let's get back to the point. You've told me what your father didn't want you to do when you came to New York. What was it he did want you to do?"

Gil avoided her eye. "He wanted me to make sure that you weren't in the city when he got here; that, if possible, you didn't even know he was expected. 'We will try other ways to remove her from the scene first,' he said, 'but you will be our final hope.' "

"Other ways," she echoed, her hand moving toward the gun she had stashed at the bottom level of the epergne, under a pile of grapes. Then she realized what he meant; something that had already occurred to her as a possibility. "The conference in Hawaii?"

He nodded. "And, before that, the conference in Palm Beach."

"That one seems to have passed me by," she admitted, "but, of course, I get so many invitations I'm afraid I don't pay as much attention as I should to each one."

"I know," Gil said sadly. "You are a very popular lady."

She was struck by an alarming thought. "Not the conference in Nepal?"

He saw the expression on her face. "Oh, it's a legitimate conference. My father merely persuaded them to alter some of the arrangements. We had hoped you would go along there with your—your friend and, once you were there, we would have contrived to keep the two of you there for as long as we needed—an airport strike, a landslide, a flood, nothing drastic. 'I want everything to be as pleasant as possible,' my father said."

Suddenly, she was worried. "Peter hasn't come back, and I haven't heard from him. Are you keeping him there as—?"

"As a hostage for your good behavior?" Gil laughed.

"Maybe we should have, but nobody thought of that. Besides, it could have repercussions afterward, which might be awkward. No, Professor Franklin is staying on of his own accord. Apparently he is enjoying himself very much there."

As I thought, Susan said to herself, dallying with some local maiden or maidens, no doubt provided by Martillo. Not—to do Peter justice—that he wasn't fully able to find local maidens with whom to dally for himself.

Irritation made her blunt. "What were you supposed to do to keep me here? Seduce me?"

Gil turned so red Susan knew she had hit the mark—although probably his instructions had been seduce only if necessary. She had known Martillo was despicable, but using his own son. . . . On the other hand, where would he find a likelier lad?

"Susan, how could you think such a thing of me?" Gil cried.

"Even if you succeeded, that still wouldn't get me out of town, would it?" she mused, thinking she had misjudged him. Then she understood. "The Cape Cod cottage!" That had been intended as their little love nest. "Then there is no Senhor Ribeira?"

Gil blushed even redder. "There is, only he doesn't know about any of this. However, there is a cottage in Cape Cod. And it is as I have described it—at least so it was described to me. And it didn't have to be—I mean it wasn't supposed to be anything—anything improper. Just a pleasant vacation with a friend, because I wanted to become your friend, Susan; that was why I waited so long—too long—to ask you to come away with me. I wanted to establish a—a relationship first, and the news of my father's arrival wasn't supposed to get out so soon."

"That's what comes of having a free press," Susan said.

"It certainly does! Oh, you're being sarcastic. You Americans are always being sarcastic."

He got up from his chair. "Come with me, Susan. We could have such a good time, and not just during my father's visit. We could stay up there weeks, months. I won't mind the cold if you are there with me."

But it isn't friendship that keeps people warm, she thought.

"And afterward, my father promised me that I could stay in New York as long as I liked if I . . ." The words trailed off. He put out a hand toward her. "I really want to be your friend, Susan, not just because of my father or because you are a famous artist. . . ."

She eyed him, unmoving, but not unmoved, although she wasn't about to let him see that—at least, not yet. He dropped his hand. He was so young. She'd bet Peter's abominable snowwoman, or whoever she was, was young. It wasn't fair, but life wasn't fair; if you wanted things equalized you had to equalize them yourself, with a gun—or in other ways.

"Are you going to speak out against my father when he arrives?" Gil demanded. "Are you going to make false accusations—oh, I know you think they're true, but—are you going to make accusations?"

"I haven't made up my mind," Susan said. Really, she thought, when you looked at the whole thing objectively, they were going to an awful lot of trouble just to keep her away from Martillo. If she accused him of killing her father, he could simply deny it, tell the same story he had told Gil. Who would there be to disprove it? All the officers who had been with him at the time had vanished, she remembered; and, if there had been any civilians around at the time, she would bet they had gone the same road.

Certainly the media would pick up the story and try to make a case out of it, but surely Martillo had encountered bad publicity before; surely he would know that if stories like that would alienate the United States government from its friends, the United States government would have few friends left in South America. Perhaps, snug in his own little world for nearly twenty-five years, Martillo lacked the thick skin, the insulation most tyrants develop against external criticism. Internal criticism could be dealt with, of course, as he had already dealt with it.

"I am sure that I could convince you that my father did not kill your father, that he was your father's good friend, if only—" he made a move to sit down "—if only I didn't have to sit in those abominable chairs of yours. Isn't there anyplace at all that's more comfortable? You said . . . the bedroom?'' There was no doubt at all as to what he meant.

Nor was she in any doubt as to what she wanted. "The bedroom has been cleared,'' she said, "but there aren't any chairs there. Only the bed . . .'' It was then that she remembered the Snoopy pillowcase. Oh, what the hell, she thought. "This way,'' she said.

Gil took a deep breath and followed her.

Susan had forgotten to turn on the answering machine, and, during the early hours of the morning, the phone rang several times. The first two times it rang, she didn't answer. The third time, Gil was already asleep. She got up and unplugged it without waking him. His head looked very young and innocent on the Snoopy pillowcase. "Susan . . .'' he murmured, stretching out his arms, "Susan . . .'' As she went back to bed, she saw the crystal on the windowsill glowing as if it were illuminated from within. That's very powerful moonlight, she thought.

She awoke to a vague sense of disappointment. Not that she hadn't enjoyed the night. Gil had been tender and loving; and in return she had made full use of all that Peter had taught her, eager to prove that experience and knowledge counted for more than youth. She had proved it to Gil, she knew, from the way he had responded. But, even more, she had proved it to herself.

Oh, Peter, she thought, I do miss you. Gil may be young and strong and handsome, but he isn't half the man you are. So what if Peter had been dallying with some Himalayan damsel? It only meant that when he came back he would have added some Nepali knowhow to his repertoire. She could forgive him his transgressions, if, indeed, you could account what he—and, in her turn, she—had done as transgressions. Where, after all, was the sin in enjoying yourself, as long as you came back home in the end?

She drew up the blinds. As the sun's rays hit the crystal on the windowsill, it sparkled until it seemed to be ablaze. Flashy, almost trashy, she thought, compared to the quiet glow the moonlight had brought out in it the night before. Or had it been the moonlight alone?

Michelle chose that morning to come in early. She was scandalized to see Gil emerge from the bedroom, yawning. "It'll be breakfast for two, Michelle," Susan said, "and make it a hearty one," for she was already familiar with Gil's appetite. Although cooking was not, as she had told Alex, Michelle's strong point, she could usually be trusted to produce an acceptable breakfast if she was in a good mood. She was

172

not in a good mood now. "Boy young enough to be her son," she muttered as she stalked off into the kitchen. "Some folks just ain't got no shame."

I suppose if I'd spent the night with an old goat like the Professor, that would be all right, Susan thought—or less un-all right, anyhow. What had made her think of the Professor right then? No reason at all, except that his had been among the messages on her tape that she had dismissed as unimportant the night before.

"I hope I haven't caused you embarrassment, *querida*," Gil said, trying to put his arm around her.

"Not a bit of it," she said, drawing away, as angry plates clattered in the kitchen. "But there's no point upsetting her any more than she is already." At least, not if we expect to get any breakfast, she thought.

"You're so kind, so good," he said. "You even worry about the feelings of someone like that."

Susan gave him her saintliest smile. "Come into the dining room and we can eat and talk. That is," she added, as a smell of burning wafted out from the kitchen, "if there's going to be anything fit to eat. Excuse me for a minute." She stuck her head in the kitchen doorway. "If you dare to serve that—whatever it is—to us, I warn you, that's going to be it!"

"It?" Gil repeated. "What is 'it'?"

"Something drastic," she told him. "You wouldn't want to know the details."

"I know what we do to disrespectful servants in La Pradera," he said, "but I didn't think you were permitted to do anything like that here."

This morning, Gil didn't seem to mind the dining room chairs, whereas she would have welcomed furniture a little more accommodating to the person, for it had been an exhausting night. He sat there, devouring huge quantities of the slightly overcooked bacon and eggs, pale toast, and buckwheat pancakes that a sternly disapproving Michelle set before them, pausing every now and then to look at Susan with a sticky, seraphic smile. "Susan, it was so—so wonderful. Never before have I made love to an older woman—that is to say, a woman older than myself. All at once, I begin to understand the French.''

Oh, dear, Susan thought, I hope I'm not going to have him on my hands afterward. But then, after all, would that be such a bad thing?

''Susan, I have been thinking, and I have come to the conclusion that my father was wrong about wanting to avoid you. I think he ought to talk to you. I am sure that, once you spoke to him, you would believe that he had nothing to do with your father's death. Besides, I want you two to know each other. I know you will have much in common.''

''I've wanted to meet him all along,'' she said, thinking and that, at least, is no lie. ''He's the one who wanted to avoid me.''

Gil nodded, his mouth full. ''It has seemed to me that he was going to an awful lot of trouble not to meet you. But Leon Yepez said to me after we all had dinner at the von Schwabes that on no account was I to let you get anywhere near my father. Not that Leon doesn't like you, you understand; he thinks you are a most delightful lady. But he is my father's man, and after what happened to our last ambassador to the UN . . .''

''I understand,'' Susan said. She remembered what had happened to the last Praderan ambassador to the UN. Not that anyone knew exactly what had happened to him after he was recalled, but they could make a pretty good guess.

The phone rang. Michelle clomped in. ''It's Mr. Peter.''

''Tell him I'll call him back later.''

''But he's calling all the way from Nee-pal.''

''Well, then, I'll call him back all the way to Nepal.''

''Suit yourself,'' Michelle said, clomping out, the strength of her tread, as always, increasing with the depth of her disapproval. In another few minutes, the people downstairs would be complaining.

''Oh, Susan, Susan,'' Gil said. ''I'm so happy.'' He half rose from his chair and reached for her across the table. ''I never knew what love was before.''

She fended him off. ''Michelle will be coming back, and

she's devoted to Peter. And you're getting butter on your sleeve.''

"I understand," Gil said, subsiding. "You don't want to offend the feelings of a faithful old servitor, no matter how ill-behaved. I honor you for it.''

Susan didn't point out that Michelle would probably be— no doubt was, since her shadow was hovering just outside the doorway—far more offended by being called a faithful old servitor than by any unseemly behavior on Susan's part, but she wished Gil wouldn't tell her that he loved her. It made her feel not exactly guilty, but not exactly innocent either.

"Tell me," she said, "how are you going to arrange for me to meet your father, if his schedule is so tight?''

Gil looked abashed. "Well, perhaps it is not quite as tight as I led you to believe. You see, the date when he is going to give his speech at the United Nations has been officially announced, but not the date when he is arriving in this country. I, myself, do not know exactly when he is coming. All I know is that he is planning to slip in unobtrusively beforehand, so nobody should know when he gets here.''

"That's surprising. Most heads of state enjoy the fanfare of an official arrival. And doesn't diplomatic protocol demand it?''

"My father is not like most heads of state," Gil said proudly. "He is a quiet, retiring man. Even back home he avoids ceremony, whenever possible.''

"But he is going on to the White House afterward?" she asked, thinking that if, by some mischance, she didn't get him here, she would have one more shot in Washington. She had a feeling it would be easier to crack the White House than the Praderan Mission.

"As you say, there is the matter of diplomatic protocol. He would not want to offend your president, who is a very good friend of his. But the diplomatic community here is another matter. He will attend only private or strictly Praderan functions. So what I have to do is get you into one of them. Which will not be easy.''

She gave him an encouraging smile. "You're a very resourceful young man, Gil. I'm sure you'll be able to do it.''

"I must," he said. "I would not want to fail you." And he gave her one of his melting looks. "This is what I was thinking—the Labarcas are very close to my father. Not only are they good friends, but Florencio is an associate of his in the economic sector."

"You mean the Praderan Government does business with Florencio?"

"I suppose so," he said. "I am an artist; I do not understand these things."

"Doesn't he have a finance minister, a minister of economic planning, a budget director?"

"Those are honorary positions," Gil said. "My father takes care of such matters personally. If you want a thing done right, you must do it yourself, he always says."

"If you want to make sure something is done," Cristobal Herrero had written, "you will do it yourself. If you want to make sure a thing is done right, you will find the right person to do it."

"I thought a head of state had to delegate authority," she said.

"As I have told you," Gil said, a trifle impatiently, "my father is no ordinary head of state. Anyhow, while he is here, he will undoubtedly have dinner with the Labarcas, and Margarita is a great admirer of yours. You should have heard her sing your praises after that dinner. Over and over she said how much she would like to meet you again. I am sure that she would be glad to invite you at the same time as she invites my father. After all, it isn't as if there wouldn't be other guests there—the Yepezes, certainly, and some business associates. Perhaps he will not even notice you. But that's right—you want him to notice you."

Actually I don't, Susan thought, but Gil doesn't have to know that. "But won't Margarita tell people that I'm coming? And, if your father knows that I'm going to be there, won't he refuse to come?"

"Don't worry," Gil said, "she is also an admirer of mine." He blushed a little. "What I mean is, she knows the story about your father and my father, and she would be glad to get everything cleared up so that we can all be friends.

Especially if I convince her that you are going to be a regular client of hers and wear her jewelry to—to all sorts of fashionable places. Margarita is a businesswoman before anything else.''

Susan gritted her teeth. "I'd be happy to wear her jewelry. Tell her—'' it was hard to force the words out ''—that I think she is one of the most talented jewelry designers around.''

"I will. It will make her very happy.''

In the foyer, Gil kissed her goodbye before she could stop him. Not that she wanted to, except that Michelle was in the act of letting a workman in, and it was a little embarrassing.

"He's her nephew,'' Michelle took it upon herself to explain, ''and he's settin' out on a long journey to distant lands, maybe never to return.''

"That didn' look like no nephewly kiss to me,'' the workman said.

"They're a very close family,'' Michelle said, as she led him away. "Besides, I don' see what business it is of yours, anyways.'' Or yours either, Susan thought.

"I'll call you just as soon as I find out what's happening,'' Gil promised.

"If I'm not here, try again.'' Susan had no intention of spending the whole day in the company of the workmen and Michelle. "And messages aren't necessarily reliable.''

"I know,'' Gil said, looking in the direction where Michelle had disappeared. "You North Americans put up with so much from your servants. After you have met my father and we are all friends, you will come back to La Pradera with us, and you will have a whole staff of servants to whom your slightest wish will be as a command.''

"I'm not so sure I'd like that, either,'' Susan said.

"You'd be surprised to find how easy it will be to get used to it.''

Actually, Susan thought, I'm afraid I wouldn't.

He took her hand. "Will you have dinner with me tonight, Susan, a proper dinner, not sandwiches—although your sandwiches were delicious. We can go to a restaurant and then afterward . . .''

"I really wish I could," she improvised, "but I'm having dinner with a couple of old family friends. I couldn't possibly disappoint them."

She took a chance. "Perhaps you'd like to come along. I'm sure they'd be delighted to meet you. Their lives are so dull, poor things."

He smote his forehead. "What an idiot I am! I was forgetting; there will be all sorts of arrangements to be made before my father's arrival. Leon and Isabella are probably expecting me to dine with them, so that we can discuss our—er, plans. Perhaps I can come up here afterwards."

"Perhaps," she said. "We can talk about that when you call."

After he'd gone, she went to her room and phoned Nepal, not expecting Peter to be in his room, since it must be around six in the evening there, and the likelihood would be that he was having a few post-conference or pre-dinner drinks. However, he turned out not only to be in his room, but likely, he told Susan in a feeble much-put-upon voice, to be there for some time. It seemed that two days previously he had started out into the foothills with a few of his colleagues in search of an abominable snowman, and had had an accident.

"Peter, are you all right?" she asked anxiously. What was she going to do if it turned out he was gravely injured and expected her to rush to his bedside?

Fortunately, the question did not arise. He had only sprained an ankle tripping over a rock, and had been forced to turn back. Apparently his colleagues had not felt his injuries were serious enough to compel them to turn back with him. "And it'll be just my luck to have them run into a snowman while I'm laid up here."

"Oh, Peter, people have been looking for the snowman for years and nobody's ever found him, except the Chinese, and they have no documentation; and it's my belief they made the whole thing up."

"That's what I've always thought, too. Chances are this expedition will turn out to be a wild-goose chase," he said, sounding much cheered. "Oh, I got your message when I came back. Sick as I was, I called you right away, but there wasn't any answer. I figured you must be out somewhere at a party, having a good time." He sounded very sorry for himself.

She remembered her visions of him in the embrace of some Himalayan houri, while all the time he was limping his way back to the hotel—probably not literally limping; he must have had some kind of transport. Still, she should have felt ashamed of herself for leaping to conclusions and, from there, into Gil's arms.

"Actually I was home," she said. "I was so tired, I just unplugged the phone and went to bed. Oh, Peter, I've missed you!"

"I've missed you too," he said. "Well, the conference is over, so there's no need for us to go on missing each other. I understand the airlines have facilities for invalids, so I'll start back tomorrow—and we'll see each other in a couple of days."

For a moment, she felt so happy that nothing else mattered. Then she remembered a lot of things that did matter—that mattered a lot. And it wasn't as if Peter wouldn't keep. "Do you think it's wise to start out now, Peter? There's so much going on in the apartment, with workmen all over, hollering and thumping—" she opened the door so the sounds of hollering and thumping could be heard clearly in Katmandu "—and not a comfortable chair to sit on in the whole place."

She went on to describe the miseries she was enduring and that he would be forced to share with her, if he came back now. "I'd been staying with Alex," she said, to forestall any suggestion of a hotel, "but I realized that nothing will ever be finished if I'm not here all the time to watch. I can't ask you to come back and go through that along with me."

"If it weren't for my ankle," Peter said, "plus some severe bruises and contusions I didn't mention because I didn't want to worry you, I wouldn't dream of leaving you to face all that alone. As a matter of fact, the doctor did say that it would be better if I had at least a week of bed rest before I started back, but I was so anxious to see you . . ."

"It would worry me if you traveled while you were in that condition. You rest in bed until you're completely well," she told him, wondering whether there would be anybody resting in bed with him. And who am I to cast the first stone? she thought.

She was about to hang up, when she remembered. "Peter, did you call me more than once last night?"

"Actually, no. I meant to, but the doctor shot me so full of pain-killer, I fell asleep."

After Peter had hung up, to the accompaniment of the strange clunks and noises that were, she supposed, the normal concomitant of overseas calls, Susan began wondering. There had been three calls in all. Who else would have been calling her between two and three in the morning?

◊◊◊ **XXV**

Mimi did call later in the morning to inform Susan that she and Gunther had had a sudden urge to go to her house in Bermuda. She was calling from Bermuda now. "But don't worry; we'll get back before the season really gets started," she said. This, of course, was intended as a pleasantry; without Mimi, the season—at least in her mind—could not start at all.

"The hurricane season has already started," Susan observed. She didn't need Mimi now; she could afford to alarm her.

"Don't be silly. If there's a hurricane scheduled, naturally we'll come back to New York. Unless," she added musingly, "we stayed here and had a hurricane ball. I've never given a hurricane ball. It would be a real challenge. Lots of seaweed, of course, and fishnet. A costume ball, I think, and all in aid of some really worthy cause, nothing trivial."

"How about survivors of the hurricane?" Susan suggested. "And by way of costumes, the guests could dress in whatever they happened to be wearing when the hurricane struck. Or, better yet, what they were wearing after the hurricane was over."

"Well, perhaps it would be better to hold the ball up there. At the Plaza. Donald and Ivana have been so sweet, I think we ought to do something for them. Oh, by the way, I got both of your messages, which is why I'm calling. Not that I wouldn't have called anyway. I wouldn't want to have you worrying about where we were. Was it something urgent?"

"No, it wasn't urgent at all." I really must be better prepared for occasions like this, Susan told herself, thinking fast. "It was just that I was wondering if you were going to the Castellan Club lunch today."

"Oh, dear, how naughty of me. I completely forgot all about it."

So had Susan until the moment before, which did not stop her from saying, "Oh, Mimi, how could you!"

"I feel so guilty," Mimi said, not sounding guilty at all, "but I can always have lunch with them after I get back. I'm sure they'll forgive me."

Since Mimi was the richest of the rich ladies who made up the Castellan Club—an organization dedicated to raising funds for providing aid and comfort to the poor concomitantly with entertainment and amusement for the rich, Susan was sure they would.

"I have a wonderful idea. Why don't you fly down here and stay with us for a few days? It'll do you good to get away from New York. And we'd so love to have you. And that handsome young boyfriend of yours, Gil what's-his-name, if you think he'd like to come." Mimi never gives up, Susan thought.

"I wish I *could* join you, Mimi, but Peter's on his way back from Nepal."

"Oh, is he? You'd better return Gil to stock, then. I know Peter isn't the jealous type, but still he's never really had reason to be jealous before. Or has he? You're a deep one, Susan."

"I keep telling you, Mimi, Gil is not my 'boyfriend,' " Susan said, making the quotation marks very clear. "And I wish you wouldn't joke about it."

"I'm sorry. I was just funning. I know you're not the type to do that sort of thing."

That should make me feel small, Susan thought, but it didn't. It made her feel large, expansive, smug.

As they were exchanging farewells, Susan remembered something. "By the way, Mimi, you didn't happen to call me rather late last night? Early this morning, actually—around two or three?"

"Heavens, no! We're in the same time zone as New York here, you know. Gunther and I were snug in our little beds, snoring away. I wouldn't dream of calling anybody up at that hour unless it were a matter of life and death or New Year's Eve. Or, possibly, if I were drunk,'' she conceded. ''But why do you ask?''

''Somebody called around two or three in the morning. I'd forgotten to leave the machine on, and I was too tired to get up and answer.''

''Probably a wrong number. It happens all the time. People are so inconsiderate. The phone company ought to do something about it. Trouble is, you never know if it's a local wrong number or a long-distance wrong number, so you don't know which phone company to complain to. Things haven't been the same since AT&T broke up.''

As she hung up, there was a click. One of the workmen trying to make a call on another extension, Susan supposed.

Even through the shut door, the hammering and the hollering outside increased in intensity, accompanied by crashes and bangs and the sound of rock music. The smell of paint began to pervade the room. I don't have to put up with this, Susan thought. ''I'm going out,'' she told Michelle. ''I'll be back in a couple of hours.'' She had no intention of coming back until late in the afternoon, but no point in giving Michelle ground for protest in advance.

Might as well do something useful, like locking the stable door after the horse has already decamped, she told herself; and she bundled up the scrapbooks and photograph albums, to take to her studio. When she got down to the lobby with her burden, she found Adolfo standing there—unusual because, as a rule, he kept out of the residents' way, so they could not seize him and make their complaints vocal. ''Residents who wish work perpetrated upon their premises must fill out work orders in writing,'' one of his under-the-door manifestoes had proclaimed. ''Oral objections will fall upon deaf ears!''

There was a strange expression on Adolfo's face. Had the doorman told him that a young man had spent the night in her apartment? Although, since one doorman had been on duty when Gil arrived and another when he left, there would have been no way of anyone's knowing, unless they were deliberately spying on her. The idea disturbed her, not only because she didn't like the idea of being spied on per se, but because it was likely to put a crimp in her future activities.

"I will get her a cab," he said, thrusting aside the doorman in the performance of his duty (and the expectation of a tip). "Are you sure you know what you are doing, Miss Melvilly?" he asked, as he flagged down a cab and opened the door for her to get in.

"Going to my studio to paint," she said. "As I do most days. Do you have any objection?"

He shook his head sadly. "Oh, Miss Melvilly, Miss Melvilly," he said, as he closed the door so gently the driver, muttering to himself, had to get out and bang it shut. Really, Susan thought, I must speak to Mrs. Acacia about him, after I've killed General Martillo. But perhaps after the general's death Adolfo will go back to his own country and there won't be any need to speak to Mrs. Acacia.

She couldn't help paying close attention to the traffic on her way to the studio. No sign of a black Mercedes or a blue Chevy but there were at least three green Dodges.

Once in the studio, she tried to paint, but found it impossible. She was in no mood for art. Instead, she found herself looking through the albums at the snapshots of her mother, her father, herself as a child and then as an adolescent. What a handsome man her father had been—tall, blond, athletic. He would have aged well, she thought, had he been given the chance. How old would he have been when he died? Forty-nine? Fifty? If she had known of his death at the time, she would have mourned him, but she would not have regarded it as an untimely end. Fifty would have seemed like a ripe old age to her.

Enough of this! Nostalgia was a destructive emotion. Since she couldn't paint, she had better get herself out of the studio and to lunch. She hadn't planned to join the ladies of the Castellan Club, but it was too late to make a date with anyone else, and she did not feel like eating alone. So she joined them, and, as she listened to them discuss the plight of the homeless and the latest fashions, she understood how revolutionaries are born.

All seemed quiet when she returned to her apartment late in the afternoon, but, as she inserted her key in the lock, there was a sudden burst of noise, as if the sound of her return had galvanized the workmen into activity. Before she was fully inside, Michelle had already started complaining. Not, however, because of the length of Susan's absence. She had further grounds for grievance. "From the moment you walked out the door, the phone's been ringin' off the hook. Every time I start doin' somethin', there it goes again. I hardly had any chance to make any calls myself—and there was Lorenzo up in the Bronx, worryin' hisself sick 'cause he couldn't get th'ough to me."

And, to forestall Susan's obvious next remark, "I cooden leave the machine on, 'cause the workmen wooden let me, awright? Said they were expectin' calls from the contractor and their suppliers. I heard their end of some of them calls and, lemme tell you, it was no contractor and no supplier they were talkin' to—leastways it wasn't no buildin' supplies they were contractin' for."

"I hope you made a note of all the calls that were for me."

"Those that got th'ough. An' I don't need ta make no notes; I got a pheromonal memory." Susan gave an inward groan. "There was Mr. Turkel—you know, Miss Jill's husband."

"Mr. Mackay," Susan corrected her, as she had done many times before, to no avail. Husbands and wives were supposed to have the same last name, and, if Jill refused to take Andy's, why, then, Michelle would give him Jill's.

"Where was Mr. Mackay?"

"I tol' you, on the telephone."

"Did he say whether he was calling from Washington or New York?"

"No, he didn'," Michelle said firmly. Pheromonal memory, indeed! Andy would never have omitted so essential a piece of information.

"And then there was your brother and your sister-in-law and a lady with a squeaky voice, and the upholsterer an' "—

she reeled off the names of several of Susan's acquaintances—"an' a man from the gov'ment."

"What government?"

"The gov'ment of the U.S. of A., what else? If Ida meant another gov'ment, Ida said another gov'ment, awright?"

"What branch of the U.S. government?"

"I disremember," Michelle said, in a tone of voice that said, Haven't I remembered enough? What do you expect—miracles at my salary?

"Did he want me to call him back?" Susan persisted.

"All of 'em wanted you to call 'em back, 'cept the upholsterer. He said he would call you back as soon as the chairs were ready, which might not be for some time, 'cause the plane carryin' the fabric you ordered got hijacked. And the squeaky-voiced lady said it was no use callin' her back, 'cause you wooden be able to reach her on this plane, and anyhow she was going to be on 'nother one. I know it don't make sense, but that's what she said, awright?"

"Did she leave a name?"

"No, she didn'," Michelle said, "an' I know that for a fack, 'cause I remember positively askin' her what her name was and she said somethin' like names don't have no meanin' an' anyhow you'd know who it was. I gotta suspicion she was one of them witches who hang out at your brother's apartment." She looked accusingly at Susan.

Susan had the same suspicion, but there was no point voicing it. "I haven't the least idea who it could have been," she said.

"Did Mr. Frias call?"

"No," Michelle said. "Nobody who give that name, anyways."

"Somebody who gave the name of Gil?"

"Not that, either."

It seemed to Susan that Michelle looked guilty, but then she always looked guilty. Oh, well, Susan thought, even if he did call and she "forgot," he'll call again. Chances were, if he did call, he wouldn't call until late. And, even if he called early and got a busy signal, he'll call again. I can't sit around waiting for him to call like a lovesick teenager, even if my motives are different, she thought. I might as well return some of my other calls. Find out what Andy wanted, for example.

As soon as Michelle had left, she called Jill's apartment. Only a recorded message in Jill's voice. She called Washington. Jill answered in person. "Hi, Susan, has Andy gotten in touch with you yet?"

Susan explained about the message. "So, if you'll tell him I'm on the phone," she said, knowing that Jill was not likely to get off the phone without urging, "I'll talk to you later."

"Oh, he's not here. He's in New York. He went there specially to see you. 'On a matter of business,' he said, by which he meant it was none of my business. 'But I'm her business manager,' I told him, 'her agent. Her business is my business.' "

"What did he say to that?"

"He just laughed. 'You might as well tell me whatever it is now,' I told him, 'because she'll only tell me afterward.' 'Not if she knows what's good for her,' he said, 'and I think she does.' "

It sounded ominous. What business could Andy possibly have with her? Susan wondered. Probably he was just teasing his nosy wife. Yet, that wasn't like Andy. And he wouldn't say he was going to New York specially to see her, unless he meant it. What could it be? Could it have anything to do with Alex and the SEC? But Andy didn't operate in that area. As far as she knew, anyway.

"Tell me, Susan, is it true that you got your tip on Consolidated Adhesives from a medium?" Jill asked.

"Something like that," Susan admitted, wondering if she had overestimated Andy's discretion, as well as his lack of connection with the SEC. "How did you know?"

"Spirit voices," Jill said, and laughed uproariously. "Well, I'd better hang up, in case that clicking means Andy's trying to reach you. Really, Susan, you ought to get call waiting."

"I wouldn't dream of it. I think it's rude."

"Then get another line. You can afford it."

Susan hung up, but half an hour passed and the phone didn't ring. There's no reason why I shouldn't ring Gil, she thought; I certainly know him well enough now for a casual call. Chances are he won't even be there. And, if he is, he might not have spoken to Margarita yet. But Susan wanted to talk to him all the same, to make sure that matters were progressing; that he hadn't changed his mind; not because she wanted to hear his voice.

She dialed his number at the mission, prepared to have the phone ring without being answered. This time it was picked up. "Yes?" a man's voice said.

"Gil?"

"I am sorry, but Señor Frias has gone out." The English was unaccented, but a little stiff, as if the speaker were more accustomed to speaking another language. "Did you wish to leave a message?"

"Would you tell him that Susan Melville called?"

"Susan Melville. . . ." the man repeated, and there was a sound almost like a sigh. "Yes, I will tell him." A pause. For a moment she thought he was going to add something more, but all he said was, "Good night, Miss Melville," and the phone clicked and clicked again.

Probably a member of the mission staff, getting things ready for *El Presidente*'s arrival. There had been something familiar about the voice. Yet, she had never, to her knowledge, met any of the mission staff aside from the Yepezes. Ambassador Yepez spoke with a strong accent; moreover, he was hardly likely to be answering any of the mission phones.

Who else, then? Possibly she'd met some member of the staff without realizing he was a Praderan. Or possibly she just imagined she had heard the voice before.

She called the Tabors' apartment. Sister answered. Fortunately, because Serenity tended to wax mystic on the phone. During the week Susan had spent with the Tabors after Tinsley's return, she had gotten to know Sister a little and to discover that the girl was less a seeker of enlightenment than a pursuer of personal advantage, which made her, like most pragmatists, a lot easier to deal with. Both Alex and Tinsley were out for the evening, she informed Susan. And they had gone out together. Alone together.

"No New Agers?"

"No New Agers," Sister said. "Call me psychic, but I have a feeling that there aren't going to be any more New Agers around here, now that Fée's gone."

"Fée's gone?" Susan was surprised. She had assumed that Fée had settled in for the duration.

She said as much to Sister.

"I kind of think she's gone for good. Judging by what I happened to overhear, anyway. She packed her bags this morning and she had some words with Mr. Tabor; then the Professor came, and they went away together in a cab. A little before the subpoena came."

"Subpoena? Somebody subpoenaed Fée?" Somehow it seemed like sacrilege—*lèse majesté*, at the very least.

"The SEC. I know, because Mr. Tabor opened it, and made remarks. Oh, by the way, she left something for you— a couple of packages."

"Would you mind opening them and telling me what's inside?" Susan asked, knowing full well that Sister already knew what was inside, but the amenities if not the proprieties must be preserved.

"Photographs," Sister said, after a decent interval. "All of her, either taken some time ago or retouched a lot. And a note. It says—" paper rustled—" 'I'm afraid you're going to have to work from memory, but these may help. I'll be in touch, though perhaps not in this life.' "

Some people never give up, Susan thought. Is she going to keep on pursuing me not only in this life but in all our lives to come? But perhaps in a life to come I will be a portrait painter and there won't be any problem. "Don't bother to open the other package," she told Sister.

Around nine o'clock, Gil called. After some words of love which she found embarrassing, yet at the same time reassuring (she didn't want him to lose interest in her yet), he said, "Susan, I have wonderful news! Florencio Labarca is giving a dinner tomorrow night for my father and some friends."

"Then your father is expected here tomorrow and not next week?" She wondered whether there might still be a chance to ambush El Presidente at the airport and save a lot of trouble.

"I told you he would slip in unobtrusively. As a matter of fact, he arrived this morning while I was away. Naturally I didn't tell him where I had been." Actually, Susan thought, he'd been where he was supposed to be, only either he'd left things too late or his father had arrived too soon.

"I managed to get a word alone with Margarita, and she says she'd be delighted to have you come to dinner as her guest. It will give her someone to talk to, she says, because all the other guests are going to be businessmen and their wives."

"I'd be happy to come," she said. "I hope I won't cause her any embarrassment." Embarrassment is going to be the least of it, she thought, but it was automatic with her to keep up the social pretenses, even when the pretenses were, as in this case, more like antisocial.

He laughed. "Margarita thrives on embarrassment. It adds spice to her life, she says. Florencio probably won't like your being there, but you won't mind if Florencio is angry, will you, especially since it will be Margarita on whom he will take out his anger, not you. He is very correct."

"Maybe it won't be all that bad," Susan said, thinking, if her mission were successful, no, *when* her mission was successful, Florencio was going to have more to worry about than an uninvited guest.

"And, I am truly sorry," Gil went on, "but I am afraid I will not be able to see you tonight, after all. I have just had dinner with my father, and he expects me to spend the rest of the evening with him. I hope you will not be disappointed."

"Certainly not. I mean, I understand. It's only natural your father should want to spend his first night here with you."

"And there will be other nights."

She gave a noncommittal murmur.

◊◊◊ **XXVI**

Susan went to the Labarcas' dinner alone because, Gil had explained, "My father will expect me to accompany him there. Besides—" and he'd given a boyish laugh "—in case things should happen to go wrong, and he gets very angry, it might be a good idea for him to think that it was Margarita's idea for you to come and that I had nothing to do with it. There is no sense asking for trouble. And, after all, she is not a Praderan and I am."

"That's very sensible of you, Gil," Susan had told him. She'd been glad to find out that he had this practical streak. He was going to need it.

Just before she set out, there was a call from Andy, but she let the machine take the message.

The high rise in which the Labarcas lived on the Upper East Side of Manhattan adjacent to the river was one of the most opulent buildings in the city, with a lobby that looked like a set for a big-budget science-fiction movie. While it couldn't have been more than a dozen or so years old, it had the kind of security that had been already obsolescent in her youth and that, she had thought, was non-existent today. There were two uniformed doormen in the lobby, one to open the door and one to escort her to the concierge's desk. As she gave her name and destination, she noticed she was being scrutinized by a hidden camera. There had not been that sort of invasion of privacy in her youth when TV was still an entertainment medium and not a security device. Perhaps it was still an entertainment medium as well. Who knew who might be lurking in some cubbyhole deriving perverse pleasure from watching visitors attempt to gain entrance? She resisted the bourgeois temptation to pat her hair.

Upon getting the go-ahead from upstairs—which was done very discreetly; she saw the concierge speak into a phone but could not hear what the woman was saying—the second doorman escorted her to an elevator and entrusted her to the charge of a uniformed elevator man (When had she last seen a uniformed elevator man? When had she last seen an elevator man?) who whisked her up to the Labarcas' forty-fifth floor penthouse so rapidly there was a faint whistling in her ears.

The elevator opened on a small, softly lit, thickly carpeted foyer, with an atmosphere of quiet elegance that was shattered by the sounds of banging and thumping, interspersed with shrieks in Spanish and English in a variety of voices, ranging from falsetto to basso profundo. Could the Labarcas' apartment be in process of renovation? At seven in the evening? When they were expecting guests? Not likely.

The elevator man looked embarrassed as he pressed a button outside one of the two doors and chimes sounded, barely audible through the din. "There is, I believe, some difficulty with the plumbing," he felt it incumbent upon him to explain, as he pressed the button a second time.

The shrieks stopped, although the banging and thumping continued. The door opened. A middle-aged woman, dressed in the kind of maid's uniform more often seen on the stage than in a private home these days, stood there, cap askew, face bloated with emotion. She was about to speak when she was thrust aside by Margarita, truly splendid in a scarlet metallic sheath, topped by a headpiece with waving ruby and gold antennae that rose high in the air. She looked, Susan thought, like a boiled lobster.

"Susan, I'm so glad you could come early!" she cried, embracing her guest with such fervor that her antennae hit the top of the doorframe, and several small gems popped out and rolled down the hall. She appeared to pay no attention. Indeed, there were no discernible gaps in the construction. "Come to my workshop; there are some sketches I want to show you before the other guests arrive." Taking Susan's arm, she led her past the thickset blue-jowled man who stood by the door, regarding them both with generalized suspicion.

"Not that he speaks English," Margarita whispered, "but it's as well not to take any chances. We want to make you a real surprise for Pago," she went on, as soon as they were out of earshot, blithely overlooking the fact that, at the very least, Susan was not likely to be a pleasant surprise for "Pago."

They went down a wide corridor even more sumptuously carpeted than the foyer outside and, after passing several open and half-open doorways that offered glimpses of almost palatial interiors, entered an alcove which led into a large room furnished half as sitting room, half as atelier, cluttered with papers and armatures and gems—possibly the real thing, possibly fake stand-ins. All sorts of tools and equipment, presumably involved in the craft of jewelry, but, in some cases, rather sinister in appearance were lying about. It looked like a part-time torture chamber owned by a rather slovenly sadist.

There were crystals here, too, in abundance, heaped in piles on the windowsills and on tables. Susan wondered whether Margarita, too, was a New Ager, or whether the crystals were part of the impedimenta of her art.

"Forgive the mess," Margarita said. "I don't usually let people in here, but I know you, as a fellow artist, will understand." And, hospitably sweeping a pile of catalogues from an easy chair she added, "Do sit down. I know you're surprised to find that I work out of my apartment, but Florencio insists. The materials I use are so costly that I need to have top security. Since this place is like a fortress—full of UN people, you know, and they're not very popular—he says I can't do better than work up here. Sometimes I find it oppressive to live and work in the same place, but an artist must suffer for her art, don't you agree?"

"Not if she can avoid it," Susan said.

Margarita clapped her hands. "Oh, you're so droll. I know we're going to be great friends."

Susan smiled and murmured something polite and incomprehensible.

"Don't be surprised if Florencio's surprised to see you. All I told him was that Gil was bringing a friend. And, since Gil will be arriving with Pago, it's only natural that his friend should come earlier to look at my sketches. Then, afterward, while the men are having their business meeting, we will sit with the wives and I can show them my sketches, too, although I am sure they will not appreciate them. What do they know about art?''

All the while she'd been talking, the banging and thumping had continued to be heard through the door. Now the shrieking started again. "My servants are very high-strung," Margarita explained. "Of course, if this place had been properly built, you wouldn't be able to hear them. You won't believe the price Florencio paid for this apartment! Fantastic! And yet the walls are like paper and the floors like cardboard, and everything is so shoddy it falls apart if you so much as look at it. And now—'' she threw up her arms in despair ''—wouldn't you know, something's gone wrong with the plumbing. The superintendent's trying to fix it. Good of him, he tells me, since it's after hours. But I didn't ask him to work after hours. I asked him to call a plumber.''

Although she couldn't have cared less about the Labarcas' domestic problems—she had enough of her own—Susan was a dutiful guest. "Why didn't he call a plumber?''

"He claims he did, but that while he was en route he got called away by an emergency event and they haven't been able to get hold of another one.''

"An emergency event?'' Susan repeated.

"That's the way he put it. His English isn't the greatest. Neither is his personality. Two of my maids are having hysterics and the caterer's threatening to quit. Not because of the super, though. The thug at the service door—they always come in pairs, you know—insisted on searching his people as they came in.''

"I'm glad the one at the front door didn't insist on searching me,'' Susan said, conscious of the gun that occupied almost the whole interior of her evening bag.

Margarita laughed merrily. "My dear, even a thug

wouldn't dare. I had to promise them—the caterer's people, I mean—a bonus before they'd so much as set foot in the kitchen. They're in there now, making hors d'oeuvres in what I can only describe as a very sullen manner.''

She started taking long rolls of paper out of a wooden cabinet that consisted of a series of front-to-back pigeon-holes. She unrolled a paper, frowned at it, and cast it aside. ''Would you like a drink?'' she asked over her shoulder, ''or would you rather wait until we join the others?''

''I'd rather wait,'' Susan said.

''Good.'' Margarita unrolled another paper and shook her head. ''Because if you take a drink, I'll take a drink, and I'm always spilling things on my sketches.''

She unrolled another sketch and gave a sigh of satisfaction. ''Now, what do you think of this? One of my more conservative pieces. Just my personal opinion, of course, but I think it's absolutely you.''

She kept hold of one end so it wouldn't roll up as Susan looked at it. Susan wished it would roll up. The figure in the sketch, whose features bore a decided resemblance to Susan's own, wore a blue and silver headpiece—sapphires and platinum, Margarita pointed out—that made her look like a genteel owl.

Susan swallowed. ''It's lovely,'' she said, ''really lovely. The ears or tufts or whatever those are on either side of the head don't actually move, do they?''

''Just a little,'' her hostess said. ''All my conceptions are motiles. Not mobiles, you understand, *motiles*.''

''Surely work like this is too—too precious to be exposed to the hazards of being worn. It belongs in a museum where it won't be exposed to—to wear.''

''This is living art,'' Margarita said. ''If it's not worn, it dies.''

''I see,'' Susan said.

''Already people are beginning to copy it—in expensive materials now, but soon you will see cheap knockoffs of it in every subway car.'' Susan could just imagine, especially during rush hour. She was glad she did not ride the subways.

''Some artists would resent such a thing, but me, I glory

in it, because it means my art will be reaching out into all strata of society, permeating the world with my visions, filling—"

She was interrupted by a crash outside. The shrieks rose to a crescendo. Then a silence. "Oh, dear," Margarita said, "I'd better go out and see what's happening. The other guests will start arriving any minute now. Here are some more sketches to keep you amused while I'm gone." She thrust several rolls of paper at Susan and rushed out in a wave of agitated feelers, leaving a trail of rubies and diamonds behind her. Susan picked them up and placed them tidily on a table. She didn't know how Margarita attached the gems to her constructions, but, if she used glue, no wonder the bottom had fallen out of Consolidated Adhesives.

Margarita's sketches would, indeed, have amused Susan, if she hadn't realized that she would be expected not only to buy one (or more) of the pieces, but to wear it. She did rather like one where the protrusions on top took the form of gold snakes with emerald eyes and quivering ruby tongues. If I bought that, she thought, I could go to a fancy-dress ball as Medusa. Or, better yet, I could give it to Tinsley for Christmas. But would I really be discharging my obligation to Margarita if I don't wear one of her constructions myself? It was an interesting ethical question.

The noises outside started up again, although in more subdued form. Ten minutes, twenty minutes passed, and Margarita did not return. What am I supposed to do, Susan wondered; just sit here and wait? There were magazines around, but they all seemed either to deal with jewelry or be in Spanish, or both. Besides, Susan thought, I didn't come here to look at magazines. And, reminding herself of what she had come there for, she fought back her irritation.

The noises outside had been dying down so gradually she hadn't been aware of the silence until the doorbell chimed. The guests were arriving. It chimed again, and again. And still Margarita didn't return. I could wait here forever, Susan thought. Perhaps I'm meant to; perhaps this is a trap and I've been locked in here until . . . Until what?

She went over and tried the door. It was unlocked.

She looked outside. No one was in sight except for a burly blue-shirted man, presumably, since he carried a tool kit, the building superintendent, walking down the hall away from her. How much all building superintendents looked alike from the back, she thought.

The chimes sounded again. A woman in maid's uniform—perhaps the same one she had seen before, perhaps another—appeared in a doorway halfway down the hall and stared at Susan. "I was wondering where Mrs. Labarca was?" Susan said. "Señora Labarca?"

The maid said something in Spanish and walked away. No way of telling whether she understood or not.

Margarita appeared, looking harried. One of her feelers was drooping. "I'm so sorry to have left you for so long, but people kept coming, and Florencio insisted that I had to greet them. But Pago should arrive here very soon, and, as soon as he gets here and everyone has gone through the obligatory toasts—I'm sorry you'll have to miss them—"

"Not at all," Susan said.

"—I'll send Gil back to you, and he'll take you in and introduce you when the moment's propitious."

The chimes sounded again. "I have to get back." And she hurried off, antennae bobbing, all except the defective one, which hung forlornly down to her shoulder.

Susan retreated into the workroom, closing the door behind her. After a few minutes, she opened it and peered out again. The coast seemed clear. In the distance she could hear voices and the clink of glasses.

I'm never going to have a better chance, she thought. She checked the gun in her handbag—an automatic gesture; she knew it was there—and loaded. Then she followed the sound to an archway which opened into a vast room where the guests were assembled—perhaps thirty, all told, including the host and hostess, the caterer's people and a few more of what Margarita had described as thugs, for even here, among his close friends and associates Relempago Martillo was well-guarded. A lot of his close friends and associates looked like thugs, too, she noted.

She posted herself on one side of the archway where she could not be observed readily by anyone inside the room. However, even if she had been standing in clear view, they would not have seen her, for all of them were facing away from the archway toward President Martillo.

She saw him then in the flesh, for the first time. He was standing with his back to a set of sliding glass doors that appeared to open onto a terrace, a glass held high in his hand, obscuring most of his face. Although he was wearing a dinner jacket rather than his customary uniform, his black beard and his commanding figure were unmistakable. Today he was not wearing dark glasses. She opened her bag and took out her gun.

Then, he lowered his glass and she lowered her gun as she saw his face—familiar to her from more than his pictures. Although almost thirty years had passed, his hair was dyed black, and he had grown a beard and mustache, she recognized him immediately. "Daddy!" she said. "Daddy. . . ."

He looked frozen for a moment; then he took a step toward her. "Susan?"

That was the last word he ever uttered. Cold wind rushed into the room as the terrace door slid open. A shot rang out from behind him and he crumpled to the floor.

The burly, blue-shirted figure who had looked like Adolfo from the rear and now looked like Adolfo from the front and was, in fact, Adolfo, stood in the terrace doorway, shouting in Spanish, his face congested, his eyes dilated. If Mrs. Acacia saw him now, Susan thought inanely, she'd fire him on the spot no matter what his capabilities.

But Mrs. Acacia would never have the chance to fire him. A couple of the thugs came at him from one side; Gil from the other. Before any of them could reach him, there was another shot . . . and he joined his general in death on the rug.

Someone grabbed Susan by the shoulder. She whirled, raising her gun.

"Don't shoot me, Susan," the young man in the uniform

of the catering service said. It was Andy Mackay. "Hurry, we've got to get you out of here before the local law gets here." And he hustled her toward the back of the apartment, just as there came a thundering knock on the front door, and a voice called, "It's the police! Open up!"

Just inside the kitchen door, Andy put out his hand. "Give me your gun."

She started to protest, thought better of it, and handed her gun to him. He slipped it in his pocket; then led her through the kitchen, where people were milling about in various stages of pandemonium, to the service entrance, and pushed her outside.

Finally she found her voice. "What are *you* doing here?"

"Never mind. At least for the moment. When I have a chance, I'll come by your place and explain things, so far as I'm able. Meanwhile, remember, you were never here. You've been home in your apartment all evening, watching television or reading a book. The first you heard of this was when you heard it on the news."

"But a lot of people saw me here."

"They're going to have other things to worry about," he told her.

He beckoned to an efficient-looking young man who was standing on the service landing. "Take her home and see that she stays there until I give you the word."

"But—" Susan began.

Andy tapped the pocket in which he had put the gun.

"Oh, very well," she said crossly.

✧✧✧ XXVII

"The hardest thing for me to understand," Andy said to Susan, "is how it was possible for Adolfo Reyes to be superintendent of the Labarcas' building and of this one at the same time."

She laughed. "Obviously you've never lived in a New York City apartment. The one thing common to superintendents here is that they're never around when you're looking for them."

It was some weeks after President Martillo's assassination. Susan and Andy Mackay were having dinner together in her apartment, comfortably seated on the new dining room chairs—new to her, that was—that she had bought from an antiques dealer; for, she had discovered, the only way to get immediate delivery on furniture was to buy it secondhand.

It had been Andy's suggestion that they eat up there, rather than in a restaurant. "There are still some things that need to be cleared up," he told her, "and I don't think a restaurant is the right place for us to talk about them."

No need for her to ask why. As Peter was attending a conference at the University of Pennsylvania (a legitimate conference—she'd checked—not that a conference in Philadelphia was likely to be illegitimate), they'd have the apartment to themselves; no risk of being overheard, unless Andy's people had bugged the place; or being happened upon by some friend, who might attempt to join them or, even worse, mention the encounter to Jill.

Jill was back in town now, and very curious to know what had been going on, "behind her back," as she put it, since she refused to accept the fact that it was no concern of hers.

After all, it was her husband and her client; she had a right, she told both of them, separately and together, to know the score. As Andy observed, "If she had any idea I was up here having dinner with you, and she hadn't been invited, she'd blow a gasket."

But of course Jill couldn't be told the truth, not only for reasons of national security or whatever—he hadn't been explicit, and Susan knew better than to press him—but because Jill was Jill. "Thank God she never knew that Martillo was supposed to have killed my father or it would have been in all my press bios," Susan said. Jill had no conception of a decent reticence when it came to publicity—or anything else, for that matter.

As for the fact that Praderan despot Relempago Martillo had in truth been New York blue blood Buckley Melville, it had been suppressed—"for the good of all concerned," Andy had said vaguely. Her father's body had been taken back to La Pradera and buried as Relempago Martillo with full honors, despite the rather dubious circumstances of his demise.

"You're sure you have no objection?" Andy had asked when he informed her of the arrangements.

Much good it would do her if she did object, she had thought. "Well, I didn't really think there was much chance of getting him buried in the family plot in Woodlawn," she told Andy.

"Actually, he is buried in your family plot in Woodlawn; at least, there's a tombstone up there with his name on it and the date of his death twenty-seven years ago, as well as the date of his birth, together with a suitable inscription. You can go up there and see it, if you don't believe me."

But she had known without going that the tombstone would be up there, looking at least fifty years old, for among the faults of the people whom Andy worked for was a tendency to overdo. She wondered what their idea of an appropriate epitaph had been, but was not curious enough to go up to the Bronx and see for herself.

Later that same week, an enterprising reporter from *Today* had confronted her with those early reports about her father's death in the Praderan counter-revolution. She had looked at him blankly and said what Andy had told her to say: that her father had died of a fever in Brazil a couple of years after his arrival there; that his body had been shipped back to New York and interred quietly to avoid further scandal. "So you see," she had finished, "there must be some mistake. Perhaps another man with a similar name . . . ?"

And, when the reporter had asked what, as a matter of general interest, had happened to the money Melville had taken with him—"the alleged money," he had hastily added, on seeing her expression—she'd told him that she knew nothing about it; but that, if he was thinking of referring to it or to her in any way in connection with a story on the Martillo assassination, he would do well to take up the matter with her lawyers, Wycherly, Weinstein and Flake, beforehand. She didn't need to remind him that Wycherly, Weinstein was the same firm that had in the recent past won huge settlements for several clients in libel suits against the media. And she was gratified to see that her name did not appear in connection with the Martillo story in *Today* or anywhere else, although whether this was the result of her own efforts or Andy's work behind the scenes, she had no way of knowing.

She felt no compunction about disavowing her father. Had he not been the one to disavow her, in a manner of speaking, first? She was thankful to Andy and his agency for not letting the truth get out, whatever their motives might have been, for she was under no illusion that they had gone to all this trouble for her sake alone, or, indeed, for her sake at all.

Bad enough to have had a father who'd been a defaulting financier. To have him resurface as a Latin American dictator would really be pushing iniquity to the point of infamy. Black Buck Melville was all very well. He was an ancestor; the centuries had lent him romance and respectability. But to have one's own father guilty of deeds that would make Black Buck's look like high jinks at a Sunday school outing was too much. "Truth does not always serve the ends of justice," Cristobal Herrero had written. "Justice does not always serve the ends of truth."

She could not hope to escape media attention entirely.

Once the truth about Gil's identity came out, the very fact that she had been acquainted with him had caused her a certain amount of annoyance. When reporters approached her, as they approached everyone in New York who had known Gil Frias, she informed them that she'd been barely acquainted with the young man. "Better talk to Sonny Fothergill," she advised. "After all, he was the one who put on the exhibit of Señor Frias's paintings that brought him to New York in the first place." She knew that this would cause Sonny embarrassment because, while some of the smaller galleries were known to put on shows in return for subsidies, Fothergill's was supposed to be above that sort of thing; and she was not averse to embarrassing Sonny, with whom she had an old score to settle.

The media did manage to nose out the fact that Gil had been to dinner at the von Schwabes' apartment along with the by-now notorious Labarcas, and the only slightly less notorious Yepezes (who, since the ambassador could not be sent to jail, had been declared *persona non grata* and asked to leave the country), so that Gunther as well as Sonny was given cause for some embarrassment. "I understand he beat Mimi up and she's filing for divorce," Jill reported, with considerable relish, if questionable accuracy. "Oh, Susan, why didn't you ever introduce him to me?"

"Gunther? But you've met him a lot of times, and you've always said—"

"You know who I mean—Gil Frias, of course. When I saw his picture in the papers—"

"You got an invitation to his opening. You said you had to stay in Washington."

"Well, I wouldn't have, if I'd known what was going to happen," Jill said. "Still, I can hardly blame you. I don't suppose you had any idea of what was going to happen, either." Lucky she never got to meet Fée, Susan thought.

Gil had had to be told the truth, if only so that he should not feel himself responsible for his own father's death. And then, of course, he had heard Susan call the man he had believed to be his father "Daddy." Others there must have heard her, too, but no need for her to be concerned about them. Andy had told her at the time that, even if they had noticed, they had other things to worry about. Although she was not entirely satisfied, she had to be content with that assurance.

Gil had gone back to La Pradera. "As a grieving son, he would naturally be expected to accompany his father's body back home," Andy explained.

"But the Praderan people don't know that Gil is Martillo's son," she objected. "That's what he told me, anyway."

"That was the official story. It was pretty much an open secret, though. And, in case there were a few people in the hinterlands who weren't aware of his identity, they are now."

"But how did you—how was Gil persuaded to go back? He likes it here. And it would seem to me that there's no reason for him to go."

Not that she wanted him to stay, of course. As a matter of fact, his departure would remove a source of potential awkwardness. But it piqued her just a little that he should be so ready to leave.

"There's every reason for him to go back," Andy said sternly. "In the first place, he has a duty to his country. In the second, he was given to understand that his visa would be revoked if he didn't."

She shouldn't have been gratified to learn that Gil had returned to La Pradera because he had no choice, but she couldn't help it.

"In the third place, if he didn't go home and a new government was established that wasn't too sympathetic to the current regime, he might stand to lose the handsome allowance he's getting, as well as his claim to inherit whatever of Martillo's fortune isn't stashed away in Swiss—or, more likely, Bahamian—banks. Morally, I suppose, the money should go to you and Alex. And, speaking of Alex—"

"There's no question of morality when it comes to that money," she interrupted. "We'd be happy for it to go to Gil, and I'm sure I can speak for Alex."

Was Andy looking at her quizzically, or was she just imagining it? That was the trouble with guilty secrets; they bred paranoia, or, worse yet, the fear of it. Was there such a thing as paranoiphobia? if there was, she had it.

She might not be able to change the subject, but at least she could turn it. "Why is it so important for Gil to go back now?"

"He's needed as Martillo's heir apparent—to keep things stable until a new democratic government can be established." One that would be as favorably disposed toward the United States Government as the old was implicit. After all, just because Martillo had turned out to be a drug trafficker and an imposter didn't diminish his country's strategic importance.

"But Gil doesn't know anything about politics," she pointed out.

"He'll learn," Andy told her. "Your father did, didn't he? Anyhow, this is just for the interim, until we—a suitable leader can be found. In the long run, creative people make poor politicians. They tend to have ideals."

The evening before he left, Gil came up to Susan's apartment to say goodbye. "I'm sorry I must leave at such short notice," he'd said on the phone earlier in the day. "I'm sorry to have to leave at all, but my duty to my country comes first. I'm sure you understand."

And she told him very solemnly that, yes, she understood.

"I know this is the way my father—my real father, I mean, not your father—would have wished it."

She could see that his real father was going to become enshrined in his mind as some kind of hero-cum-saint. Better that, she thought, than that he should know the truth, as Andy had told it to her. She saw no reason to disbelieve that the real Relempago Martillo (*né* Alberto Frias) had been a two-bit terrorist, who had been the prime bungler in the former ruling junta's regime; and who never would have been able to carry the counter-revolution through to a successful conclusion, let alone rule the country efficiently for twenty-five years. It took a Buckley Melville to do that.

If only Daddy had managed to preserve at least the semblance of honesty, she thought, he might have stayed up here and become president of the United States. But then she would have had to fill the role of the president's daughter, and she did not think she would have found it a congenial one.

"I see you finally got the place fixed up," Gil said, following her into the living room. "It looks very nice. I like the curtains."

"There's a lot that still needs to be done," she said, "but at least I can live in it, thank God."

"I wish that I could have said goodbye to you properly," Gil said, with a sidelong glance in the direction of the bedroom, "but they are waiting for me downstairs to drive me back to the mission. In fact, I had trouble stopping a security man from coming up here with me. From now on I will never really be alone." Not that he ever had been, she supposed.

"You know, of course, that Florencio has been arrested, along with most of the other people who were at the dinner party," Gil said, as they sat down in the newly recovered chairs. The fabric had turned out not to be the one she had carefully chosen back in the old days when such choices had seemed a matter of importance, but she'd had too much on her mind now to do more than give the upholsterer a piece of it.

"The papers said Florencio was head of some kind of drug ring," she said, "and those other people high-level drug dealers from all over South and Central America."

"It was one of the largest Latin American drug cartels," Gil corrected her, a note of what sounded almost like pride in his voice. "And only deputy head. My father—your father—was its actual head."

She knew by this time that the president of La Pradera's reputation as a staunch foe of the drug traffic was as much a sham as he himself had been. This news had not surprised her. What had surprised her was that the United States Government apparently should have been taken in by him. Or, perhaps she shouldn't have been surprised by that either.

Gil sighed. "Once I wouldn't have believed that my father could possibly have been involved in anything like that, but, now that I know the man whom I thought was my father was your father and that, instead of my father killing your father, your father killed mine, I can believe anything."

"There was a time when I wouldn't have believed anything like that about my father, either," she said, "but that was a long time ago." This time, they both sighed.

"I'm glad they didn't arrest you, along with the others," she said.

Gil looked surprised, and a little affronted. "But naturally not. How could anyone possibly think I would have anything to do with something like that? It was obvious that the only reason I came to the party was to be with my father; and that the only reason I came to New York in the first place was for my show."

That wasn't the real reason he had come to New York, of course, but she was sure that in time he would come to believe it—if he didn't believe it already. Just as well nobody knew that the main, perhaps the only, reason Gil had been sent up to New York was to help make sure she never had a chance to get close enough to his "father" to recognize him as her father, should all the other schemes to get her away fail. The man who'd taken on Martillo's identity had been afraid that, despite the passing of the years and the change in his appearance, she would know him for her father.

And he had been right. She had recognized him. At the same time, if it hadn't been for Gil, she might never have gotten close enough to identify him. In which case, she rather than Adolfo would have been the one to kill him. So that actually things had worked out for the best after all.

Down in the street an automobile horn honked, Gil got up. "Goodbye, Susan. I hope that, after the elections are over and things have settled down, you will come to La Pradera. After all, it is, in some small part, your country, too."

"What about the strikes, the mudslides, the Communists?"

He gave her a smile that was only a pale reflection of its once brilliant self. "Let us hope that, after the elections are over, they will disappear along with . . . all the other bad things.''

Rather too much to hope for, she thought, but it was best for him to feel that way.

"I will write to you, Susan, I promise. And you will write to me, won't you?"

She had promised she would, thinking, he'll forget about me after he's been down there a little while. And then, perhaps not. They would share more than the memory of a night together; they would share the memory of two fathers, each, in a sense, assassinated by the other, if you consider Adolfo as the surrogate of the real Martillo.

Gil kissed her. "I will come back to New York one day, I promise. And, until then, whenever I see Snoopy—who is carried, in Spanish, by *el Tiempo de Ciudad Martillo* as well as by several of the provincial papers—I will think of you."

She had already removed the Snoopy pillowcase and replaced the linens on her bed with a set of purest white. No more colored or patterned sheets for her ever again, she thought.

As his hand was on the doorknob, "Wait a minute," she said. "I have something for you."

She went back to the bedroom and brought out the crystal Fée had given her and gave it to him. "To remember me by," she told him.

"I thank you, and I will treasure it always, although I will not need anything to remember you by. You will always be in my heart."

He's a Latin, she told herself, and young. One must make allowances.

She felt a little empty inside after he left, but she didn't know whether it was because he had gone, or the crystal had gone, or even her hatred for the man whom she thought had killed her father had gone. If she had been younger, if she had been less in possession of herself, if she had had any vestige of Latin blood, she might have cried a little. As it was, she went back into the bedroom with dry eyes to call Katmandu and find out what was keeping Peter.

✧✧✧ **XXVIII**

"I've already realized that it must have been Adolfo who searched my apartment," Susan told Andy over the dinner she'd ordered from a local takeout food place—nothing too aggressively gourmet, for she knew Andy prided himself on his simple all-American tastes. "But I still can't understand why. What did he hope to find out from my apartment? Or was he deliberately trying to frighten me into doing something, and, if so, what?"

Andy's mouth was too full of potatoes for him to speak, so he simply shook his head to indicate ignorance of any answer or answers.

"I could very easily have gone to the police. It isn't likely that they'd have found out who'd ransacked my apartment—not with their record—but it was a possibility. He would have been out of a job, one job anyway—because that was something even Mrs. Acacia couldn't have overlooked—and under suspicion at the very moment you would have thought he'd want to be least obtrusive."

She spoke of Mrs. Acacia without rancor, for that lady was no longer chairman of the co-op board, having resigned under pressure and been replaced by Fred Burney. "Out of the frying pan into the fire!" one of the residents was heard to say. Not that Burney's proposal to turn the basement recreation room into a soup kitchen for the homeless had any chance of finding favor with his fellow residents, but the very idea that he should come up with something like that did not make for a good neighborly feeling.

"Now that both Reyes and your father are dead there are a lot of questions that are bound to remain unanswered,"

Andy said. "Your father obviously didn't dare to confide in anyone, and Reyes didn't seem to have anyone to confide in. He did talk to Toribio, his assistant—"

"Toribio? Oh, that must be Wilfredo."

"—who assures us he thought Reyes was crazy when he claimed Martillo was really an American named Buckley Melville."

"Put like that, it does sound a little crazy—Yes, finish the potatoes if you have room for them; I'm certainly not going to eat any more—Imagine, me the daughter of a South American dictator!"

And they both laughed. Bad taste perhaps, but there was no one to overhear them—as far as she knew, anyway.

"Toribio says he just humored Reyes for the sake of his own job, which makes sense. The things I have to pretend to believe for the sake of my job." She hoped he'd say more about his job. It was the first sign of indiscretion he'd ever shown. But he went on, "Is that apple pie? Great. My favorite."

"I suppose Adolfo didn't really want me to participate in any demonstrations?"

"No reason to suppose there were any demonstrations planned. In fact, I doubt that there are enough Praderans in New York to mount a respectable demonstration."

"Gunther von Schwabe—you know, Mimi's husband—claims that you can hire demonstrators in New York for anything; that they have standard rates, plus extras if it's raining, or they're required to dress up, in kaftans, yarmulkes, whatever."

"And double rates for violence, I suppose. Well, that would be the local police force's headache."

"I thought you worked with them," Susan said.

"Sometimes we do," he told her, "and sometimes we don't. This is excellent pie."

"Another thing I can't understand is why, as soon as he'd escaped from the country, Adolfo didn't simply denounce my father publicly? Or why he didn't do it later, after he came here?"

Andy looked at her as if she had been slow on the uptake.

"Don't you see? They *were* on the same side. Your father couldn't have worked the impersonation all by himself. Some of Martillo's men would have had to be in it with him, especially the officers. Those who wouldn't go along with him would have been killed off early in the game. Then he would have gotten rid of his co-conspirators, one by one, until eventually there would be no one left who shared his secret. He couldn't afford to trust anybody."

Andy chewed and swallowed. "From what we can piece together, Reyes was one of your father's most faithful henchmen, with a hand in most of the worst things your father did at the outset. Possibly, he was the one who killed off the real Martillo's family. That had to be done, because they would have been bound to recognize your father as a fake instantly."

"That seems so—so cold-blooded."

"That's what revolutions are all about. Your father would need Reyes to help him get rid of the others. Apparently it never occurred to Reyes that, once they were gone, he would go, too. Something must have happened to make him realize that your father was going to kill him next, and he managed to get away in time. But he could hardly denounce Martillo as a fake without sticking his own neck out. He was hated every bit as much as his boss. But, from that time on, according to Toribio, Reyes lived only for revenge. The only thing he wanted out of life was to kill your father. And, in the end he got his wish."

"But why was he waiting for him here in New York? What made him think my father would ever come back here?"

Andy shrugged. "He knew this was where your father had come from. Maybe he used to talk about going back home some day. Maybe there was no place else for Reyes to wait. There's no way of knowing what was in his mind."

But there is, Susan thought. If Andy got in touch with Fée . . . but that was ridiculous. Fée put on a good act, a terrific act, but that was all it was—an act. And that strange voice that had spoken in Spanish at the séance—to think that could possibly have been the real Relempago Martillo, trying to tell the world that the man who was passing himself off as Martillo was an imposter would be to make her as gullible as Tinsley and her crew. If she told Andy that Fée might have the answers, he would laugh at her, and she would deserve to be laughed at.

In any case, Fée was gone, taking with her the SEC investigator who had pretended to be one of her followers, trying to get her to betray the source of her arcane knowledge (i.e., inside information), and, in the process, coming to believe in her—or, perhaps, government salaries being what they were, deciding to throw in his lot with her. Whatever the Professor's motives had been, he had vanished as completely as she had, according to Andy.

"Everything else apparently having failed, he figured he might be able to find out the truth about what was going on from you or through you. But he kept getting in our way, so we told him to get lost until we were through with our current—er—project. And so he got lost all right. I'm told that nobody's been able to find hide nor hair of either of them. They took a cab to Grand Central, and, after that—nothing."

He didn't seem concerned about their whereabouts. Susan gathered that he felt such matters were outside his province.

"Maybe they went to another planet," she suggested, smiling to show it was a joke.

Andy laughed, to show he knew it was a joke. "It's easy enough to disappear on this earth, especially if you have enough money, and this Fée—whatever her real name is—appears to have been loaded."

"You mean you don't know what her real name is?"

Andy looked annoyed. "I imagine if we'd tried to find out we wouldn't have had any trouble. But it was none of our business." That there was a lot he could say about the efficiency of other government agencies was implicit in his tone but discretion prevented him.

She wondered whether she should tell him about the package of photographs of Fée that Sister had turned over to her. Perhaps there was a clue in them, but she decided to let sleeping seers lie.

"My guess is that they're headed somewhere well south

of the border, where the restrictions on trading are less stringent. It looks as if the old geezer did pretty well for himself, doesn't it, specially since he was slated for retirement anyway."

Susan wondered whether it was an out-and-out elopement or a simple business relationship, or perhaps a combination of the two; and whether they were going to stay wherever it was they had gone to or come back to New York on another plane, in every sense of the word. Would Fée continue to channel or would her mysticism take another form? Would she remain in this life or pass on to another one or lead several lives synchronously, as the Professor had said she was wont to do, and would he lead them along with her?

And what do I care? Susan thought. Our lives aren't likely to touch again, especially since, now that Fée was gone, the heat was off Alex as far as the SEC was concerned. They seemed to have stopped their harassment after their warning that whatever it was he had been doing he had better not try it again.

As for the photographs of Fée, Susan had put the package high up on a closet shelf. Not the shelf where she kept her guns, because she expected to be using them again very soon for during her brief sabbatical, the UN personnel had been up to their usual tricks. This was a shelf she used for dead storage, where she kept things she never expected to look at again, like the set of Snoopy linens.

There had been another crystal along with the pictures in the second package that Fée had left for her, a larger, more brilliant crystal than the first. She put it on the windowsill in her bedroom. It was even more decorative than the first had been and, when Peter came back, which he did two weeks later, it had seemed to inspire him to new heights of ardor.

She asked Andy why Gil hadn't been killed when the rest of his family was massacred, but he had no answer. Perhaps, he suggested, since Gil had been too small to remember his real father, whoever had done the actual killing had taken pity on him and put him in an orphanage along with the many other children who had lost their identities in the war. Later, her father, aware that he would be destined to spend the rest of his life alone, never daring to let anyone get close to him, had "adopted" the child. Just like her father to have chosen that particular child; he'd always had a sentimental streak.

As far as her father himself was concerned, apparently he hadn't had any trouble passing for Martillo. The two men had been of about the same height and build and, although Melville had been a dozen or so years older than the man whose place he had taken, he had been an active sportsman, so had probably been in much better physical condition. The true Martillo had gone into exile wearing a hairline mustache. The false Martillo returned with a full beard and bushy mustache (both dyed black from their original light brown). No one except Martillo's nearest and dearest would ever have recognized him as an imposter, so he had gotten rid of Martillo's nearest and dearest, and for twenty-five years he'd been home free. But had it truly been home? Or, for that matter, free?

She couldn't imagine how her father had ever managed to pass himself off as a native Spanish speaker. "When he left, he couldn't speak a word of any language except English. He hated foreigners." How galling it must have been for him to have become a foreigner himself!

"I suppose he started to learn the language when he threw in with Martillo," Andy surmised. "At the beginning, he never gave press conferences and his speeches must have been rehearsed over and over again until his pronunciation was perfect. Over the years he could have practiced until he could speak without an accent. It can be done, you know."

She remembered *Pygmalion*. But who had been her father's Henry Higgins? Probably someone who'd been disposed of as soon as his talents were no longer required.

It would have been too much to believe that it had been simply coincidence that had led Adolfo to take either the job at the Labarcas' or the one at Susan's building, Andy told her. "He must have hoped to get access to your father through one or the other. Since he must have known about the drug connection, Labarca would seem to be the likelier prospect, but it wouldn't be easy to bug his apartment or tap his phone. That was something a fellow in Labarca's line of work would always be on the lookout for. You would be a much easier prospect. But he still couldn't be sure that you were the right Susan Melville, and, even if you were, that you accepted the fact that Martillo was Martillo and that he had killed your father; or, if you knew he was really Buckley Melville, and, if so, if you were in contact with him.''

"So many 'ifs,' " she said. "I could almost feel sorry for him.''

"He—I got all this from Toribio—thought that if he had a chance to search your apartment, he would find something to give him a clue, and, now that you tell me about those scrapbooks and family albums of yours, I guess he did.''

He looked at her with disapproval. As if there were something wrong in keeping scrapbooks, she thought. Lots of people keep scrapbooks, and hadn't it been his own wife who had given Susan hers originally? Nothing wrong with family albums either, even though she had forgotten the existence of hers until they had turned up; until Adolfo had turned them up.

Then the awful truth struck her. "You don't mean to tell me he deliberately flooded the apartment upstairs just so that I'd be forced to give my keys to him?''

She couldn't help feeling that, if so, all his other atrocities paled beside this one.

"I wouldn't be a bit surprised," Andy said cheerfully. "Plumbing mishaps seem to be his specialty, although he was pretty good at botching up almost everything. Every time he had to come up to your apartment to fix something, Toribio tells me, he tried to install a bug, but, instead of transmitting to his lair in the basement, the way it was supposed to do, it wound up coming out of that old coot—what's his name?—General Van something or other's hearing aid. Which would have driven him mad, if he hadn't been mad already.

"You'd think Reyes would have had better luck with a phone tap, since you can do that from outside the apartment, in the basement. Any halfway competent building super ought to be able to install a phone tap, but he didn't get yours right—kept getting all the neighbors instead of you—until that weekend before you came back to the apartment, just in time for him to hear young Frias tell you that his father was going to be at the Labarcas' the next night. From then on he didn't need you."

So, in a sense, she had been responsible for her father's death. Well, at least he hadn't died by her hand.

But by whose hand had Adolfo died? She asked Andy. "One of those thugs that was guarding Martillo, of course," Andy said, as if she should have known better than to ask such a silly question.

"But I didn't see any of them fire at him."

"You may not have noticed, in the confusion. Anyhow, he was behind you."

But there couldn't have been anyone behind her, or she wouldn't have been allowed to go on standing there. Oh, well, she supposed someone could have come up behind her after Martillo was shot. In any case, she could see that this was an occasion when it was better not to ask questions.

She remembered something else that had been bothering her. "So much else has been happening I never got a chance to ask you why you were trying to get in touch with me in the days before my father got killed. It didn't have anything to do with all . . . this, did it?"

"It has to do with that gun you were carrying to the party," he said.

She'd been hoping he wouldn't have the bad taste to bring that up. "I always carry a gun when Peter's away," she told him. "A woman alone, you know . . . I'd always meant to apply for a license, but somehow I never got around to it."

He gave her a reproachful look. "Oh, Susan, Susan, you lie so well. Unfortunately, from your point of view, we'd been keeping an eye on you for some time. Not a close enough eye, as it turns out—we couldn't afford to go to the expense of a full-scale surveillance—but an eye nonetheless."

"Oh," she said.

"I was trying to warn you to keep away from Martillo, but I didn't think there was any urgency We'd hoped to bag him at that dinner, but, since his visa hadn't been approved yet, we figured he wasn't going to be able to make it. It never occurred to us to keep a watch out for an elderly American citizen named Buckley Melville quietly entering the country on his own passport, which, it turned out, he'd kept up to date—maybe just in case; maybe because he'd been using it all along; who knows? So, we had no idea that Martillo, the man who called himself Martillo, was already in the country until he showed up at the Labarcas'. The rest you know about—anyway, all you're going to know about it."

They'd been keeping an eye on her, had they? So it was true what the liberal media had always claimed: that government agents were forever spying on honest citizens. Then she remembered that, technically, at least, she was not an honest citizen. However, they would have had no way of knowing that unless they had been spying on her in the first place.

She could not afford outrage. "How long have you been—er—keeping an eye on me?" she asked.

"Long enough," Andy said.

She looked at him with a question she dared not voice.

"Democracy is a wonderful thing," Andy said, "but sometimes it has its drawbacks. Sometimes the law doesn't always work the way it should; sometimes it doesn't work at all. And there's nothing we can do about it, except hope for a miracle."

"But miracles never happen nowadays," she said.

"They do, more often than you might think." He grinned at her. "How do you like being a miracle-worker?"

"Sometimes the end justifies the means," she quoted, "and sometimes the means justifies the end; but, where there is no end and no means, there is no justification."

"Very true," Andy said. "By the way, Susan," he went on, "in case you ever get tired of painting full-time and would like to take on some freelance jobs the agency might have an occasional assignment for you. The rate of pay wouldn't be high and the hours would be irregular. But I think you'd find the work very worthwhile."

She had difficulty speaking, but, even if she could have found her voice, she would have had no idea of what to say. "You don't have to give me an answer now," he said. "Just think about it."

The phone rang. "Excuse me," she said, getting up, "I have to answer it."

"Of course," Andy said. "I'll just have another piece of pie while I'm waiting. Oh, there's only one piece left."

"You might as well finish it," she told him.

She took the call in the bedroom. It was Tinsley. She sounded excited. "Listen to that," she cried.

Susan listened. "All I hear is barking, Tsung, I presume. Nice to know his lungs are healthy, but—"

"You're not listening carefully. He's not just barking. He's barking words. He's talking."

"Don't be silly," Susan said.

"Listen carefully."

Susan listened carefully. The barking *did* begin to sound like words: "Buy General Mo-tors. Buy General Mo-tors."

She was not going to have any part of this. "All I hear is barking," she said, and hung up.